THE FOUND LADY OF AZANIR

A L ROJO

THE FOUND LADY OF AZANIR

Copyright © A L Rojo 2026

The moral right of the author has been asserted in accordance with the Copyright Amendment (Moral Rights) Act 2000.

All rights reserved. Except as permitted under the Australian Copyright Act 1968 (for example, fair dealing for the purposes of study, research, criticism or review) no part of this publication may be reproduced, stored in a retrieval system, or transmitted in any form or by any means, electronic, mechanical, photocopying, recording or otherwise, without the written permission of the publisher.

 A catalogue record for this work is available from the National Library of Australia

https://www.nla.gov.au/collections

Title:	The Found Lady of Azanir
Series:	Shifters of Azanir
Volume:	Book 2
Author:	Rojo, A L
ISBNs:	978-0-6488690-8-5
Subjects:	FICTION: Romance/Paranormal/Shifters; Fantasy/Romance; Romance/Fantasy; Fantasy/General

This story is entirely a work of fiction. No character in this story is taken from real life. Any resemblance to any person or persons living or dead is accidental and unintentional. The author, their agents and publishers cannot be held responsible for any claim otherwise and take no responsibility for any such coincidence.

Cover concept by A L Rojo
Cover design and interior formatting by Katelyn at Design by Kage

A L ROJO

SHIFTERS OF AZANIR
BOOK TWO

ALSO BY A L ROJO

The Pack of Farrowline Series

The Heart of Farrowline
The Power of Farrowline
The Strength of Farrowline
The Pride of Farrowline
The Duty of Farrowline

Shifters of Azanir Series

The Lost Lady of the Darkwoods
The Found Lady of Azanir

AUTHOR NOTE

The Found Lady of Azanir contains themes of abuse, violence, trauma, explicit language, discussion of maternal death, and adult content. This novel is intended for adult readers.

Please head to www.alrojo.com.au for all content warnings and information on all of my novels.

TERMS

Azanir - The realm of the Azanite

Azanite - Shifters of Azanir

Zaric - Language of the Azanites

Azar - Nobility and Royals - An Azar is born into this ranking. Only other way to become an Azar is through binding and finding a mate within this ranking.

Thal - Workers/Commoners of Azanir - A Thal is born into this ranking. The only way to elevate a Thal's status is to complete their training in the Drengar Academy or mate with an Azar.

Drengar - Hunters that protect the realm - Drengar are the only ranking in society an Azanite can work towards. The title holds status in Azanir as they are the protectors of the realm.

Medir - Healers - A Medir is born with the power of the Sun Gods to heal. They can be born of any ranking.

Wraiths - Demons that haunt the night. Wraiths hunt the Azanites for their energy which they need to cross into our world and form shape.

Prologue

Ten years ago...

Bored and lonely, I walk through the lair humming a tune Meryl sings when we are out in the garden.

My human maid loves music and while the beasts of Azanir don't care much for it, I find it hard to get my brain to not play her songs in my head. Today was a busy day of learning about the courts of Azanir, from the royal family in the capital to the battle-hardened BlazeAzar's high in the north to the Riverland close to our border and the reclusive Cavelands in their mountains.

Today's lesson focused on the academies around the realm where beasts go to learn to become Drengar or Medir or academics. It was a little boring but the music in my head kept me entertained. I still have no idea why I'm learning about these places. It's unfair if you ask me. It's not like Father will let me go to see any of them. I've already asked a number of times to go to the Drengar Academy in the BlazeAzar lands where my brothers are trainers. Each time I ask my father if I can go and visit Luka and Emmet the idea is squashed really fast.

It makes me sad.

I barely know my brothers. They're so much older and when they do come back to the lair, they never seem to know how to interact with me. Mostly they're just bossy, telling me to learn my studies and be on my best behaviour. When I was much younger, they'd get grumpy when I tried to follow them around so I think that's why they keep their distance now. In my defence, I was just trying to connect.

It never worked.

I'd like to get to know them and I believe I could if I were able to visit them. I know that I'm not as strong as other Azanites and that I'd need to have some of the Drengar come with me to keep me safe but I still don't think it's fair that I'm always kept separate from everyone.

I'm fully aware of what the court thinks of me and what they say behind my back. I've heard some of them speak about how I am strange and how it's odd that my beast can't take control. I even heard one group of younger females talk about how no Azar lord would want me mating into their lairs and having their younglings. Which is fine by me!

The group saw me eventually and hurried away, probably not wanting to incite the wrath of my father's beast. They're never quiet when they talk anyway. I always hear them when I'm out in the garden.

Meryl always tells me to ignore it, which is easier said than done. She tries to distract me. My Meryl. I don't know what I'd do without her.

Running my hand along the stone wall, letting the beast under my skin feel the bumps and grooves like she likes to, I slow down when I hear raised voices coming from my father's sitting room.

'We need to understand her better, my lord.'

I stop moving.

I know that voice and the sound has every hair on my body stand on end.

'How would you like to understand my daughter better, Medir Leon?'

I can't understand my father's tone but it has my heart beat harder in my chest. They're talking about me.

Ear straining, I step as close as I can to the slightly open wooden door and pray to the Sun Gods that the males in the room don't scent me.

I can smell four males. My father. Medir Leon, who scares me more than the idea of a wraith demon. A male that smells like sand and another who seems familiar, even if I have no idea who he is.

'I say we take her to the Medir academy. Keep it quiet that she is there and we have her sleep for a time, record her dreams and see if they're actually of any use. It has been years since she has had a dream like the one she had the other night. We have only a handful that actually came true over the years. It could just be an active imagination of a small female. Yes, some of her dreams helped us to prepare for a number of wraith attacks when she was younger, however they seem to have stopped. Now, a great deal of them seem to be just nonsense. Some were even about humans being some kind of answer to a problem,' the Medir finishes and I stand with my back hard against the wall and try to control my breathing.

I feel sick. What Medir Leon has just said has my legs turn to stone. I'd run if I could get them to work.

'We need proof of these dreams. I'm not comfortable bringing her back to our academy with just your word. No offense, Lord DarkwoodsAzar,' the one that smells like sand says. He sounds old and I'm dying to sneak a peek and see who he is.

'We also have to get to the bottom of why she's having these dreams and why she can't shift yet,' the other male says and the noise that comes from the room has me quiver.

I know that beast.

'You don't need proof and you don't need to get to the bottom of anything, Master Medir Tamor. I'm not sure what I want to do. She's my daughter. I need time to think this through.'

'We came here at Medir Leon's request.' The sand male sounds offended, probably by my father's tone.

'Yes, he did.' My father growls and if I liked Medir Leon, the monster, I'd feel bad for him. Except I hate the very air that he breathes so despite my fear I smirk. Which dies when I hear a small commotion.

I react on instinct and sprint down the hall just as the door is flung open. Back pressed against the stone wall, I clap a hand over my mouth to muffle the sound of my heavy breathing. I've managed, somehow, to get around the corner.

All I can hear is the pounding of my heart in my ears so I miss what is said next. Realising that the two mystery males have left, I begin to shake uncontrollably when my father aggressively demands that Medir Leon to remembers his place.

I chance a quick glance around the corner to see them both huddled together.

'They mustn't find out about her parentage, Leon. I'll be shunned and called before the King!' My father sounds scared and I feel my heart drop to my feet.

My father is never afraid. He is the most formidable male I know. A pillar of strength and leadership. A commander. The Lord of the Darkwoods.

'I know, my lord. No one needs to find out that she's part human, but we cannot keep the dreams a secret much longer. Not after what she said the other night about the sacred text. If what she says is true, it will be stolen. She said it has—'

'I know what she said!' my father snaps, shutting the insufferable male up. Every word they speak further drains the colour from my face. I feel cold. Sick. While, I have no idea what they're speaking of, I still feel the fear of their words, like deep down, I know something momentous is going to happen. Something that I wish I could remember. An image flashes in my mind, like a memory, one of fire and sitting on a strange seat in an enclosed cage with small windows.

Dizzy, my legs lose all strength and I slide down the wall and hit the stone floor, hard. Too much runs through my mind. Words. Images. All of it has my head spinning until I hear, 'she can never find out that her mother was a human. No one can. My father secured my mating with the Lady Celina many moons ago and we still rely on her family for many things in the Darkwoods. We cannot have war with our neighbours. The Riverlands are important. All who know have a stake in this secret, including you, Leon. I'll remind you of that.' My father's threat is clear. 'Maybe I should find her a mate. A less important male of the realm. That is what I should focus on. Find a family who would turn a blind eye to her oddness in order to gain standing by mating into our family. Pretend there is a connection and then bind them. That should be our next step.'

'Maybe you're right, my lord. It happens often enough. Not many feel the mating dance anymore. But what if she says those things again after a dream, especially about the one with the humans? Even a lower family will ask questions.'

'Leave that with me. I'll begin to enquire. I will manage this situation and if I can't, we will consider sending her to the Medir academy.'

Their voices trail off as they get further away and I'm left crying, thick, painful tears on the cold hard stone. My entire life turned upside down and shattered in the space of a handful of moments.

I feel lost and confused. They want to send me to the Medir academy to be studied. To be sent to sleep for my dreams.

Fear like nothing I have ever experienced before pulses in my veins and the need to run becomes the only thought in my mind.

I'm not safe here and I never will be.

I need to leave and never, ever, return.

Chapter One

Present Day

A THUNDEROUS ROAR CONSUMES the darkness, keeping me from blacking out. Exhaustion pulls at my bones, demanding that I shut down.

I flicker in and out of consciousness, each blink is longer and harder to open my eyes from. The only thing keeping me from slipping into the darkness and welcoming it's embrace is the heat coming from the paw I'm laying on. The rain evaporates before it can hit my body.

My mate, or the male who will be when I work through my shit, holds me safely against his leathery underbelly so that I'm fully protected from the storm raging around us.

I'm soaking wet and yet, I don't feel cold. I feel his heat. His power. It pulses through my body, healing me from the ordeal of almost drowning, keeping me alive. Keeping me from that endless void trying to pull me into oblivion.

A dragon shrieks in the night and I force open my heavy lids to see the line of male Drengar flying in formation through the night sky. Something whispers in my mind that it's a formation I've seen before, dream and memory collide in my head, making it hard to focus.

Another male roars his displeasure and I shiver as the skin on my arm ripples as if the normally quiet beast is responding to the call. I can still feel her in my mind, sitting close. Closer than I've ever felt her. She saved my life only moments ago and retreated the moment she called for the male holding me protectively to his chest. I feel like I don't fit inside my own body, it's so foreign and odd. A sensation I'm beginning to remember I've felt before, as a youngling maybe. Which is weird and confusing. I'm half human and half Azanite—an abomination. I can't shift my form. A few weeks ago I couldn't even make a puff of smoke.

Everything has changed. My life has taken a turn that I could never have imagined.

Since giving up everything to save my foster brother's life, I have transferred fire to a dagger, I've protected myself with a fire ball that left the interior of a minivan charred and damaged, and I've heard my beast in my mind, telling me to give her control so that she could save my life.

A sharp noise has me push myself up on shaking arms, knowing that there's something wrong and manage to look over the edge of the dragon's 'hand' and see the ship we were sailing on being thrown around by the rolling waves.

Unsure if I'm hallucinating, I try to understand what that sound is. The relentless siren is so loud that it reaches me all the way up here.

'Wilder?' I know that he probably can't hear me and then again when his voice slips into my mind, I have no idea why I continue to doubt the power that is Drengar Wilder BlazeAzar Medir.

My future mate.

Mate.

The male who owns the other half of my soul. A male so powerful that he holds every title of the people of Azanir.

Drengar- Warrior.

Azar- Noble.

Medir- Healer.

I was so frightened of him when we first met. I couldn't even look at him longer than a few heartbeats. Now, I'm clinging to his paw, knowing that there is nowhere safer.

'Wraiths.' That voice. Nothing in this world can compare to the low timbre and the power that rushes my system every time it comes into my mind. Wraiths are the monsters that hunt my kind for their fire and life. The mention of them has me gaping in horror at the ship below, imagining all the humans down there, trying to survive against a horde of demons.

Memories of being held captive in an office in Satmark assault my mind. I watched demons tear into human flesh and if I close my eyes I can see it happening so vividly. There are no words to explain that kind of horror.

'We have to help them,' I whisper.

Fucking hell, I need to say it with my beast. It's the only way to communicate effectively and is so foreign to me that I have to remember the instructions Wilder has given me on talking in my mind. *'Wilder, we have to help them!'* I practically scream, unsure which way is up and which was is down at the moment, I'm all over the place.

'Never fear, Astgeer. You are with the Drengar. No wraith will survive this night.' His tone makes me shiver in panic and need.

I quickly look over at the two dragons on Wilder's right and watch in absolute rapture as they arch up into the sky, shrieking their battle cries and dive, headfirst toward the ship.

Chapter Two

They're beautiful. I didn't run away from Azanir, from my homeland, because of the lack of beauty.

There aren't enough words in both the human tongue and Zaric, the language of Azanir, to fully describe an Azanite beast. There are stories and movies that humans enjoy with dragons and they do an okay job of describing the lizard like body and the mighty leathery wings. I'm still convinced that some human has come back from Azanir and given this information. I think if the King of Azanir knew that the human world had details of what an Azanite looks like he'd be very enraged.

They don't have it all right though. They understood the scales of shiny steel-like skin, a smooth underbelly and the long tail, but what the humans don't seem to get right is the ends of the whip-like tail. They are covered in spikes that point out in multiple directions. As does a two horn-like appendage at the top of their heads. Those spikes follow the line of the spine all the way from the horns to the tail.

An Azanite is not a beast you can ride like some human stories like to romanticise. They're dangerous, deadly predators. Fire breathing. Razor sharp claws and teeth. Monsters like that belong in nightmares, not love stories.

Despite all of that, they are absolutely stunning to behold.

Alistair and Viktor dive at the ship, both letting fire rain on the vessel. Frightening shrieks fill the world, the sound has been part of my nightmares for as long as I can remember.

Wilder keeps us high above the battle raging between dragon and demon. I watch the smoky wraiths as they shoot towards the two males continually diving and dodging around the now burning deck.

Heart in my throat, I see three wraiths fly at Alistair and the prince beats his monstrous, leathery wings to manoeuvre himself away from the demons that slam into his body. They latch on and my nails dig into the paw under me.

'We have to help them!' I can't take it. I can't do nothing. I can hear the screams of people fighting for their life against monsters that are not fully corporal. Why aren't we down there helping?

'I will not risk you.'

I don't understand what his growly words mean until I'm practically hanging from his hand, watching in horror. 'You won't—' fuck it, I need to remember to use my beast, *'you won't go down and help because I'm with you?'* I practically shout at him in my head and give myself a headache.

'Yes,' he growls back and the annoyance and rage that sweeps over me is consuming.

I feel so helpless.

Viktor has my full attention as he sweeps past Alistair, his fire blasting the wraiths attacking our prince.

The demons on the ship are still wreaking havoc and while I can't really see the humans, I can see what appears to be guns shooting rows of fire at the horde of demons. It makes me feel a sense of pride knowing that they're fighting back. That the humans of Azanir know how to defend themselves.

It's still not enough though.

'Then drop me on deck or in the water or whatever. We can help! I know you want to. I can feel your beast. I can feel the way your paw is twitching to be part of the fight.' I'm not lying, he is practically radiating fury. I can feel his need to get involved, his beast isn't keeping quiet. Wilder is just hovering high in the storm, not doing a thing while we watch.

Felix is hanging back too and I know it's because of the little child he has safely in his grasp. It must be killing him to not get involved.

The smaller dragon roars and Wilder snaps at him in reprimand. By smaller, I mean a tiny bit in the length and wingspan to that of the black beast that holds me firmly like he is worried I'm about to jump from his paw and go fight demons like some kind of Drengar.

Something changes and my skin ripples under the electric energy in the air.

I don't know what happens to make Wilder arch back. His roar shakes my bones. Before I can process, he dives.

My stomach flies into my throat, wind whips my hair back and I grit my teeth and hold on tightly reminding myself that only moment ago, I was shouting at him to help.

'Hold on Astgeer, it's going to get hot.'

Fuck me. The moment those words come into my mind, hot is what I become. His masculine tone. His promise of death and destruction. The way his voice caught as if he's excited about the idea of killing wraiths has me forget for a moment that we are plummeting through the sky, at breakneck speed, toward a boat load of humans and wraiths.

There are so many of them. I can see the deck. I can see the humans fighting. I see the door to access the lower decks covered and secured, keeping everyone safe and I can see the mass of wraiths, shrieking their displeasure.

Wilder pivots just before we smash into the ship, his wings effortlessly manoeuvring us through the sky. Viktor is close, ducking and diving and setting the world aflame.

Even with Wilder keeping me close to his chest, safely tucked under him, I still feel the heat and the power of the fire that shoots from his throat. The force of it wipes out so many of the enemy and leaves me gaping like a fool. That's when I notice what had Wilder enter the fight.

Alistair, the prince of Azanir and the commander of this wing of Drengar is on two legs, completely naked on the deck, fighting his way through the wraiths like butter. If I wasn't so scared, I'd have time to appreciate the view. An Azanite male is taller than the average human guy. They are bulky, incredibly muscular and tanned. So deliciously tanned. However, at this point, I couldn't care less that he is naked. All I care about is why he is putting himself in such danger.

'What the fuck is he doing?' I demand. We already have enough to deal with going back to Azanir with my history, we don't need to come back without the freakin' prince. Sun Gods, we'd be fucked if he died. I'm already afraid that the king is going to kill me for being an abomination. I don't need to add on that trauma of his second son being killed. It would definitely mean my death.

'He's getting the book.' Wilder sounds about as happy I feel hearing that. *'It could be what is drawing this many wraiths.'*

Confused, I go to clarify and watch Wilder eliminate most of the demons on deck. A stream of terrifying smoky-like demons suddenly appear from beneath the turbulent ocean and climb the side of the ship. Hundreds of them appear, like a never-ending sea of death. It's probably the most terrifying thing I've ever seen and I was kidnapped, attacked and then witnessed wraiths eat people only a handful of days ago. So frankly, that's saying something.

Viktor calls a deep sound before he drops from the sky and lands on the deck in his human form. The male just shifted mid-flight, and holy Sun Gods, I've never seen anything like it.

Wilder banks and twirls, making me forget all about the males fighting naked. He dodges about ten wraiths that shoot towards us and then uses his fire to clear the path for the Drengar on deck. It doesn't even make a dent, there are just more and more coming from the ocean, no matter what Wilder does. Even Felix gets into the action, the way he flies past, clutching Roxy to his chest. I know that Wilder has sent the young human girl to sleep using his Medir powers and she is resting peacefully and safely with Felix, unaware of the dangers going on around her. But knowing all that doesn't stop the shiver of fear creeping down my spine at the thought of being forced to sleep. Not that what Wilder has done is anywhere near comparable to what happened when I was young.

Little Roxy was the reason I jumped into the ocean. I had dreamt what happened so many times and I honestly thought that it was my ending.

I know that I'm probably in for a massive 'talking to' when this damn night ends. Not just from the male who has just wiped out twenty wraiths with a flick of his tale and a blast of fire, but by the two who disappear through the doors on the ship. I'm probably going to hear it from the one he flies by, at speed, past the other side of the ship, killing a mass of demons scaling the side as well.

I feel so helpless.

'We need to do something. I need to get Roxy to her father. I don't want to risk her little life. Not after Serafina nearly died saving it.' That was not Wilder's voice and I look over to the younger male flying back around the ship, unsure why he's included me in this conversation. Maybe it's to show me how pissed he is that I dove into to the ocean because each word is like a whip.

'Once we get the book off the ship, they should follow us.' Now, that was Wilder. *'We just need to ensure safe passage for our prince.'*

I want to shout that the Drengar can defend themselves. All I can think of is the humans below deck and the ones fighting valiantly at the doors, keeping the rest safe by sacrificing themselves.

My next thought is both frightening and yet, clear as day. Only a few days ago, the Drengar told me something that helped when I was kidnapped by those fucking pricks who thought they could use me to open the sacred text of the Azanite.

I'm gonna be in so much trouble.

'Wilder, I have an idea,' I say hastily, afraid he'll catch on and stop me. *'Felix, if this works, get Roxy to safety and then we may need your help.'* I have no idea if either of them are listening and I send a final warning to Wilder to get ready. Shooting off a quick prayer to any Sun God who may be listening to 'please not let this be the worst mistake ever', I slice my hand over the closest claw and watch as the blood pools in my hand. The cut is deep. Painful.

All hell breaks loose.

Chapter Three

I'm in big shit from my future mate. His red eyes blaze as his long, lizard neck bends down so that we are face-to-face. His monstrous wings push harder and faster from the shrieking swarm of wraiths who are now flying at us. The mass is like one of the waves that had me nearly drown to death only moments ago.

'Would you stop doing things like that!' Wilder is mad.

'Well, it's working, isn't it?' I fire back and watch as the dragon narrows his eyes at me, the fire in them promising retribution before he pulls away to focus on flying us from the vulnerable on the ship. *'It's working.'*

Wilder banks left, blocking off my view of the ship.

'Don't sound too happy about it. And yes, it has. They're coming for us. All of them.' Swallowing the ball of anxiety that blocks off my airway, I've not thought this through properly. I've never been one to think before I act. I blame my foster brother for his bad influence. Van would be hooting and egging on the wraiths like he was a Drengar himself. I miss him with a furiousness that has me wishing he was here now. He'd be on my side no matter what.

Wilder veers suddenly and I fly back and whack into his paw just as a mass of white smoke zooms past. I didn't even hear the tell-tale shrieking that the demons make. The storm hasn't stopped. Lightning cracks through the sky.

'Hold on, Serafina.'

Doubt is the next thing to whack me in the face and for a moment I fear that I've placed my future mate in terrible danger. We are swarmed by wraiths and Wilder roars a sound that matches the thunder that engulfs the world. His fire follows and for a moment the night is illuminated.

I sit, gaping at the sight. Wraiths cover my view of the ocean, their mass thick and solid despite their incorporeal bodies.

Holy shit! *'Uhm…Wilder.'*

'They are off the ship and following us. The others are close. Nothing will happen to you.'

The noise that comes from my throat is completely involuntary. *'I'm not worried about my safety. I'm worried about you. I should have thought this through better.'*

Wilder's beast growls in my head. It is a sound that sets me on fire. It's halfway between a scoff and a reprimand. Very male and very frustrating.

'So, you can worry about my safety but I can't worry about yours?' I fire back, annoyed at his arrogance. Damn fool.

His laughter fills my mind. *'My mate has teeth. While I'm not happy you're bleeding mate, you did the right thing,'* he says and then spirals downwards so quickly that I lose every thought that came to mind. I scream. Not because I think we are going to plummet to our deaths into the violent ocean but because three wraiths latch on to the underside of Wilder's paw.

Their hands materialise into sharpened claws as they dig into his skin. If he feels it, he makes no show. He just keeps fighting and flying at a speed that has the rain hit me like little needles against my skin.

That isn't my main concern right now though. My attention is stuck on the wraiths now climbing higher, their mouths wide with their hollowed-out eyes locked on me. Not that I know if they have eyes or can see. I just know that they are definitely looking at me. I swear the one at the front, who doesn't seem so incorporeal anymore, is smiling.

I have nothing to defend myself with, I'm drenched to the bone and bleeding. The bastard things just keep coming, like a horror movie and not one that Van and I would've laughed over. It's like that movie with the cave and the goblin monsters and the humans who were trapped underground in the dark. They ended up attacking each other and going crazy. The idea of never seeing the sun again had my heart pounding and a pillow over my face while Van and my other foster brothers pretended to not be shitting themselves too.

Not wanting to distract Wilder, I scurry backwards on his paw and look around for some kind of answer as the wraiths crawl closer and closer. That's when the sound of wings beating furiously and the rush of wind has me whip my head to the side to protect my face. When I look back at where the wraiths are still heading straight for me, all I can see is the dragon who has flown under Wilder, the beast makes a sound that shakes my bones.

He is hanging upside down, his neck extending and then as his head gets closer, I swear it winks at me.

The wraiths shriek as if they're overjoyed at being so close, they have no idea that Felix is behind them.

Stunned, I watch as a small fireball shoots from Felix's mouth.

It will take out the wraiths and me!

Wilder closes his hand the moment Felix's fire gets to his paw and the last thing I witness is red flame before the entire world goes black.

I breath through the panic.

I can hear multiple dragons screaming their battle cries and the horrifying sounds of wraiths. Wilder isn't listening to my pleas to open his hands and my fear of distracting him has me shut my mouth, curl up against his warm paw and pray to the Sun Gods that he will be safe.

Squealing a little when Wilder moves quickly and I'm thrown sideways, I try to sit back up and get thrown again so I just stay on my side, curled up against his claws.

I wait. In the darkness, wishing I could help.

Wave after wave of pure ecstasy and pleasure ripple through my body.

There is no logic. No thoughts. Nothing. There is only my skin rubbing against hard muscle. A hard, all-consuming length buried within me. My moans are loud. My heart is pounding. I'm hot. On fire. His mouth explores my body, while his hands do the same.

I'm falling.

Running. I know that I need to keep going. That I need to run faster. They are going to get me. I'm going to die. Then I trip and I'm engulfed by smoky darkness.

Screaming for help, I hit the bitingly-cold wood floor and jump wildly to my bare feet with a small cry of pain. Trying to keep my composure, I look up and see the wooden wall open, my stomach drops. I feel like I've been here before. It's so fucking cold.

Taking a small step forward, I stop as someone steps through the door.

A sound I've never made before rips from my throat and I smash through the wood and fall forward until I'm on my back screaming in agony. Someone is speaking to me, apologising for what they have done and all I want to do is escape the fire burning me from the inside out.

Standing in a grand, golden hall, I don't care about the face-less people around me. Something bad is going to happen.

Something that I need to stop!

I gasp awake and sit up to the sun on my face and the ocean greeting me with its distinct, calming sounds.

Rubbing the sleep from my eyes, I marvel at the clear blue sky and the peace of flying.

I must have fallen asleep and feel immensely guilty when I look over at the three dragons flying beside us. Alistair. Viktor and Felix.

Alistair is a deep brown.

Felix is more of a reddish-brown and Viktor is black like Wilder but with more of a blue-like tinge.

They're all so beautiful as they fly effortlessly through the air. So grand. I take a moment just to admire the view. To take in the magnitude of the male holding me close to his chest.

They all look well despite the drama of last night. Hopefully it's the last time we have to deal with any more storms and wraiths as we continue our journey to Azanir.

I need the four days we have left to wrap my head around my next move. I have so much to consider and I'd kill for a shower and a good night's sleep.

I don't know what has the lightbulb go off in my mind but I hurry across Wilder's paw and peek down at the calm ocean and see...only water. Why are we still flying and not back on the ship?

'Uhhh...Wilder, where is the ship?'

'We are heading straight for Azanir, Astgeer.'

'Straight to Azanir? Why? It's like four days away.'

A four day flight to Azanir is long, even for an Azanite dragon. Just open sea and nowhere to stop or rest.

The next voice that comes in my head is Alistair, the second son of the King of Azanir. Alistair AzanirAzar-Drengar. Wilder must have been projecting what I'm saying to the others.

Mind connecting through your beasts is a gift only given to those who are connected in a fundamental way. I have learnt, through my time with these males, that they're bound together. I can speak to Wilder because of our mate connection, even though we haven't 'officially mated' yet. We have to have sex to form the last part of this bond. However, speaking to one another in our minds has been something he and I could do very early on.

'It is best that we try to get home as quickly as possible. Wraith attacks typically happen within days of each other. We risked too much having our sacred text, and you, on a ship full of humans in these waters.'

Hearing that wraiths attack like that has me shudder.

I lean over and study the brown dragon flying just ahead of everyone. Technically, Alistair is the commander of this wing of Drengar, however,

I know that the others protect him just as much as they all try to protect me. I can see the golden book that I blame for throwing me into this mess in the Prince's paw, which reminds me... *'Roxy?'*

'She is safe. Felix made sure of it before he left the ship. Your trick worked with getting the wraiths off the vessel and we took care of the swarm of demons, so they should be safe for the remainder of their journey.'

I slump back in Wilder's paw and take a deep breath, I didn't realise that I was holding so much tension.

No longer distracted, I remember my hand injury and smile to myself when I see it's all healed.

'Will you all be safe though? Four days is a lot of time to be flying. Wilder?' There is a pause and it does nothing for the well of anxiety that blooms in my chest. *'Wilder?'*

'Trust me, Astgeer. Don't worry about a thing.'

Chapter Four

Worry is all I do until I get so tired and weak that I can't hold my head up. We have been flying for days with nothing in sight except sky and water.

The four dragons don't stop. As the sun falls on the third day, they don't slow down. All communication has ceased, even Felix has stopped telling crude jokes.

They're exhausted. We haven't had a break in days. No food. No water and no sleep. Even I feel the pull to pass out and I'm only laying on Wilder's paw, refusing to allow him to send me to sleep. The trauma on my body after the near drowning and the lack of water and food is making it hard for me to do anything but lay still.

'Please Astgeer, allow me to send you into a healing sleep. I can't accept your suffering,' Wilder begs for the hundredth time.

I reply in the same way. *'You and the others can't rest so neither will I.'* I could do with a big glass of water though and a burger and fries. And a piece of chocolate cake.

'Please Serafina.'

'No.' I won't budge. I won't sleep while they risk their lives to get us to Azanir. *'Stop it, Wilder. Save your strength,'* I snap when I feel his healing power heat me from the inside out. I feel instantly rejuvenated and shout a

few choice words in my head so that he knows how I feel about him putting himself in more danger wasting energy on me.

He just grunts and I swear if I could, I'd set his underbelly on fire.

For hours, I lay there, humming a tune to try and chase away the rollercoaster of emotions and thoughts that plague me. These last few weeks have been full of trials and near-death experiences and I keep reliving every moment.

My eyes burn but I refuse to rest. I've never felt so disorientated in my life.

So powerless.

For ten years, I've lived in the human realm trying to find answers. Trying to find a place to belong, and while I was happy, I *didn't* find it. Yes, I found love with my foster family. Van, Scott and Brent and with my Laney, but running away fixed nothing.

Then, meeting the incredibly arrogant and pig-headed, gorgeous and protective Drengar changed my life again. I could never have imagined what would happen once I met the four males who threw me back into the world of wraith demons and dragon shifters.

This much quiet is not good.

I have to fight the tears that beg to be released and no one needs that right now.

I remember the day I ran from Azanir so vividly. I can recall every detail. Every emotion I felt sneaking through my father's lair, avoiding the warriors patrolling the grounds. I heard that I was half human and half

Azanite—an abomination. I listened to my father as he tried to work out what to do with me so that I wouldn't expose his lies and his deception. I was going to be sent away so that my dreams could be studied or given to a 'fake' mate so that I could be controlled.

A little delirious, I watch the three dragons fly and wish I wasn't a burden. Wishing I wasn't what I am.

All this leads to the next unhelpful thought bouncing around in my head. I wonder if my days are numbered with Wilder. If he will still be as devoted when he learns who I really am and that I'm keeping a massive secret from him. Wilder comes from the mighty house of the BlazeAzar. They have as much power and influence as the royals.

I can only imagine how they'll react when they find out.

I'm falling.

I'm surrounded by male heat. My body is on fire, in the best possible way. I've never felt this connected to another in all my life. It's ecstasy. It's pure happiness.

I'm falling.

Agony. I'm being ripped apart and nothing will ever be the same.

I'm falling and the world is on fire.

Screaming, I call out for Wilder but there is only destruction and death. A large figure blocks out the night sky and I watch in horror as it falls against the stone wall of the lair jutting out before me. My heart breaks in two and the agony of it has me wail into the night.

Someone grabs me and I'm spinning and then standing in a cold, swaying room screaming in rage.

This time when I fall, I know I will never wake again.

I blink awake, my mind groggy and full of nightmares. The moon shines brightly, illuminating the world. I hate myself for falling asleep.

Turning on my back, I haven't got the strength to understand what Wilder is saying. He says something about being almost there, but 'there' means nothing. I just want to sleep.

My head is pounding. The world is spinning.

The paw I'm lying on has been shaking for a while now and I whisper my worry to the male who owns my heart and get back the feeling of his power reaching into my soul and calming me instantly.

That's until I hear the tell-tale shriek of an imminent attack.

Chapter Five

The next few minutes are a blur as Wilder dips and dives.

Once again, fire fills the world. The noise of four dragons fighting and wraiths attacking is a sound that will haunt me for the rest of my days. I'd give anything not to hear it again but somewhere in my sleep deprived and delirious mind, I know that I won't be so lucky.

Trying to push myself into a seated position, I scream when Wilder banks left as if he has been injured and we plummet toward the ocean at a breakneck speed.

'Wilder!'

Frantic, I hold on tightly to his paw and shout his name again. This time out loud. My fear isn't even for me, it's for him. The idea of Wilder getting hurt makes my chest tighten.

'Hold on.' Wilder's beast is the one who responds and just before we slam into the water, the dragon spirals and pulls back.

I quickly look over at the smoky missiles that fall into the ocean.

Wilder flies high, climbing up and up and I get a good look at the battle raging around us. Viktor and Alistair are close now, their bodies between me and the demons. Felix flies around us all. His energy is infectious as he takes out wraith after wraith like he is enjoying himself, except, I can see the fatigue in his movements. In all of their movements.

The Drengar are running out of energy. The last few days have been too much and I cry out when Viktor is too slow to evade an attack, and before my eyes, is overrun by demons who eat Azanites alive.

'Viktor!' My shriek is gobbled up by the noises around me and with my heart in my throat and my poor, abused body shaking, I watch in fear as Alistair and Felix follow the blue-black dragon as he falls towards the sea. Fire engulfs the male fighting for his life. 'Viktor!'

Wilder is still lifting us higher as if he's getting me away from what is happening as fast as he can, but like the others, it's not as quick as I know he can move. They're exhausted. This is bad.

This is really, really bad.

Losing hope, I'm about to go out of my mind with anxiety when the distant sound of dragon's roaring grabs my attention.

Head snapping to the horizon, all thought leaves my mind.

'Wilder?' A new kind of fear wraps around my heart.

Coming towards us is a wing of Azanite dragons. Big males with teeth snapping and red eyes blazing. The speed in which they move is breathtaking.

Five of them descend on our battle with wings and claws and fire. They zoom past Wilder who sits just out of reach of the battle and I get the best view watching the newcomers eliminate the horde of demons.

'Sit back Serafina,' Wilder states and I do instantly.

The sight of Azanite Drengar has my heart pounding. It means we are close to Azanir and I'm not ready. Every decision I've made up until this point comes into question. I don't know what kind of reception I'm going to get.

I'm not ready.

'Wilder.' Panic takes over and while it's completely unfair to burden Wilder with more of my shit, I can't help but reach out to him for reassurance.

'You are with me, Astgeer. Nothing will hurt you while you are with me.'

Sun Gods, who says things like that and why does it have me melting into a puddle of desire and lust?

'What if...' I can't even finish what I wanted to say because one of the new Drengar flies low, his long neck craning upwards to get a good look at what is in Wilder's grasp.

I scurry backwards and hug myself so that I'm not so easily seen. The rumble of warning that comes from my future mate has every hair on my body stand on end. His paw shakes with the sound. I feel his body tense as if ready for battle again and I swallow the bile that rises in the back of my throat at the impending danger.

I'd rather face a horde of wraiths than an Azanite shifter.

The Drengar are warriors in every sense of the word. Before Wilder can fully react and I vomit all over his paw, Alistair is there in an instant, putting himself between the two dragons with a low sound in his throat that has the other one fly off to his wing.

Viktor and Felix pull in close until I'm completely out of view and I don't fight it when Wilder closes his paw a little more to keep me hidden.

We continue to fly towards a place I ran from ten years ago.

Chapter Six

I HAVE NOTHING LEFT in me.

Shivering, I can only nod when Wilder instructs me to hang on. *'We are almost there, Serafina.'*

I want to tell him that's the problem. My past has come back to haunt me during this trip and I find myself regressing into that scared adolescent that walked the walls of my father's lair all alone and isolated from the world.

I had no friends. No allies, except a small handful of humans who treated me with affection. However, even that was limited. I was an Azanite Lady, they were human servants. I find myself thinking of them now.

My maid, Meryl. The young woman who helped her with my hair and cleaning the rooms and the man who brought us food every mealtime and tasted every dish before I ate it. Meryl was the only one who spoke Zaric, as only top ranking servants or humans who hold positions of power are allowed to speak the language of the Azanites.

It's been so long since I thought about the people who treated me kindly and not like I was a pariah, like something was wrong with me.

It's sad really, I couldn't communicate with them properly and they were all paid to be there but their smiles and gestures of friendship meant so much more than any relationship I had with my 'mother' and brothers.

Then there is my father.

My memories of the Lord of the Darkwoods are all twisted in negative and positive moments. It's so freakin' confusing. I hate him and everything he did to me. The secrets and deception. The way he locked me away and forced me to sleep to steal my dreams. Yet, for so long, I tried so hard to please him. To be the perfect daughter.

A long forgotten and buried memory surfaces and I drift in and out of oblivion. I was standing on the roof of the lair, watching everyone fly in the crisp morning sky together. Massive beasts enjoying the sun and me on two legs feeling the pull to join them. A single tear slips down my cheek at the memory of what happened next.

The burning under my skin when I was younger had me constantly crying for answers and peace. My beast was always so ready to take over but never able. It would hurt so much. The need to stretch my wings and feel the wind was debilitating sometimes. I would cry and shout on the roof of the lair until my dad would come and pick me up. He would shift with me in his arms, and much like Wilder is now, he'd carry me in his paw and lift us up to join the others. It always bought me so much joy. In those moments, I felt loved.

It's what made everything else hurt so much more.

Too lost in my own mind, I barely register the massive cliff that welcomes us back. It's too dark and the never ending pull to find shelter is making my bones hurt.

Before I can clarify where we are, Wilder slows and I watch as the courtyard under us gets closer. The massive space is big enough for multiple Azanite beasts to enjoy the space. At the moment, it's quiet, only the torches of firelight illuminate the space. Night isn't a time for socialising and everyone except the Drengar on-duty would be out at this time. The lair across the courtyard is massive though and has my full attention. Whilst it is dark, it's hard to miss the extravagance and grandeur of the place. The lair could house most of Azanir. The many windows of the stone building hints to the numerous levels. The golden floor of the courtyard catches my attention and I brace myself for the moment Wilder pulls back his wings and gently steps onto land with his back legs. The others land around us.

'I'm going to place you down now Serafina and shift. It will be but a few moments and then you will be in my arms and safe.'

I nod, despite the fact that he can't see me. I find my legs unable to work as Wilder sits me down gently on the golden stone floor.

Everything hits me pretty hard the moment I'm out of his warm embrace. My eyesight is a little fuzzy, I gape at the sight of males running from within the monstrous lair towards us.

So many Drengar. I squeak an embarrassing sound when arms wrap under my body and hoist me upwards.

Wilder's scent wraps around me and I can't help but curl into his chest to bury my face into his solid body.

Voices shout. Someone demands to know what's going on and I try to hide from reality. If I don't see them, I can pretend that they're not there.

Felix, Viktor and Alistair are standing close. The prince is helping to block me from sight and I could kiss him.

'What is the meaning of all this! Alistair? You're back from the human realm. You sent no word.' That voice, my skin ripples under the sound of it. The power wakes up my silent beast and it could mean only one thing. I swallow the ball of trepidation that sneaks up my throat and threatens to choke me when Wilder bows slightly with me still tucked against his body. He wobbles a little when he does and I pull back instantly.

Damn he is gorgeous, and for a moment I forget about the volatile, dangerous situation I'm currently in. With those obsidian eyes, his chocolate skin, cut jawline, and the scar that runs down his face and over his throat, he's the most panty-soaking male I've ever laid eyes on.

For days I've spent time with the beast and now, I get the male. I see the exhaustion on his handcrafted face and try to get him to put me down.

'You can barely stand.'

I quickly look to the others and see that they're in the same state. They're practically swaying as if they may collapse at any moment.

'I'm never too exhausted to hold you, my love.'

'Sweet talking won't get you out of this. Put me down. Now! Please, I don't want to face any of these males...' I want to say that I can't appear weak even though I think I might pass out at any moment, but I lose my words. I need strength right now and as if he reads my mind, Wilder places me on my feet, all be it reluctantly. He keeps me close though. I don't fight it, if he let me go, I'd topple right over.

'What has happened? And who are you trying to hide with your scent, Wilder BlazeAzar? That smells like an Azanite female! What is happening!'

My entire body freezes as I become the centre of attention and I get a good look at the crowd of warriors in the courtyard.

Wilder growls protectively, his beast in his eyes as they turn red and for some reason I know, deep down, that he's responding to my instinct to fight or run the fuck away.

Shit.

Chapter Seven

'Sire, we found the prince and his wing not far offshore, they were under attack from a horde of wraiths,' someone says. The voice sparks a memory but I have no energy to follow it in my mind. The edges of my vison are darkening. 'I haven't been able to identify the female Wilder BlazeAzar is holding. He was carrying her over the seas.'

'Over the seas?' The King repeats as if it's the most absurd thing he has ever heard and I don't blame him.

I finally get a good look at the male who rules over the shifters and humans of Azanir. He is an older version of Alistair. The same pale blue eyes and tanned complexion. Alistair's jaw is a little more defined and his hair is much darker though.

Azanites age very slowly and live longer lives than humans so while the kings hair has streaks of grey it doesn't give away how old the male actually is. The King is huge though, as big as every other Drengar here. Muscle heavy arms. Taller than the average human.

It hits me that here I'm not going to be looked at as some kind of freaky tall chick like I was back in the human realm. The amount of comments I got for my height bordered on bullying in my neighbourhood. But here in Azanir, I'm shorter than even the average female, thanks to my half-human parentage.

The King has kind eyes though and he looks to his son with concern and relief that he is back. It makes my chest ache. They're all wearing the leathers of the Drengar, even the King.

'I found it very strange too, my king,' the familiar voice states.

There's a great deal of testosterone in this courtyard and I wish Van was with me so bad right now. My foster brother would know what to say to break the tension. He'd make some wise-arse remark on the sausage party happening right now to make me laugh.

I miss him so much. I miss Brent and Scott, and my Laney. I will regret the way I left them for the remainder of my days.

Another guttery growl from the male holding me securely under his arm, draws me from my wayward thoughts. *I'm about to rip his throat out, Alistair.* I don't know why Wilder is including me in his conversation and by the way Felix grins, I can tell that he is speaking to us all.

'Thank you, Drengar Darkwoods. We will tell our own story,' Alistair barks to the male who was speaking to the King.

His words hit me so hard, I swear I stop breathing as I finally pay enough attention to the male who was talking.

Holy. Fucking. Shit.

Emmet.

My gasp is involuntary and every male standing in the courtyard looks sharply over at me.

Drengar Darkwoods.

I find myself staring at my brother with so many emotions that I nearly whimper.

How did I not recognise him, Emmet hasn't changed much since I last saw him and that was nearly a year before I ran away. I didn't have much of a relationship with my siblings. My 'mother' always kept me separate from them as if my half human status was infectious.

I never understood why she hated me until I heard the conversation between my father and his advisers. I wasn't her child. She made my life so hard, as if it was my fault that my father was unfaithful, something I can't wrap my head around now that I've met Wilder. We haven't even secured our bond yet and I could never imagine being with anyone but him. It brings back memories of what I heard in that conversation between my father and that damn arsehole of a Medir who influenced and worked with him to keep me asleep. They were discussing 'finding' me a mate, someone they could manipulate and control. The questions that invade my mind around this makes my head ache. Can you fake a mating? Is that how my father cheated?

I haven't even been back here for a few minutes and already I wish I could run back to the human realm.

Emmet.

My brothers are much older than I am so they were off training in the Drengar academy for most of my childhood. Luka is fourteen years older than I am and the gap between Emmet and I is sixteen years.

His green eyes narrow in my direction and I want to avert my gaze but can't.

He doesn't recognise me.

I remember as a youngling that I used to wish for his eyes. Eyes like our—

his— mother. Both he and Luka got the green eyes. I inherited the grey, dove wing colour of my father. I really wanted to be like the boys, I wanted to be like my 'mother'. It was another thing that set me apart from them.

'Father,' Alistair states, breaking the spell Emmet has over me and I'm finally able to look away. 'We'll answer all of your questions, but right now my wing and I are in need of rest and respite. It has been a long and arduous journey to get home, including two battles with the demons of the night. And,' Alistair begins to unfold the cloth covering our sacred book, his demeanour is completely different to the male I met in the human realm.

Viktor and Felix don't say a word. Alistair isn't their companion and commander here, he is their prince. Everything has changed.

The entire energy in the courtyard changes when the covering falls away and the golden text is revealed. 'We found it, Sire. We found the stolen book of Azanir.'

Voices fill the night, the King steps forward to embrace his son and honestly I didn't know a father like the scary looking King of Azanir would be so openly affectionate. 'You did well, son. All of you did. We are indebted to you all.'

I can finally breath now that I'm not the centre of attention and relax a little beside Wilder. Until I hear, 'Serafina?' Emmet's tone is sharp, like he just worked it out and blurted my name.

My stomach hits my feet and I slowly look over at Emmet once more and see the shock and confusion on his face.

'Hey Emmet.'

Chapter Eight

Fucking hell.

Hey Emmet.

What a complete and utter fuckwit. You'd think I'd have something profound to say. I haven't seen him in eleven years and all I can come up with is, *hey Emmet*. I don't think I've ever said hey to him in my entire life. Our greetings were forced bows and weird, awkward conversations on the weather and my studies.

Again, everything goes quiet and I'm the centre of attention.

'But you...what...we lost you,' Emmet says the last part so quietly that I almost miss it. He takes a single step towards me.

Wilder loses it. He pulls me firmly behind him and for a moment all I can see is his, Felix, Viktor and Alistair's backs. They all moved so fast that I'm surprised I don't have fucking whiplash.

'Step aside, Wilder BlazeAzar. That is my sister and you have no right to step between her and I!' Emmet shouts, he leaves out a few of Wilder's titles on purpose, I'm sure of it.

I'm beginning to think that these two don't like each other very much. That should be fun. My brother. My future mate. All one big happy fucking family.

Sun Gods.

The tension in this courtyard is so thick I can barely draw enough air into my lungs. I manage to see everything through the gaps of the thick bodies of the Drengar.

'You will not approach my mate, Emmet Darkwoods.' The way Wilder speaks has a different note to it, like an echo, and by the way every male in the courtyard flinches I can only imagine it's because he has just projected his words into all of their minds.

The power of my future mate stuns me and my jaw hits the stone floor. I didn't know anyone could do that.

'Mate?' Bewildered is an understatement to the tone in Emmet's voice.

'Lady Serafina DarkwoodsAzar is under my protection,' Alistair states in his princely voice, and again everything goes silent.

I can't take much more of this. I need to sleep. I need to go inside and get out of the darkness. My skin is crawling.

Feeling a little exposed and raw, I check to see if anyone is behind me. I study the wall that separates the courtyard to the massive fall down the cliff the King's lair is built upon.

The capital city of Azanir, Katthwaite, sits on the top of the flat mountain of Kattikate. The cliff overlooks the vast ocean that separates Azanir from the human realm. The mountain sticks out over the water like a giant blade, a warning of the power of the Azanites. The lair of the King of Azanir and the other Azar, who call the capital home, sits on the top layers of the mountain.

The city runs down the side of the mountain. I've always wanted to see it and now that I'm here I wish I was anywhere else.

'She does not smell like you, Wilder,' Emmet persists, not caring what his prince has just said and I think I'm about to hyperventilate. 'Step aside, now! As the ranking member of the house of the Darkwoods, I demand that you move away from a female of my house. She is an unbound female of the Darkwoods and is under my protection. Not yours. That is the law of our people, Prince Alistair. Sire, I demand that Wilder BlazeAzar and his wing step aside, now!'

It's like hearing my father. Emmet has truly turned into the arsehole. He hasn't said hello back or seemed at all concerned that he hasn't seen me in eleven years. All he wants is to throw his power around and reclaim a female of his house. Such an Azar thing to do.

'Alistair, I think this needs to be explained now,' King Oswald states, all friendliness long gone. The book seems to be forgotten and I have an overwhelming need to pipe up and remind them that the book they were all so worried about is safely home. That we should be talking about that, not me.

'Your Majesty,' Alistair states, 'Our story is long. Lady Serafina was a catalyst in us retrieving our sacred text and ensuring the safety of my wing on our journey. For that, I have offered her the protection of my name and our house. I really must insist that we head inside. The Lady Darkwoods needs to be taken care of and while their mating has not been consummated, Lord Wilder BlazeAzar and Lady Serafina are within the mating dance. He cannot step aside and hand her over to the house of the Darkwoods, his beast will not allow it. I will not allow it. It'll do more damage to the Lady and we all don't want that. We owe her everything, and Azanir should show her the respect she deserves—'

'Sire!' Emmet says forcibly, cutting Alistair off. The King of Azanir sets his gaze on me and I feel like I'm about two feet tall.

'You'll remember your place, Lord Emmett DarkwoodsAzar.' Alistair is all formal and serious. 'I'm speaking, and I'm your prince. My word is as binding as my fathers.'

Holy fuck! Is it bad that I think I fall a little in love with Alistair?

I want to shout, 'you tell him Al', but keep my mouth shut and try desperately to not look so smug.

Wilder throws me a small glare over his shoulder that has me bite my lip to keep from smiling. The big, gorgeous male winks before turning around and all thoughts of Alistair leave my mind to be replaced with dirty thoughts of Wilder and how his thick, muscle heavy body would feel on top of mine.

Emmet looks as if he's swallowed a lemon. I probably should feel bad, he is my brother after all, but I barely know him and he's acting like a real dick.

'I will not—' he begins and swiftly shuts his mouth when the king says, 'I don't think this is the time. The prince is right, the female needs to get inside. We can all smell her exhaustion. I will send messengers to the corners of the kingdom. We will assemble tomorrow to hear this tale.'

My gaze is fixated on the big, furious, red faced male glaring at Wilder like he is a wraith demon. Emmet opens and closes his mouth a few times, obviously weighing the pros and cons of arguing with the king and then shuts it firmly. He looks like his mother. It's fucking terrifying.

Throwing an intense look his shoulder, Emmet nods to the three males of his wing. The group turn and walk away without a word. They shift at the end of the courtyard and I watch as the four dragons fly into the night.

A deep sense of dread washes over me as I watch him go.

I'm so tired.

The King's mighty sigh is what draws my attention back on the males around me. 'Looks like we will be receiving an audience from the Lord of the Darkwoods first thing in the morning.'

If I didn't know any better, I'd say he doesn't sound too excited at the prospect of my father coming here. It says a lot.

If I wasn't so mind fucking-ly numb, I'd probably fall to my knees and scream and cry that I want to go home.

All of that slips away though when Wilder's hand reaches behind his back to grip mine. He takes it into his calloused embrace and I feel instantly calmer. Secure.

'Let's get inside,' the King states and when I look up at him, I discover that he's staring. 'I feel I need to be sitting when I hear this story. Take the Lady to the guest suites and meet me in the meeting rooms.'

Stunned that the king doesn't seem to care that the four Drengar are swaying from exhaustion, I go to tell him that they need to rest but am stopped when Widler grabs my hand and Alistair bows and says, 'certainly, Your Highness. The Lady will stay in my quarters with us for now, so that she is comfortable and not too far from Lord Drengar Wilder.'

King Oswald gives a gesture like he is happy for us to do what we want before he throws me one last questioning look and walks back toward the lair. The row of warriors follow swiftly behind.

'Well, that went well,' Felix states like a true smartarse and if I wasn't sick with anxiety, I probably would've laughed.

Shit is about to hit the fan and I now for a fact I'm not going to be able to dodge it.

Chapter Nine

'You can't be serious!'

Shuffling from one foot to the other, I watch the four males have an argument while trying not to vomit on Alistair's pristine floors.

'When am I ever not serious, Felix?' Viktor snaps back and the poor human servants who were fussing around the rooms quickly scurry away at the tone of the scary males voice. I don't blame them and half wish that I could scurry the fuck away too.

Watching them leave has me contemplating how far I'll get if I follow.

'This is so typical,' the poor male declares. He isn't happy that they've told him to stay with me in Alistair's rooms while they go and speak to the king to debrief him on what happened.

'I'm not leaving her alone up here and you shouldn't want her to be, Felix!' the prince states calmly, he's moving around the quarters, taking off his weapons and placing them in a cabinet against the left wall. Wilder is close, he is doing the same as he places his on top of a table between two closed doors to my right. Viktor is with him, they all look tired.

Felix is pacing the large living space we're standing in. When we first walked in here I was stunned to see the architecture and design. The males took me to the very far section of the lair. We went up multiple steps and down countless hallways until two big double doors were opened and I was led into this sitting room. It's unsurprising that the prince has such lavish quarters but I seem to have forgotten how extravagant everything is here in Azanir.

I feel awkward standing in the middle of the open room, with richly upholstered chairs and couches scattered around a deep mahogany table, watching them all speak about me like I'm not here. The energy is tense and the way Felix is speaking has me wrap my arms around my middle.

He's angry about staying here with me. It kinda hurts my feelings.

Wilder drops a dagger onto the table loudly and Felix shuts his mouth. I watch the mighty male finish what he is doing and then turn and walk toward me, his eyes fixed on the younger male across the room. They never drop. Felix shuts his mouth and scowls and I can only imagine what my future mate has just said.

'I'll be fine here on my own...' I begin to tell the group, lying through my teeth. The idea of Wilder and the others leaving me here, despite knowing we are safe, is making my stomach churn.

Wilder draws his attention from Felix and fixes those black eyes on me, they're soft and full of things not spoken between us yet. *'Felix will stay with you, Astgeer.'*

'If he doesn't want to—'

'He does, don't you Drengar Felix?'

I peek over at the younger male who wraps his arms around his chest and nods once. I'm not convinced and I'm sure Wilder isn't either because he makes a noise in the back of his throat that has every hair on my body stand on end. Felix just rolls his eyes and slumps down in one of the armchairs.

'We won't be long, we will go and speak to the king and then be right up. Try to rest, Felix will show you to my room and you can sleep. Food has been sent for.'

'Your room?' I question, unable to keep the way my brow rises at what he has just said. Wilder just gifts me one of those male arrogant smiles before he kisses my forehead and goes to leave.

'We'll be back,' Alistair announces before throwing Felix a warning look that I'm glad I'm not on the receiving end of.

All three males head to the doors and I quickly turn and say, 'what are you going to tell him...about me?'

The trio share a look and I'm left biting my lip in worry.

'We are going to tell him the truth, Serafina.'

Sun Gods, I don't think my poor heart can take much more. Telling the truth doesn't come naturally. In all honesty, it terrifies the shit out of me. I've learnt from such a young age to keep my secrets after everything I've experienced. Memories flood my mind and with them comes a wave of panic. I remember the conversation where my father was advised to send me away to the Medir academy. If the King finds out about my dreams I will be sent away, to be forced to sleep.

'*Astgeer?*'

Blinking up at the male staring down at me, I realise that everyone is waiting for me to answer. My fight or flight reflex is on overdrive. 'I don't want to be locked away,' I blurt out.

There's a heartbeat of silence as my words settle amongst those in the room.

Wilder holds my attention. He takes a single step towards me, his gaze is intense and heated. *'Do you think I would allow anyone to do that to you?'*

Shaking my head, I *do* know deep down that Wilder will protect me but years of conditioning and trauma can't be overridden by a few sweet, simple words. *'They said they'd take me to the Medir academy to be studied and...'*

Four male Drengar growl in unison which confuses me deeply. They shouldn't have been able to hear me, I'm not strong enough to connect with them all to be able to speak directly to them, am I?

Chapter Ten

I sit across from Felix, watching the handful of humans who move swiftly and efficiently in and around the sitting room. They leave trays of food on the mahogany table. Two women pour tea and lay out plates, all without looking directly at me.

One elderly male with grey hair and black trousers and a red tunic stands near the door, he's the only one who addresses Felix in Zaric. He too doesn't look in my direction. I'm a Lady of Azanir. I'm off limits.

Untouchable.

It infuriates me and my knee bounces rapidly as the minutes tick by. Felix doesn't even acknowledge the humans, he only nodded once to the older man's question if we wanted our food. All he's been doing is tracing the same pattern on the armchair over and over, his brow furrowed and his energy hostile.

The poor women who are setting a feast on the table keep glancing at each other. They wear black loose flowing pants and a shirt that buttons up the front with gold buttons. Not dissimilar to the uniform worn by the humans in the Darkwoods. My maid, Meryl, wore a deep brown tunic every day while she worked. I asked her once, in my naivety, why she didn't change. I think it was when I was being dressed for some event I was excited to be attending. I couldn't understand why she couldn't put on one of the many shawls or use the fabrics the human dressmakers would bring to my rooms on those random occasions. I used to watch her admire the different silks and leathers. All she ever wore was that brown tunic, like every other human that worked in the lair. I remember the way she smiled fondly at me and told me to keep my innocence. I had no idea what she meant until later in life when all that 'innocence' was drained out of me by nightmares and tra uma.

Now I know she had no identity working under Azanites. Everyone wore the same thing. Just a body doing a job. Not a face. Not a living, breathing individual.

Many years later as I laid under a mountain of blankets on my bed at Laney's, I shed a tear for the woman that raised me. A woman who meant so much to me. Someone I didn't know very well. I was a job for her. On those rare days off, she left to go 'home' and I never asked where that was or who was waiting for her when she did. I realise that having a role in the lair of the DarkwoodsAzar would've been a privileged position, but I wonder if I meant as much to her as she did to me. I wouldn't blame her if I didn't, I was the rich, whinging lady of the house.

Watching the human women working now makes me sad. I hate that they look so similar. That they keep glancing at Felix then quickly look away in case they get caught. I know what they're both thinking. Felix is exceptionally handsome, his dark blonde hair curls around his face and accentuates his masculine cheekbones and jawline.

I wonder if their shared anxious frowns have anything to do with them feeling the energy radiating off him right now. I know I sure can feel it.

Felix is pissed, with a capital P, and I'm beginning to believe that it's not just about being left out of the meeting with the king. It's like he wants to speak his mind and get something off his chest.

'Felix,' I state, afraid of his response and yet needing to ask him what is wrong. I wait until he faces me. Those blue eyes fall to my face and I kinda regret speaking. 'Are you angry with me?'

The Drengar cocks his head a little as if listening or remembering something before he sighs and replies with a curt, 'yes.'

Fuck! That hurts.

I open and close my mouth, unsure how to respond. The old butler bows just as I find something to say and informs Felix that he only needs to ring down for anything he might need. Not what 'we' might need. *He* might need. It's what I was dreading by coming back here. Becoming invisible. Powerless.

However, right now all I care about is Felix.

The humans depart silently, leaving us alone. The brooding male says nothing more and I don't really know what I should do. I know I need to fix this. Felix is my friend. He was the only one in the beginning to show me any kindness and his companionship has become truly important to me. The idea of him being angry at me has my appetite evaporate and my tired eyes heavier. I can't think of what I've done wrong.

'Felix...I—'

'What you did by jumping off that ship was reckless, Raff.' He cuts me off and I sit stunned at his harsh tone. 'The events of the last few days were all because of the decision you made to jump off the ship, during a storm, into the ocean and putting yourself in danger.'

Fuck! He's angry.

Gobsmacked, I watch him excuse himself and stomp through the room. He disappears behind one of the many doors.

I know what I did was reckless but I never expected to survive the ocean. I dreamt that it was the way I was going to die. I was okay with it even as I floated in the darkness, not knowing which way was up or down. For Roxy, for that small little child, I would've gladly given my life.

I guess, I didn't truly think of my actions and what that would mean to the males that are now so important to me. I admit that I didn't think of Felix and how that would affect him. I grieved Wilder in that water but I never really thought of how my actions spiralled into the four day ordeal that ended with us now in this situation. Exhausted. Starving. Unprepared for what has happened tonight.

I'm not an idiot. I know that Emmet is flying to the Darkwoods to tell my father that I've been found. I know that they're going to come here and demand that I go with them. I also know that I won't have much of a choice when the time comes. The only option I have is to complete the mating dance with Wilder and consummate our union. While the idea of him and I finally having sex, to do it for the wrong reason is like a bucket of water over my arousal.

The events of the last few days come crashing down on me and I curl up in the chair, just wanting to disappear. I feel as if my world is spinning out of control and there is nothing I can do to stop it. I just saw my brother for the first time in eleven years.

I've returned to Azanir and already I feel small and not in control.

Chapter Eleven

The butler comes into the apartment for the third time. I haven't moved from my position, all curled up in the armchair feeling sorry for myself. The first time he walked into the room, he stopped short at the sight of me alone, without a male around, and quickly bowed and hurried out.

The second time, he didn't leave as fast, instead he bowed, didn't step into the room, eyed the mountain of food on the table that I haven't touched despite how amazing it smells, frowned deeply, opened his mouth twice and then left.

Now, I found myself smiling against the knee I'm hugging when he appears at the door once more. The poor man appears to be surprised once again that I'm still on my own, in the exact same position, and then his focus lands on the food.

I watch as he battles with himself to figure out what to do. He seems to decide that speaking to me is worth the risk. 'My Lady, is there something else you'd like to eat that I can bring up for you?' he says in perfect Zaric.

My heart sinks into my butt. I didn't consider that was the problem until I look over at the food still piled high on the table. I should have put the poor guy out of his misery when he first came in but I didn't want to get him into trouble or make him uncomfortable by speaking to him.

'There's nothing wrong with the food, I'm just waiting for my friends to come back before I eat.' I'm not. The idea of eating right now has me want to throw up, but I lived in this world long enough to know that the sight of untouched food in front of an Azanir would be an insult to the cooks of the castle.

One time, when I was young, my 'mother' hated the food at dinner. It was a rare occasion where I was allowed to sit at the table with them. It was only our family at the time so really it shouldn't have been a big deal. However, everything is a big deal when it came to that evil beast. She made a massive scene and had the two human cooks come up to the dining rooms and apologise to the lord of the lair. She berated them and told them to pack their things. Even in my youth I remember thinking how dramatic the whole thing was. Now as an adult who understands the high paying and privileged position that they lost would've been a massive blow to them and their families, I see the entire situation differently.

With that in mind, I emphasise that I'm just waiting for the others to come back before eating.

The butler nods once, clearly uncomfortable, and just before I think he's going to back up and leave me here alone again, he flicks his gaze to the door Felix disappeared behind and asks, 'is there anything I can get you, Lady? Some fresh clothes maybe? I can send up a few maids to assist with a bath, if you'd like?'

The offer takes me off guard and I find myself biting my now wobbling lip, feeling the back of my eyes burn with emotion. It's been a long couple of days and I finally uncurl myself and look down at the mess that is my outfit. The idea of a bath is almost enough to have the tears spill down my face. I know I probably stink and my skin feels all weird after the ocean and then being out in the elements for four days.

'Actually, I'm fine to bath without a maid, if you could point me in the direction of the bathing room or one of the rooms that I can use, I can get clean myself.' This is half the reason why I'm just sitting here. I don't know what is behind the various doors and I don't have the energy to deal with any kind of mistake I might make by entering any of Alistair's private rooms. Azanites are weird with their stuff. We love to nest and horde and keep our things in a certain way. Possessive would be the right word.

Butler guy takes a moment before answering. I think I've confused him with my response. 'Lady, I haven't confirmed which room you'll be using with his Lord Drengar Alistair.' The poor guy looks torn between wanting to help and not wanting to get in trouble with the prince.

'Right. That's okay, I'll figure it out.' I hate how small my voice sounds. How unlike myself I feel.

The human bows excessively as he steps from the room. That's going to get old very quickly. I forgot how much everyone bowed all the time.

Sighing heavily, I realise that I need to get up off this damn seat and start working out what I'm going to do.

Take control.

Yes! I'm going to work out a plan and not sit around waiting to hear what's going to happen to me when the others get back. That's not who am and I won't let this place change me! I refuse!

Stomping around the large room, adamant that nothing will stop me from being myself, I give myself the best talking-to.

I will find the bathing room myself. I don't need any help!

Ten minutes later, I stand back in the sitting room with my arms around my chest, grumpy that I wasn't able to find the room I was looking for.

I peeked through a few doors before my bravado waned and gave up in case I did something wrong. I found a huge dining room with an open balcony behind glass screens that made me quickly shut the door because of the sight of the heavy darkness. Damn beast under my skin controlled my reaction to that.

One was Viktors room, I know because it smells like him. I quickly shut that door.

The other was some weird weapons rooms that gave me the creeps. That's when I gave up. I made a point of ignoring the door Felix went through. I've decided that I'm angry at him too now. For leaving me out here and for not showing me around and…for being angry at me!

Huffing and puffing with no way to release my frustration, my foot starts tapping on the stone floor and I know I'm being petulant. It's hard not to be. Deflated, I'm about to slump back into the armchair when Wilder's voice creeps into my mind, soothing all the aches and fears.

'Astgeer, what's wrong?'

Chapter Twelve

'*Nothing,*' I reply easily in my mind now. I don't have to focus as much anymore on using our connection to converse.

'*It's not nothing, I'm trying to focus on this very mundane conversation about sacred text and the fate of our race and how I will not help in any way, meaning my family will not help, without the guarantee of your safety. Yet all I can focus on is your emotions.*'

Smiling to myself despite everything he has just said, and how serious the conversation he is having with the king sounds, I sit down heavily and look around. I should be looking for the exits, not wondering how much longer he will be.

Damn, I've got it bad.

'*I was looking for a bathing room and I don't know where to go and the corridor is pretty dark,*' I confess. I feel the need to beat myself up for how pathetic that sounded.

'*Where is Felix? He can show you to my rooms.*'

'*He...*' I hesitate, not wanting Wilder to get involved. I don't want to see Felix right now which is what will happen if Wilder starts having a go at him.

'*He went to freshen up and I don't want to disturb him,*' I reply instead.

Wilder's response is a small growl that I can't really decipher.

'Why do you have rooms here too?' I didn't scent him behind any of the doors I've checked out and glance down the creepy corridor. I bet its down there.

'You're in Alistair's wing of the lair. We all claimed rooms when we became a wing. I typically head home when we come back. I don't stay in the capital. My family usually insist that I head back to our lands. I still have a place here in case it's needed.'

The mention of his family brings up some pretty strong emotions that I really don't have the energy for right now. The thought of meeting the BlazeAzar's freaks me out just as much as the idea of seeing my dad again does.

They're going to hate me when they find out I'm half-human.

'Astgeer, you're thinking too loud again.'

Pushed out of my raging thoughts, I quickly ask, *'did you hear what I was thinking about? Can you read minds?'* Fuck, that's all I need.

'No, my heart. I can only feel your emotions. I have told you I can't read your mind. You are anxious.'

'Right.' I don't believe him. He does that a lot. *'Why do you not work for your family. The BlazeAzar's would have one of the biggest Drengar armies in Azanir, wouldn't they?'*

'Yes, we do. I have four brothers, Serafina. Two command my father's army. One is a leader in the Drengar Academy and I travelled a great deal when it became obvious that I was a Medir. I spent time in my youth around Azanir in the many academies to learn my power. I was sent by our king to the human realm on a mission seven years ago with Alistair and Viktor. He had requested that all the council lords send a handful of Drengar to him for

this and my family chose me. Viktor and Alistair were picked by the King. It is there that we bonded. Our beasts had formed a wing and it was no question that I joined the armies of the King. Alistair is the prince, he had no choice. We met Felix two years later.'

His words conjure images in my head of the four warriors becoming friends on a mission. I'm a little envious of it.

Wilder goes quiet for a few minutes and in that time I'm reminded of the darkness and that he is actually speaking to the king right now about my fate. It has my gut churn with worry.

'Everything is going to be fine, my heart.' Wilder's voice seeps through my mind.

'Fine? You're with the King of Azanir discussing some pretty serious stuff, Wilder. My brother, who I haven't seen in ten years, is right now racing back to the Darkwoods to tell my father that I have returned.'

'See, nothing to worry about. All things we can handle.' He's teasing me and I chuckle. Rubbing at my face, it's unbelievable how his voice alone can make me feel so calm and content. Heat blooms in my chest and I wish he were here next to me so badly that my bones ache.

'Head down the hall to the room at the very end.'

I groan. Of course it's down the scary hall.

Wilder laughs lightly in my head. *'What's the problem with where my room is located?'*

'It's dark,' I confess. Fuck, I'm pathetic.

'I'll stay with you and you said Felix is only in his rooms freshening up. You're in the lair of the king. There are more Drengar here than in any other place in Azanir. Well, all except maybe the lands of the BlazeAzar. You are safe.'

'I know that, logically,' I say, slowly heading down the dark hall. The walls have been plastered like you'd find in a human home.

The Darkwoods lair is all exposed stone on the floors and walls. It's cold and uninviting. A complete contrast to the king's lair. The walls here are white. The roof is high and the stone floors are a beautiful grey. There are fire torches along the walls and if I was strong enough, I'd be able to turn them on with my beast. All she is doing is rolling under my skin.

She hates the dark. It makes me feel all itchy. Why is this hall so long!

'Tell me what you're all talking about,' I whisper in my mind as if the darkness can hear me.

'Alistair is now telling the king about the night we found you and the book in the office at that pathetic human town they call a city.'

'You mean the city of Satmark?' I chuckle, such a typical Azanite male response. The city of Satmark is a very popular and very large human city. It's where we found the sacred text. Well, it's where the human rebels that kidnapped me took me to in order to use my blood to open the book. They believed that it would be the answer to how they can possess the power of the Azanite beasts, like somehow the book will tell them how to become a dragon shifter. After the vision, thanks to that golden book, I'm beginning to think maybe they were right. Or at least onto something.

That's not an excuse for what they did.

They tortured me. They hurt me. My best friend, Miles...he betrayed me. All for a theory.

'Yes, that cursed place where they took you. Now, Alistair is explaining the role that you played in drawing the wraiths to the humans, which ultimately helped us find you. This is making me angry.'

'Why?' I smile and take note of all the rooms I pass which drops when his growl fills my head. *'What happened?'*

'I'm just being reminded of how those pathetic humans touched you. How they hurt you. It's reminding me of what happened.'

Why does his rage turn me on? Sun Gods, I have fucking issues. At least his voice has distracted me from the darkness in the hall. My beast isn't so afraid.

'Now, I'm telling them all what will happen if they push me when it comes to you.'

'That doesn't sound good.' I chuckle, those poor males are probably getting Wilder's rage as they discuss my future or something equally annoying. *'I won't go back to my father, Wilder. I will run again,'* I warn and smile again when he growls roughly in my head. I don't know if it's because I've said I will run or if he understands that I'm not joking.

Finally at the end of the hall, I push open the door slowly and shake my head. How I didn't scent Wilder from across the corridor is baffling because when I step into the room his scent engulfs me. Wilder is wild, masculine and full of fire and power. It has my skin heat and my body crave him.

'You found my rooms,' he says and I swear there is a hint of smugness in it like he knows exactly what is happening within my body right now.

Glaring, knowing full well that he can't see me, I inform him that I don't need his help anymore and that I'll be taking a bath on my own, without him in my head. His deep timbre laughter fills my mind and has me shudder.

Then he is gone and I'm left staring at the monstrous round bed in the middle of the room. Thick curtains block out the night to my right, multiple fur rugs lay on the stone floor, one before a gigantic fireplace that I'm sure when lit is a marvel to be seen. It's mostly for show, Azanites don't really feel the cold, they have fire in their blood. Except me, I feel it and I'm kinda grateful for the sight, even if, when I step into the room, I have no idea how to start it. A problem I wouldn't have if I was fully Azanite.

The place is cold and I wrap my arms around my body and try not to let the darkness of the room overwhelm me. I want to run and jump on the bed and use the mountain of pillows to build myself a little nest and snuggle up in the softness, but I smell.

It's a real battle. Sleep and comfort or searching around in the dark for another fucking door. What has my life come to?

Chapter Thirteen

'Lady?'

My squeal of fright bounces off the wall as I spin, gripping my now pounding heart and come face-to-face with the butler and three women, all dressed in black. A look of pure fear cross their faces and each fall to their knees and press their heads to the hard floor.

'Serafina! What is it?' Wilder's voice shakes every bone in my body as he shouts in my head. I swear the entire lair vibrates with his rage.

Felix is at the door, looking like some kind of Sun God. He hasn't got a shirt on and the fire in his eyes is enough to send anyone to an early grave.

'What is it!' Felix shouts, his long sword in his hand, scanning the darkness for whatever he thought he'd find in here, probably a wraith demon.

The humans tremble against the stone, the butler starts apologising profusely for frightening me. 'Please forgive us, lady.'

Opening my mouth with the intent of asking them to get up, I'm stopped when Wilder bursts through the door, his massive size and violent energy making the four humans on the floor whimper. Viktor and Alistair are close behind him and the drama of the entire situation has me cross my arms.

Wilder stomps over to me, his eyes roaming over my body and I feel his power against my skin as if he is scanning me for injuries.

I forget for a moment what my name is and that we have an audience until he is before me, towering over my smaller frame, his black eyes boring into mine. *'Are you all right?'*

'Yes. *They just scared me is all, I didn't hear them behind me.*'

Wilder turns his gaze slowly over to the cowering humans like he has just realised that they are there. It rubs me the wrong way and I push past him to bend down and touch the shoulder of the kind butler.

He flinches and I quickly snatch my hand back not wanting to touch anyone that doesn't like it. 'I'm sorry, please get up.'

'We didn't mean to upset the lady,' he says again to the floor and I'm overcome with a wave of emotion that almost chokes me. Their behaviour disturbs me on so many levels. The butler's eyes have raised from the floor and yet, he isn't looking at me.

'I know you didn't, please get up,' I say a little more forcibly with the hope that they will listen.

'Forgive us, my lord.'

That's when I realise that he's looking between Wilder and Alistair as if he is unsure who I 'belong to'.

A noise I don't normally make rumbles deep in my chest, tickling the back of my throat. Every eye in the room falls to me and I snap my mouth shut, expecting steam to puff from my nose. Pissed off, for multiple reasons, I rise and again wrap my arms around my chest in outrage.

'We understand. Leave us, I'll summon you when the lady is ready for attendants.' It's Alistair who responds and it's Alistair the butler stands for.

The women just follow, having no idea what has been said as everything was spoken in Zaric.

Huffing, I stomp over to the bed and sit down on the edge, refusing to look at anyone.

What the fuck just happened!

There's a heartbeat of tense silence as I stare at the wall, refusing to acknowledge anyone.

'We'll leave you to it. There is food out here. I'll get the servants to bring some in,' the prince says, indicating for Viktor and Felix to leave. 'We will talk later. We need to eat and sleep because everything's going to get a great deal more interesting tomorrow.'

Wilder nods and I refuse to allow Alistair's words to pull me from my anger, even though I really want to ask what he means.

Right now though, I would love to start shouting and yelling about what has just happened.

Wilder turns, not addressing me, and blows a big puff of fire into the fireplace. The flames roar to life and the instant crackle of wood helps, in a weird way, to calm me a little.

The heat chases the cold and the darkness. However, I don't think it's the fire that is making me all hot and flustered. I've become very aware of the male walking around his room, giving me some space. Something I don't want. I'm angry. I want to argue and tell him that I didn't like what just happened. I want to scream and shout. Not to be calmed by Wilder's presence. Even though there is no denying that the tension in my body has evaporated. With Drengar Widler BlazeAzar Medir, in the room, I feel completely and utterly at ease. The idea of nesting on the bed and going to sleep becomes my main focus and I realise how tired I actually am.

Wilder has lit every candle by the time he stops before me and offers me his hand.

'I didn't like that,' I say aloud, desperately trying to hold onto my rage. I don't think I sound angry though, I sound sad.

Wilder sighs in my head. *'I know, but you aren't in the human realm anymore, Serafina. You're in Azanir.'*

'I know where I am,' I snap, squeezing my folded arms tighter around myself, refusing to take his hand even though every fibre of my being is screaming at me to touch him. To touch my mate.

Wilder just waits patiently. *'I hope so. Things are different here, my heart. You need to remember that. And everything is going to start getting complicated, Astgeer.'*

'I don't like it,' I repeat solemnly and hang my head. 'I ran away from this place, Wilder. What happened just then with the humans made me uncomfortable. I don't want my life here to be like that. I don't want people speaking over me or about me like I don't have any power. I don't want this to be my life. Do you understand that?'

I'm just so...tired.

Wilder kneels at my feet and I look up hesitantly and marvel at how he still towers over me even in this position. His black eyes, eyes that scared me in the beginning, now hold so much love and devotion.

'I understand. I don't want you to live a life that gives you anything but happiness. This will take time.'

'What will take time?' I pout and then close my eyes when his large hand comes up to rest against the side of my face. My beast sighs and it's the oddest feeling. Everything that seems to matter slips away.

'You changing our world.'

Blinking my eyes open, I frown at the expression on his face. His words hold so much meaning and I'm unsure if it's all in my head but it feels as if he knows all my secrets.

'I'm not going to—' He stops me with a soft kiss against my lips.

Pulling back, I swallow the lump in my throat. 'You shouldn't kiss me. I haven't bathed in two days. I smell,' I warn and then laugh loudly when he tells me that I smell good enough to eat.

His scent invades my mouth as his lips fall back on mine. His tongue pries my lips open and I forget how to form words.

Chapter Fourteen

Finally clean after bathing in the lavish, pool-like bathtub in the bathing room attached to Wilder's rooms, I reach over the mountain of pillows I have constructed around the soft bed and pick up another of the fur covered cushions.

I spend a good two minutes finding the right spot for it and then sit back to admire my construction.

Tonight, feeling a little raw and in need of comfort, I've constructed my nest like a wall. Mostly, I just sleep with pillows stacked around me but tonight it feels different. Here, I don't have to wait until I know no one will come into my room before throwing blankets and things around me to help me sleep, which is what I had to do at Laney's.

Van and the others have no idea what privacy means. They burst into your room asking questions or seeing if you have food or if you're watching anything good. Which is why I could never truly give in to my beastly instincts to nest.

I love them and equally get frustrated by them at the same time. A small spark of longing forms in my heart just thinking of my family back in the human realm.

Shaking off thoughts of what they might be doing right now, I practically dive into my nest and snuggle into the mattress feeling a sense of freedom I haven't felt in...ten years.

Something is different tonight.

Now comfortable, I finally pay attention to the male moving around the room fixing the fire and tidying his space.

Wilder fed me when I left the bathing room and gave me the privacy I asked for while I got clean and dressed. Wilder is all freshly bathed and looking amazing as he moves around the room. Now that I'm no longer focused on my comfort, I take in the sight of his chiselled abs and his defined chest and arms. I have no idea why he isn't wearing a shirt but I'm not complaining. It's not what has me watch him in wonder though. It's the fact that he didn't make a snarky comment or seemed at all surprised when I asked him to find me more pillows. He just kept throwing more and more on the bed while he got ready for sleep.

I have no idea where he got them, probably from one of the doors leading off his room. The fact that he helped me get comfortable and make my little nest has something deep and unwavering settle into my soul.

Wilder looks up as if I've spoken aloud and I find myself caught in his gaze. Those dark eyes run over the bed and the little nest I've made us. He smiles and it's the most beautiful thing I've ever seen.

'From the moment I realised what you were to me, I have dreamt about having you in my bed. I'd like it more in my lair back in the Blazelands, but this will do.'

I feel the colour rush to my cheeks.

Damn, how can words turn you on?

Afraid that if I speak right now I'll sound like an idiot, I just pull the covers back and pat the space beside me. Wilder asked me just before I started making the bed if I'd feel more comfortable with him sleeping in one of the other rooms. I quickly shut it down. Honestly, I was so focused on what I was doing, I didn't really understand what I was saying when I told him not to be silly. Now, I'm not so sure it's the best decision. It doesn't matter we've spent many nights sharing a bed while we were on the road to Satmark. It's different tonight.

We are alone. Truly alone. All those nights on the road or on the ship, we always had the others around.

Wilder takes in the state of his bed and I eat my bottom lip embarrassed at what I've done to it.

'What's wrong?' he asks, his head tilting as if he's listening to my pounding heart.

I look at my nest and shrug. 'I'm a little embarrassed,' I confess.

Confusion clouds his face before he slips under the covers with me. His warmth hits me first. A heat that settles against my skin and has every muscle in my body relax. His scent is next, it's masculine and sinful. It has my mouth water.

I watch as he gets comfortable and turns until we are face-to-face.

We lay for a moment, just staring. My eyes track the scar that runs down the side of his face and then snakes across his throat.

'Why would you be embarrassed?' he genuinely sounds like he's puzzled by my declaration.

Shrugging, I try to find the right words. 'I guess, every time I did something like this—' I indicate to the bed— 'back home, I'd feel more out of place. I tried so hard to fit in that when I didn't, or I'd do something like this, it just highlighted that I never would. It made everything so much harder.'

Wilder brushes some of the hair from my face and I close my eyes to hide the water that's building in them. *'You're home now, Serafina. Nesting is your beast finding comfort to rest during the night. When we are mated the instinct will get stronger, especially when we're ready to have younglings. It's nothing to hide or feel ashamed about. When you're with me, you can be yourself. Completely. You no longer have to hide who you are, Serafina. My love for you is infinite.'*

His words hit a spot in my heart that has me bite the inside of my cheek to keep from breaking down into a blubbering mess. A life and future with Wilder forms in my mind and for a moment I feels as if it'll happen. That life isn't complicated and there is nothing holding us back. That there are no life-changing secrets between us. Secrets that I know will change everything once they are uncovered.

I can't be completely myself. In order to do that, I have to confess that I am human and beast.

'I don't think I've ever been myself,' I admit and the heartache in my tone is not missed by the male watching me closely. The room is peaceful with the crackling of the wood in the fireplace and the heat of our combined bodies in my little nest.

'You don't have to hide who you are anymore,' is all he says.

Leaning forward, Wilder kisses my forehead. A tear slips down my cheek and I cover it by burying my face into his solid chest. Wilder's large arm comes over to wrap over my waist and he holds me firmly against him. The weight helps me to get a hold of my emotions.

'We need to discuss what happened in the meeting with the king.' The seriousness of his tone has me want to bury my way under his body and stay there for weeks.

'Not now.' I yawn, knowing that I'm avoiding an important situation. I just don't have the energy right now. 'Tomorrow. I will deal with it tomorrow.'

Breathing him in and out, I yawn again, drawing in his warmth.

'Tomorrow,' he agrees. *'Sleep, my heart.'*

And I do.

Chapter Fifteen

I'm in a bed screaming for more. I need him to stop treating me like I might break. I need him. I want everything he can give me and I shout and yell and see stars when his magical mouth captures my breast, sending me over the edge.

My next scream is not one of pleasure and I try to tell him that everything is okay even though my body feels like it's breaking in two. He just sounds so distraught. It's not his fault that I'm dying...is it?

The next series of events that flash through my mind have me on my knees wishing I could go back to a life where all I wanted was to fit in.

I watch the lair burn and the figure in the sky falling. I scream, my heart breaks and I'm pulled backwards.

I'm bound on my knees, I blink in the darkness and watch as the door across from me slowly creaks open. Murderous rage pulses in my veins and I know that there is no going back after this.

I blink awake with a single tear dripping down my face and into my ear. The emotional residue of the dream is making it hard to find my way back to reality. The only thing keeping me from losing my shit is the all-consuming heat that surrounds me. Keeping me grounded.

I close my eyes at the way the hand that is sprawled on the bare skin of my stomach begins to move in smooth, slow motions. I can't fully remember the dreams but I know that something is coming.

Something that will change my life forever. I just don't know what it is or what it all means. It doesn't help that my entire body erupts in flames, bringing with it an insatiable hunger. The greedy beast under my skin awakens. I have no control over the way I grind my arse back against the solid, deliciously warm body curled around me.

A shiver racks my up my spine when the male behind me pushes forward, driving his hardness firmly against me. It feels so amazing and with a cloud of lust, and not fully in control over my own limbs, I moan. He surrounds me. His warmth, his scent, his energy. It wraps around my soul and has all the worry of nightmares and prophecy evaporate as I remember that I'm not alone.

'Good morning, Astgeer.' Wilder's deep, masculine voice slides into my mind and sets me alight. His hand might have something to do with it too. It has worked its way up my sleep shirt and his fingers graze the underside of my breast. Each stroke has me bite harder on my lip, keeping the embarrassing noise that wants to slip from my lips in my throat.

It's useless though because the sound is in my mind like the male touching me. He can hear it clearly between the bond that we've formed and through the mating dance we have found ourselves in.

All we have to do to complete the binding of our souls is consummate it. Something I am now regretting asking him to give me time with. Stupid me thought that it was important to understand myself better before throwing myself into a committed relationship with a male like Wilder.

His lips trail a line down the side of my face and neck and I move to give him better access. My need is almost painful. I'm drenched and burning for him to move that hand higher, or lower. At this point, I don't care. I just want to feel him everywhere, but every time I try to turn so that I can grab him, he keeps me in place with his superior strength.

I stare over my shoulder, just to get a good look at him. In my dreams, he is the main character, even when I never got to see his face. I know he is mine.

And damn me he is gorgeous. With those obsidian eyes, his chocolate skin, cut jawline and the scar that runs down his face and over his throat.

'This is torture,' I groan, grinding harder against him. I know it's for him too because the sound that comes from his throat and filters through my mind is one of desperate hunger and control.

'You have no idea, Serafina. I could grip your thigh right now and claim you as my mate.'

I moan loudly and longingly. Gone are my reservations for keeping quiet, I turn with every ounce of strength I have and know I'm only facing him now because he lets me. I throw my leg over his thigh, holding him to me as he grips my arse. He runs those black eyes over my face and then leans in to use his mouth in some very sensual ways. Who knew licking a certain spot along the side of your neck to your ear could be so arousing.

'What I would give to feel you, Astgeer. To hear you scream my name.'

I don't know why that turns me on so hard.

'I'm ready when you are.' I sigh. He touches so good.

'Because we're not taking that step until you are ready.'

'Oh, I'm ready.' I laugh. I'm so ready that I fear that I might combust. His laughter fills my mind.

'Yes, you are!' Sun Gods, I nearly climax at the roughness to his tone and what he begins to do to my neck. *'However, that's not what I mean.'*

I know it's not. I can still hate it though. I grip his face just to remind myself that he is real. We stare. Eyes locked. They convey to me so much that it's hard to form a coherent thought. All I can do is reattach our lips and feel him.

We make-out for a good ten minutes before we detach ourselves from each other, both panting. His red-rimmed eyes are full of the dragon.

Chapter Sixteen

'We must take this seriously!'

'I thought we were,' Felix grumbles, the younger male is still pissed at me, even if he's trying to hide it.

Wilder and I came into the sitting room for breakfast to find the others already up and the place full of servants. Felix was the only one who didn't greet us.

Viktor seemed to be the only one who noticed and threw me an odd look when I huffed, remembering that I'm pissed at him too, and sat down.

I'm back in the armchair, curled up with my legs crossed. I have a plate full of food balanced on my lap. Wilder insisted that I need to eat.

He is sitting on the floor resting his large frame against the front of the armchair. The way the chair wraps around my back and sides, I feel like I'm in a little, comfy nest and while the conversation between the Drengar is giving me anxiety, my beast and I are settled. It helps that the food is spectacular. Meats and pastries and the freshest juice I have ever tasted.

'That's not helpful, Felix,' Viktor warns the younger Drengar who is sitting on the long lounge across from me.

Alistair's pale blue eyes narrow towards the shit-stirring male. His jaw clenches and I know he's mad by the way the muscle twitches.

The table between us all is covered in food again. Viktor and Alistair are on either side of the table on their own seats. They aren't wearing the leathers I'm so accustomed to them wearing. Each of the males has on loose, light coloured pants and tunics. I dressed in a simple tunic and pants that Wilder had to ask one of the servants to find.

'I'm just saying that there is nothing we can do or say about the king calling the council to the capital today so why are we talking about it.' Felix is being a dick and the way Viktor frowns at him would probably make someone else stop but not our Felix, the male doesn't back down. 'They will make a spectacle of Raff and question her and there will be nothing we can do to stop them. Not even Wilder can save her from what is coming.'

The bread in my hand falls to my plate and Wilder's growl has the servants in the room scatter.

'You need to watch yourself Felix. I know there are emotions over what has happened but you will not cause my mate stress.'

I flinch at Wilder's harsh tone. I have no idea if he is pissed at Felix or at the entire situation. What Felix has said is not entirely wrong, even if it does scare the shit out of me. We all know that my father is coming. Alistair made it clear that the king was going to call all the ruling families of power to the capital to discuss the book and what happened.

'We need to all keep a level head. I won't deny that we have some challenges to face—'

'Challenges to face?' Felix interrupts, cutting off Alaistair who doesn't look too impressed. Felix laughs though there is no humour in it. 'We cannot protect Serafina without her bond being completed with Wilder. Which hasn't happened yet.' My jaw hits my crossed legs at that. 'We don't have answers to why the book opened for her after being shut for thousands of years. We don't fully understand what the vision the book gave her means. A human and an Azanite male with a youngling. You said it yourself in the human realm, Alistair, it is information that the Azar in Azanir will not accept. Humans and Azanites are forbidden to interact in such a way. Humans live and work for us. The moment Raff says those things, it will cause a problem. We have no idea why she has the dreams that she has. Unless there is something Raff would like to share with the group to make it easier for us to protect her?'

I stop breathing. Every eye in the room falls to me, even the damn butler from last night stares from across the room.

Felix's words sink in and I begin to hyperventilate.

They know.

They must, or he wouldn't have said it like that.

What the fuck am I going to do? I will be executed. I'm an abomination. The BlazeAzar family will reject me as Wilder's mate and then I will be locked away in the Medir academy to be forced to sleep. My father will be angry at me for what I did, he will agree with the Medir Masters.

It feels like something is sitting on my chest. It brings back memories of drowning and dreams of death.

Shit, my lungs feel so tight. Each breath hurts.

The plate on my lap topples over and hits the floor with a loud crack.

Two strong, firm hands manoeuvre my body around, pulling my legs forward and my shoulders down so that my head sits between them.

'Breathe, Astgeer. I won't let anything happen to you.'

Wilder sounds so sure and yet, I don't believe him. When he finds out my secrets, he will hate me for lying. I didn't tell them the extent of what the book showed me. I told them about the Azanite male and the female he was with, how it appeared that they had a child, but that was it. I didn't tell them what happened to the female at the end of the vision. I left that part out. I'm not fully sure why.

'You... can't...promise...that...' Each word is hard to get out. Felix is right.

I think I'm having a panic attack.

Wilder's power seeps into my skin, warming me from the inside out.

The males have a quick, heated discussion while I try to remember how to breath

'I'm not meaning to frighten you, Raff.'

'Well, you did!' Viktor shouts and I don't catch what happens between them. All I hear is the blood pounding in my ears.

Alistair's shoes appear in my line of vision and I feel him crouch down beside me. His large hand rests on my knee while I try to remember how to draw air into my lungs properly. Wilder is helping but there isn't actually anything for him to heal so his presence is the only way he can support right now. I'm too damn frightened to allow myself to be calmed.

'Raff, we're all going to be there with you. I know this is frightening. No one is going to hurt you. Do you really think that any of us would let that happen? You just need to be honest and answer their questions.'

'Questions?' I manage to get out.

'Yes, when the houses of Azanir convenes, you'll be there to answer their questions and tell them what happened. You just have to be honest, everything else we will work out.'

Eyes wide, I sit up a little and stare at Alastair and wait to see if he is joking. He isn't. I'm going to be called into the council of the most powerful Azanites of Azanir and questioned. Fucking hell!

Oh my Sun Gods, the air is too thin. My head begins to spin.

'Serafina! Calm down,' Wilder demands and I try. I really do. He has no idea how difficult it is. I'm half fucking human, what if that is the reason the book opened for me.

Shit, I'm screwed. I'm more than screwed. I'm fucked.

'We can't do much about the decision the King has made. The council meeting is happening, we should calm down and discuss how to handle it,' Viktor LongwingDrengar states like he has no idea how hard it is for me to function right now.

'That's if you and I are allowed in the room, Viktor. We're not Azar, remember,' Felix states and I can't believe how insensitive he is being.

Viktor's next few words are a string of curses that have the young male pale a little. 'Enough!' Viktor now has everyone's attention. 'We are going around in circles. There is nothing we can do but prepare for what is to come. We are Drengar.' His features are a great deal harsher than Felix with his straight nose and strong features. His eyes are dark brown and lined with a honey colour that makes it hard to not gaze into.

The silence that descends on the room is heavy. 'I need…I need a moment. Please, can I have some time on my own,' I whisper.

I jump up and hurry back to Wilder's rooms.

The door slams behind me, and I fall apart.

Chapter Seventeen

It's the sun beaming through the glass doors across the room that motivates me to pry myself from the floor and head outside to drink in the heat and warmth of the morning.

Last night they were covered by the heavy curtains. One of the servants must have opened them while we were at breakfast. Like most lairs this size, Wilder's room has a balcony attached to it, and by balcony, I mean a small patio big enough for a beast to shift and take flight.

Gripping the railing, I lean up against it and curse the fact that I can't grow wings and fly away. The need to get the fuck out of here is overwhelming. I know I told Wilder that I would deal with all this today but I wish I could go back to last night, snuggling into his side.

Everything Felix said was right, from not binding myself to Wilder to how they can't protect me from the council of Azar that will demand I tell them my story. They will want to know why I left, what I have been doing in the human realm and they will want to know of my vision.

The one given to me by the sacred, golden book. The same fucking book that hasn't opened in a thousand years. The one that opened for me after I was kidnapped and beaten and almost killed for my blood. The humans believed that the blood of an Azar would open it.

Joseph, the fucking arsehole leader of the human rebels, with his weird-ass white inked rebel tattoo, can go to hell. He drugged me, bound me and tried to kill me, all for the knowledge they believed they would find within the pages. When I heard him say that the human rebels were looking for information of how to become an Azanite, how to become a dragon shifter, I laughed in his face. An Azanite is born, or at least that is what I always thought. I can still hear Joseph's voice in my head, telling me that he believed it held the secrets of the Azanite power. He told me that there were stories amongst humans about there being a way for an Azanite, to have their own beasts. I thought he was a lunatic. Now, I'm not so sure after the vision the book gave me.

Closing my eyes and lifting my face to the sun, I breath in and out slowly. The vision is so vivid in my mind. Unlike my dreams, I can recall every detail and as if I've pressed play on a movie in my mind, I see it all again.

I'm in Azanir, but it looks different, like I've been sent back in time.

Standing on the top of a hill, a hill that is familiar, yet not, I watch as beasts and humans interact in the town down below. I see human women kissing their Azanite males and I watch as younglings play and laugh through the busy streets of the market.

Movement catches my eye and I look to my right to see a little girl hurrying down the hill to my right towards a woman and a male in beast form. The human lady crouches down and the youngling leaps into her arms and shifts. The mother cradles her beast youngling before placing her down on the ground. I fall to my knees, unsure of what I'm seeing as the lady kisses the mighty head of her male as he lowers it to rub against her body in an affectionate move that has tears fall down my face. The youngling bounces around the pair, clearly excited to be in her beast and then as the parents finish with whatever moment they're having, the woman stands and she does something that has me fall to my knees and weep.

Blinking my eyes open, I wipe the tear that trickles down my face. I left that part out of my retelling to the Drengar back in that motel room. I didn't tell them that the rebels were right. I watched as that human shifted her form into a dragon. It was smaller than a typical female Azanite but she did shift.

I don't know how or what it all means but there is a way for humans to become like us. I have been battling with this knowledge since it showed me.

It's a dangerous piece of information.

No Azanite, especially an Azar, would want to to hear this.

Humans are servants, maybe thousands of years ago they all lived together, ruled together, but that all changed. Our history teaches us that jealousy and fighting became too much. That humans wanted more power and began to treat Azanites, especially the females who they mated with, badly. No history lesson I have ever heard tells the story of how humans gained the ability to shift into beasts but I'm very aware that history can be manipulated.

On the other hand, if the human rebels find out that their theory of the book holding the key to an Azanite's power is correct, then there is no telling what they will do to get it back. I've seen the obsession and felt first-hand the lengths they will go to get it.

Rubbing at my cheek when a tinge of phantom pain ripples over my skin when I remember being hit by Joseph, I sigh.

This entire situation is so messed up.

The worst thing, and the one I will not admit, is that I held onto this information because it broke my heart. Saying out loud that humans can become beasts is hard to admit. I'm half human and half Azanite and I can't shift. It's soul destroying. How come a thousand years ago, a human woman can change her form and I'm left unable to connect fully with the beast that lives under my skin. And my damn father is a powerful Azar. It's childish but it makes me so mad. It just highlights that something is really wrong with me.

'Why?' I whisper and then look down sharply at my arms and watch the skin ripple and bend painfully. Sucking in a breath of pain, I wince. It's not the first time I've felt her under my skin so strongly and while a spark of hope forms in my chest at the idea that maybe I'm not as broken as I thought, when I try to connect with the dragon, I don't feel anything.

She saved my life in the ocean, mine and little Roxy. My beast spoke to me, asked me to give her permission to take over, and when I dropped the barrier between the two parts of my soul, I felt a sense of power and strength that I've never experienced. Now, nothing.

I try to do it again, with no success. She's gone back to being too far away for me to connect with.

Chapter Eighteen

I look out into the morning sky, the glistening ocean on the horizon and I map the lines of clouds spilling over the magnetic blue. There are beasts flying in the distance, enjoying the clear morning and I long to join them. To fly from my problems and forget about prophecies and books.

I want to fly home and hug Laney and get in trouble from Van, Brent and Scott for leaving. I want to go back to my shitty job and stress over shitty things that don't really matter.

Then I remember everything that happened. I put my family in danger by drawing the wraith demons to them. Van nearly died because of me.

Taking in the bright city and the way the town of Kathiwate snakes down the side of the mountain face, I know deep in my soul that running from this place ten years ago wasn't the answer to my problems. It just made me feel more out of place, more alone.

A roar from the distance captures my attention and I watch sadly as a wing of males fly toward the ocean. They must be Drengar on patrol.

I feel the pull to fly. To follow.

To feel free.

I don't have to turn to know that Wilder is behind me and I lean into his heat when he presses against my back and buries his face into my neck. Strong, comforting and steady arms wrap around my body.

'I'm sorry for how I reacted,' I say after a time and love it when he growls in my mind. His chest vibrates against my back and I love the shockwaves it sends through my every nerve.

'There's nothing to apologise for. This is a great deal for you to have to process without Felix adding to your worries.' Wilder is clearly pissed and I look over my shoulder at him when he grunts. Sun Gods, he is hot.

'He wasn't wrong though.'

'Still, he needs to watch himself.'

I sigh. 'He's just pissed at me for what happened on the ship.'

Wilder doesn't move away, he just holds me while I watch more dragons fill the sky.

'Just say the word, Serafina. I will take you from here in a heartbeat. Just tell me what you need, my heart.'

The most intense shiver shoots down my spine. 'I want to fly, Wilder.' It's a confession and a plea. 'Please,' I whisper, unable to bear the need.

'I would give you the world, Astgeer.'

His warmth disappears and as I turn slowly I watch Wilder shift.

A black dragon appears on the balcony. He stretches his mighty wings and neck like he is settling into his new skin. I watch in utter awe of the beauty and magnitude of Drengar Wilder BlazeAzar-Medir.

Wilder throws his head back and screeches his joy. It has me smile in response to his elation.

Lowering his long neck, I come face-to-face with eyes of fire. 'You're so pretty.'

Wilder snorts and I giggle as I'm bombarded with a gush of hot air. I would have stumbled backwards at the force of it but the sky has been blocked out as his wings wrap around my body, keeping me secure and in place. I lean into the massive leathery wing.

'I'm not pretty,' his voice snaps in my head and I can't help but laugh again. There is more beast than man in that tone and I bat my eyelids. *'I am mighty and powerful.'*

Raising my hand to run it up the side of his rough, scaly cheek, I bite my lip to hide my smile. Such a typical male response. 'Of course you are, big guy.'

His low growl makes me laugh and I can feel his elation at hearing the sound. *'You are mine,'* Wilder states and I agree fully.

I am his and it doesn't matter that we haven't completed our bond, I am, and always, will be Wilder's.

'And you are mine,' I remind him and squeak a small sound when he scoops me up with his monstrous front paw and lifts us off with a mighty flap of his wings. The force takes my breath away.

I throw out my arms and relish in the wave of adrenaline and pure euphoria that rushes my system.

Wilder beats those magnificent wings and takes us high into the morning sky until we are soaring above the ocean.

Flying so high that I feel as if I could reach up and run my hand through the clouds, we're already over the ocean.

Kathiwate is behind us and it feels good to be out of the city. The chill in the air has my skin prickling and just as I think that it's cold, the paw I'm sitting on lifts so that I'm closer to the smooth underside of his body.

Raising my arm, I skim my fingers against the skin of his chest and relish in the heat. *'Thank you.'*

'Always. You are my mate, Serafina. Your comfort and safety is all that matters. No matter what was said back there, there is nothing or no one in this world that can hurt you or take you from me. I will burn the world to embers before I'd allow that.'

'I don't deserve you.'

'On the contrary, love. You deserve everything this life can offer.' I don't know how he will feel once he finds out my secrets. *'And I'm going to show you.'* Wilder banks fast to the right and then nose dives towards the ocean. My stomach falls into my butt and I shout in joy at the feeling that floods my system.

Chapter Nineteen

Standing outside Felix's door, I raise my hand for the third time and let it drop. Even after everything that happened this morning, I still want to make peace with him. I need to.

I need my friend. Now more than ever.

'He probably already knows that you're at the door,' a voice says from down the hall.

Sighing loudly, my shoulders slump. 'I don't know why he's so angry. I get that what I did was stupid, but I had to save Roxy, Viktor.' I'm almost pleading with him to understand. Viktor stops a few feet away and leans his back against the wall, his thick arms crossed over his chest. He seems relaxed even though he is back in his Drengar leathers.

'I think his anger is directed more at himself than you,' he states and I truly have no idea what he means. He just shrugs when I ask if he'd like to elaborate.

'What was I supposed to do? I dreamt it. I thought I was going to die in that ocean, and for a moment, I was okay with it.'

I have no idea why the words fall from my lips and I watch as those honey-lined eyes take me all in.

Viktor is a male I used to spy on as a youngling in my father's lair. The badge on his uniform is the crest of the royal family and I'm dying to know why he left my father's Drengar. Out of all the Drengar, he's the one I feel the less connected to. I'm not sure why. Maybe because he's a face of my youth and his presence will always remind me of the past. I know it's probably not fair that I can't look at him without feeling a mixture of emotions, but he too has kept his distance.

'Do all your dreams come true?'

Taken a bit off guard, I don't really know how to respond. The way he's looking at me so intensely and the tone hints to there being more to this question. As if he knows I keep things to myself. I feel a wave of anxiety and blurry images flash in my mind. I know my dreams of late have been full of screams and immense pain, even if I can't remember a single thing about them. 'Um, not all. I don't remember all my dreams when I wake, most of them slip away. Others leave an emotional hangover and I get these feelings, like something is going to happen. It's not until I'm in the situation when I realise I dreamt it. That's what happened on the ship. I remembered all my dreams of dying in that ocean. I didn't see Wilder saving me.'

We stand in silence for a moment before he asks, 'and what are you dreaming of late?'

Opening and closing my mouth a few times, I shrug and say, 'nothing of note.' It's a fucking lie. I see the images of the falling dragon. I hear the screams.

'I know that things were said this morning that shouldn't have been. I just want you to know that what we said back in the human realm is still true. We owe you everything Serafina. You are one of us, and we protect what is ours. You saved our lives multiple times and we won't let anything happen to you. No matter what happens later today. You know that right?'

Nodding, I hope he isn't offended that I don't really feel like they have the power to protect me from my father and the laws of our people. I can tell that I haven't convinced him.

Viktor waits for a moment before he pushes off the wall and begins to walk away. He stops after a few steps and throws that honey-lined gaze over his shoulder. 'You would tell us if you're having any dreams that are worrying you, yes? You're not keeping things from us, right?'

Shaking my head is the only way I can communicate right now because if I speak I know that I'll give myself away. Viktor throws me a weird look before finally leaving and I release the breath I didn't realise I was holding. It makes me sound shady as hell, so of course that's when Alistair walks past and side-eyes me. He slows down, eyeing me suspiciously. 'You good?'

'Uhhh…yeah.' I look at Felix's door. He looks at Felix's door. We both look at each other.

'Do you need help?'

I nearly laugh at the doubt in his tone. His pale blue eyes are narrowed like I'm doing something criminal. Alistair is honestly one of the most attractive males I have ever laid eyes on. His tanned complexion, cut jawline and those eyes makes him look fake. He doesn't do much for me now that my entire mind is focused on Wilder but he'd make a female very happy one day.

'Yep,' I pop the 'p' and seriously I want to kick my own arse.

Shuffling on my feet, I look once more at Felix's door. I'm just starting to realise that I don't even know if he's in there. I haven't seen him since breakfast. Wilder and I went for a fly and then he had to go and meet some people when we got back. This afternoon is going to be hard when I'm called to the council and I just need my friend.

'Well, I'm about to call up for our mid-day meal to be served. Let me know if you need any help or I'll see you in the sitting room,' Alistair states before he continues on his way, probably thinking that I'm a lunatic as he goes.

Focusing back on what I was doing, I stare at Felix's door with a frown.

I hate the distance between us. Even the silent beast under my skin feels agitated, like she wants me to smash open the door and demand that Felix starts speaking to me again. Felix means so much to me. We spent weeks together, eating on crappy motel room beds, chatting and laughing.

That thought has a small idea bloom in my mind and grinning like a fool, I clap my hands in excitement and hurry down the hall to the sitting room where Viktor and Alistair are discussing something about patrols.

Both males look up as I approach, both frowning at whatever they see on my face.

'Actually, Alistair, I could use your help with something,' I say a little too eagerly and watch as a smile breaks over his face as I tell him my hurried plan.

Chapter Twenty

SMILING TO MYSELF AT my little plan, I begin to carry the heavy tray to Felix's rooms. It took a while to get Allistair and Viktor to let me carry it. They only stopped when I told them that it was important that I fix this on my own.

Using my elbow and my foot, I manage to get his door open and hope that this will work while praying to the Sun Gods that he isn't naked or anything.

'Felix,' I say, with my back to the room in case he isn't decent. He's hot, but I don't have any interest in what he is packing under those Drengar leathers.

'Raff?' Felix sounds perplexed and I can't help but grin. 'I'm busy Serafina.'

'This will only take a moment,' I say and I spin slowly so that nothing will fall off the very full plates and practically profess my love to the universe because Felix is sitting on his bed, exactly where I needed him to be. His rooms are almost identical to Wilder's. His blue eyes are all scrunched in confusion at whatever he sees on my face—probably triumph and my inflated ego at how wicked I'm being right now.

Presenting him my offering, I hold out the tray and say, 'I'm sorry, Felix. The thought of you being mad at me makes me feel like shit. Forgive me,' I finish and wait for him to reply. Which is longer than I would like.

His blue eyes stay fixed on me, they flick to my offering and back to my face a few times. My arms begin to shake slightly under the weight.

'You...are they chicken nuggets?

'Yep,' I chime. 'I had Alistair speak to the cooks and he asked them to make me some. I knew they wouldn't say no to him if he asked. They took a bit of time because apparently no one in the kitchens knew what they were. The butler told Alistair that they had to find one of the newer humans who came over on the last shipment of migrants. Or something like that,' I shrug. I was just too excited when I saw what the butler was carrying that I didn't pay much attention to why it took so long.

Looking at the odd shaped goodies, I smile proudly down at them. 'I know they don't look like a typical take-away nugget from the human realm but I've eaten two already and they are very good. Better actually then the take-out place you like so much.'

'Raff—'

I don't know what he's about to say but I cut him off because I don't like his tone. 'Felix, I know that what I did was irresponsible and that my decision endangered all of us, but I couldn't let Roxy die. She is a child. Like I said, I had dreamt what happened and I was content knowing that it was my end. I made the decision without thinking of you. However, I would do it again. In a heartbeat.'

Felix shakes his head and looks away and my heart drops.

He's frowning.

Fuck, this isn't working. Stepping forward, the tray shakes in my hands. 'Please, Felix. I hate being back here in Azanir. I hate that I have to face my father and brothers today and I hate that you are angry at me.'

'It's me who should be saying sorry, Raff!'

Okay, that's not what I expected him to say and I end up standing awkwardly in the middle of his rooms, trying to process what he means.

It's my turn to frown. 'I don't get it. Why?'

Felix is looking down at the furry comforter on his bed. The dude seriously needs a little nest made up, his bed looks super uncomfortable. 'I'm not angry that you saved a small human child, Raff. I'm angry that I was placed in that situation. I've been left to try and come to terms with the fact that I almost lost you. That Wilder, a member of my wing, and my brother in all ways but blood, nearly lost his mate because I made the decision to save a small child too.'

'Ahhh...okay...' I still don't get it.

'I picked her, and not you!' Felix rages, he jumps off the bed and I jump back and nearly spill the nuggets everywhere.

I feel Wilder in my head, his small growl of warning whispers in my ear but I push him away. This isn't his conversation or his argument, it's mine. He's only responding to my emotions and he slips away when he realises that I'm not in any danger.

Felix stomps to the closed glass doors that lead to his own balcony.

I'm fucking confused. 'Felix, I'm lost. You're angry with yourself for coming to get us?'

'I'm angry that I had to make a decision in the ocean. You lifted Roxy in the air. I couldn't see you and by the time I got to her, you were already sinking, Roxy wasn't. She was still on the surface. I made the decision to take her and leave you because I couldn't guarantee her safety if I dove into the water. She was barely breathing. I knew that Wilder was close, but I still made that decision, Raff. I still picked her, knowing that I could lose you.'

I think my mouth hits the floor with a thud. 'Felix—'

The male turns around, and again, sets those eyes on me. They're full of regret. 'You saved my life in the human realm. You helped us to retrieve our sacred text despite all that we put you through in the beginning. Even with your fears and all your trauma, you helped us. I should've picked you. I owed you a life debt and I should've picked you. But I couldn't let that child die.'

I think my heart cracks in two. 'Felix, you did the right thing.'

I thought he was furious at me for what I did, I never imagined that he was angry at himself for what he thought was some kind of betrayal.

'I would never have forgiven you if you had let her die. I never would hold it against you if you chose someone's life over mine. I'm not worthy of more just because of what happened with the book or me dreaming something that changed the outcome of what happened. Or because of Wilder.'

'You're a female Azanite and my friend, Raff. My guilt has been eating at me for days.'

I don't know what to say to make this better.

I step towards him. The tray wobbles. 'I'm your friend, Felix. You know me. I'm not a typical Azanite female and I don't want to be,' I reply, shocking myself. It's true. I don't want to be treated like a porcelain doll. I desperately want to belong and find my place, but not like that.

'My brother was killed in a wraith attack when I was young,' Felix declares out of the blue.

'Shit, Felix, I'm so sorry.'

I see the sadness etched on his face. My poor, sweet Felix. My heart breaks for him. 'I was there, defending our lair with my sister and mother inside. I was too inexperienced and small to do anything. It was the first time I came face-to-face with a wraith and I made the decision to stay at the door and defend it. I made the decision to not follow my brother into the streets.'

'Streets?' Trying to piece the event in my head together, I'm a little confused by that.

'My family are Thal. Our modest lair is close to the main part of town. I live in the Riverways.'

A Thal is the title used for the working Azanites. They're not noble and spend their days working on their crafts. They work closely with the humans of Azanir, which explains how Felix always seemed more comfortable around them. It also highlights that while I love all my Drengar, I still have much to learn about their lives and who they are. 'My decision in the ocean felt like making that same one all those years ago.'

Sun Gods, I feel like an absolute arsehole. 'I'm sorry to have put you in that situation. You made the right decision in saving Roxy and I know that your brother would feel the same about your choice to stay with your mum and sister, Felix.'

He gifts me one of his brilliant smiles and I'm so relieved that it's genuine and without anger. 'I'm sorry Raff. For everything. This morning I was a bastard."

I chuckle. 'Yeah, you were.' He smiles, knowing I'm just teasing. My grin drops. 'Me too, Felix. I can't tell you how sorry I am,' I state all serious now.

We stand, staring at each other, both feeling the tension release from the room. It's a nice moment until I almost drop the tray. I swear colourfully and manage to save the food.

'Sun Gods, here, let me get that.' The Drengar jumps into action and grabs the tray.

Holy shit that was too much, my muscles practically sigh in relief. 'Thank you. That was fucking heavy.'

'Did you really ask the cooks to make me nuggets? No one eats nuggets in Azanir.' My friend looks at me like I'm some kind of saviour. It makes me giggle.

'Well, Alistair asked and gave the instructions. It was my idea though.' I'm acting like a youngling and I don't care. 'And they're freakin' awesome, try one.'

Felix laughs and I feel it in my soul. We hurry to the bed.

Getting settled, we then devour every last chicken nugget on the plates.

Chapter Twenty One

Groaning, I rub at my bloated belly and curse my decisions—something that I feel I do often these days.

'They were amazing, but we should've stopped at eighty,' Felix grumbles from his position on the floor beside the couch I'm lying on.

We practically rolled ourselves from his room to the sitting room.

I'm so full I can't even nod.

'I feel so sick!' He burps and its gross and funny.

I laugh and swear at him for making the pain worse. 'Stop, I'm gonna throw up.' He and I have been laying, immobile for a while, regretting the number of nuggets we inhaled for the last half an hour.

Twenty minutes, that's all it took for us to eat maybe a hundred, each.

'Serves you both right for being so greedy.'

I glare at the male sitting in my usual armchair. I know that Felix is doing the same from the floor. We share a look, roll our eyes, and go back to groaning. Viktor hasn't stopped berating us since we moaned our way into our current positions. I think he's just pissed that we didn't leave him any.

'Wilder told you both to stop before you got sick,' Alistair states.

Wilder makes a grunting sound of acknowledgement. I swear it's like being surrounded by three annoying dads.

Attractive dads, but still, very annoying.

'Wilder, you sure you can't use your Medir powers to makes us feel better?' Felix begs.

Wilder just ignores him. The three Drengar are discussing what's going to happen this afternoon at the meeting. I raise my head eagerly and flop back down when he ignores Felix. He already told us he can't help.

'I think that's a no,' I tell Felix and get a sad nod in return.

The conversation on the other side of the room heats up a little. Wilder isn't including us in what he is saying, so I'm only half listening as I close my eyes and try to rest. I'm hoping sleep will help.

'How are you feeling about this meeting?' Felix asks.

'I have no idea,' I confess, being completely honest. 'I don't feel anything right now but extremely nauseated.' It's a complete lie. Felix finds that hilarious and laughs so hard he turns a weird shade of green. 'Stop laughing! If you throw up, I'm going to throw up!'

Felix groans and tries to roll and then thinks twice about his position and rolls on his back again. He pulls his legs up and rests them on the table and gets in trouble by Alistair so he has to put them on the lounge beside my hip.

'Will you be okay telling everyone what happened with the humans?'

'What do you mean?' Why does that question make me feel a little sweaty? Or is it the nuggets repeating on me that are making me perspire?

'You were kidnapped by humans Raff. You were beaten and drugged. I'm surprised that you can even look at one of them. You are either really good at repressing your emotions or you are one tough lady.'

Oh right. Am I repressing my emotions when it comes to the *incident* and finding out that someone I thought was my best friend could betray me...probably. Is that a healthy way to manage and process trauma? Fuck no! Has Wilder and the others tried to get me to open up about my feelings and made it clear that I'm safe to do so? Yes. Swoon. I love them.

However, at this stage in my life, I have way too much going on to even think of it. All that seems to plague me is that I'm an abomination who is the mate of a BlazeAzar and I have to see my fucking family in a few hours. What Miles, my once very close friend, did...I just can't. Not yet. It hurts too much.

I rub at the space between my breasts.

'I feel it too, Raff,' Felix sighs in sympathy.

'You do?' I ask, kinda shocked that he would understand how Miles's betrayal has hurt my already fragile understanding of myself and my worth. I see Wilder rise from his seat in my peripherals.

Felix burps again and rubs at the same spot I am. 'Indigestion,' he groans and I can't contain the laughter that bursts from my throat.

How can I wallow in self-pity with Felix around?

'I don't think that is what Serafina was feeling, Felix,' my future mate says as he steps over Felix, forcing him to shuffle over, and stands beside my head.

Sun Gods, he takes up all the energy in the room and I shut my mouth, all laughter gone, when he leans down over me. Every fantasy imaginable plays through my mind as his obsidian eyes take me in.

He is huge. He blocks out the light and I can hear Felix cursing us to get a room but I don't care because I know he is about to kiss me and I quickly make sure with my tongue that my teeth are clean of nuggets. I wonder if I'll ever not feel these butterflies for him and pray to the heavens that I don't.

'You know what I'm feeling?' I whisper just before those full, kissable lips land on mine.

I should probably be worried that he knows I'm keeping a secret or something but right now, I don't care about all that. I could speak to him with the beast so that none of the others hears my breathy-embarrassing tone, but I forget my own name in this warriors presence. I also forget why I'm fucking waiting to consummate this and seal the deal.

All I can smell is him. All I can see is him. All I want is...his lips crash into mine and I moan into his mouth as his tongue takes over my existence. His warmth invades my body, heating me from the inside.

Wilder pulls away and I catch myself following after him with my mouth. I only stop because of the smug look I register on his face. Damn, handsome male and his perfect features. His shoulder length midnight hair falls around his face and I reach out and run my hands through the strands just to keep touching him.

'Yes, you think too loud.' My gut drops into the couch and I swallow audibly.

'You said you can't read my mind,' I retort, just to make him reassure me for the billionth time that he can't.

'Wilder, we should go over some of these details,' Viktor states, drawing my future mate's attention from me from a moment. I feel like I can breathe without those eyes on me. He makes me want to confess my sins and ask for forgiveness and maybe what I can do to redeem myself.

Wilder throws me a small, smug half-grin as if he *can* hear my thoughts and I stick my tongue out and giggle as he walks back to the two males.

Hopping off the couch with the thought of maybe taking a bath and finding some sun before we are called to the meeting, I stretch and sigh in relief. It takes me way too long to realise that I don't feel like shit anymore.

'Hey!' Felix shouts as if realising that I'm up and moving and not dying of pain at the same moment I do.

Grinning widely, I hurry over to the male sitting back down with his back to me. Throwing my arms around his shoulders I kiss him on the cheek. 'Thank you.'

'That's not fair! You said you can't help!' Felix shouts

'And I meant it.'

'You're a Medir. Isn't it your job to make Azanites feel better? Didn't you take some kind of oath?'

I kiss Wilder again. My beast is starting to get a bit unbearable again. She wants him. My hands are moving over his shoulders and I have an overwhelming need to rub my cheek over his. Wilder just turns to stare at me and rests his lips on mine again in a soft kiss that melts my soul.

'I don't think Wilder is going to kiss you to make you feel better, Felix,' Alistair states absently to the book now sitting on his lap. I have no idea what he is reading but it looks serious.

'Why not?' Felix grumbles. 'I'm a good kisser!'

I think my small chuckle turns into fits of hysterics because the three males just ignore the smartass like they are used to his behaviour. I stop when a firm knock on the door has every one of the Drengar whip their heads around to face it.

Chapter Twenty Two

The Meeting Hall is silent.

All you can hear is the sound of Drengar boots on the stone and the soft thud of the slip on shoes that I found amongst the clothes laid out for me this morning. The noise just adds to the doom-ie atmosphere. As if I'm walking to my death, my heartbeat falters and changes so that it begins to beat in time with the sound of our footsteps.

There are Azanites everywhere, watching us walk down the 'aisle of doom' towards the male sitting on his throne.

The King's meeting hall is next level opulent. It's definitely a room fit for a king, a dragon king. The walls are gold, the roof is made of thick glass so that you can see the sky. The floor is shiny and the over-the-top throne at the end of the room is sitting on a podium and appears to be made of...well, gold.

Van and I used to watch a show, the kind that comes out one episode at a time at a certain hour, and this throne reminds me of that. Instead of being made of sharp objects that appear to be very uncomfortable to actually sit on, it is made of melted stone.

In my anxious flooded mind, all I can think is how much heat and fire it would've taken to mould something so breathtakingly beautiful.

A little fixated on the décor and the chair, I give myself permission to be distracted from the fucked-up situation I'm in right now.

I have to actively keep my gaze from roaming the masses of seated and standing males.

I know my father is here. I can feel it. I saw Emmet just as I stepped through the doors. The table of Darkwoods males is at the back left of the room.

I haven't seen my father yet.

The Lord of the Darkwoods is probably biding his time before he steps out dramatically and reprimands me in front of the ruling families of Azanir. There are long tables filled with males, their Drengar's standing behind them. I don't have the stomach to take notice of who is placed where. Wilder's family are here. Everyone is here.

It's probably why my neck muscles refuse to obey me. I can't look. My focus is locked on the throne.

I knew this wasn't going to end well when Viktor and Felix were told to wait outside. Felix was right, they aren't invited in because they aren't Azar and not part of the King's inner Drengar Circle.

There's just so many reflective surfaces in this place. The sunlight blazing from the roof is bouncing all over the place and all I can think about is how fucking long the walk from the door to the podium is.

I feel the brush of power in my mind and take a shaky breath. I don't dare look at the Drengar surrounding me like bodyguards. Each one stone-faced like this is nothing but a lovely stroll we are taking towards the king. Like they do this kind of thing every day. Wilder is to my right wearing those tight, black leathers. He wears them like a second skin. His face is hard. There are no emotions, no hint to the rage I can feel below the surface of his skin. I can't describe how I know Wilder is angry. Maybe it's the heat that's radiating off him or that I can almost taste his fury. Or perhaps I'm losing my mind and feeling things that aren't real.

We are half-way down the aisle when I almost drop dead of a heart attack.

'You are safe,' Wilder says quickly and I swallow the squeal of fear that tried to escape when five, massive warriors step from the crowd and take up positions around me. *'My brothers.'* They fill in the gaps so that I'm practically hidden from the many eyes scrutinising me and I peak to my right to spy a particularly large male with short, black hair and a jawline that reminds me of Wilder. I get my answer as to why when I spy the crest on his chest and quickly go back to looking straight ahead. Just a few more steps. One foot after the other. My flight or fight reflex is on overdrive. I want to get the fuck out of here so fast that every step is now painful.

I stop when the others do. We stand before the king, ready to hear what he has to say. Probably, 'kill the abomination,' or, 'kill the lawbreaker,' or something equally as terrifying.

The larger-than-life male sitting on the throne is all serious and stone-faced. His pale blue eyes are all Alistair and while they're hard in an assessing kind of way, they aren't threatening as they settle on me. The King is a huge male, maybe the biggest I've ever seen and his energy has me avert my eyes. He's all dominant predator. Everything in the room revolves around him. His energy is hypnotic and petrifying.

Even sitting, the King of Azanir is tall and his streaked grey hair just adds to the allure of the male watching me like I'm a puzzle that needs to be solved. I got the run-down of what was said last night in his private meeting with Wilder, Viktor and Alistair. They spoke about the trip in the human realm. They even told the king of how the sacred, thousand-year-old permanently-closed book, opened when I touched it.

However, they left out what actually happened after. They thought that it was best if I explained, and honestly, I have no idea what to say.

The truth?

Sun Gods, the way these Drengar reacted when I told them what I saw was enough to have me hesitate to tell the King of Azanir and the council of leading families of this realm that I saw a human woman and an Azanite male in a romantic relationship, with a youngling.

There would be a riot.

It's forbidden to have a relationship with humans, hence my fear of being back here. Azanites are beasts, predators, who love power and they all have power. Their society is founded on that.

Humans are lesser. They're servants. They are here to serve us.

But what if that's the problem? Thousands of years ago, the dynamic between humans and dragons was different. We supposedly lived in harmony. Shared power. And as a result, war and conflict broke out because power corrupts. It's one thing I learnt living in the human realm. Their history is testament to that fact. But what if that is the problem and why less and less females are being born. I didn't get a sense of there being any issues with race extinction from my unwanted deep-dive into the text.

'I guess we should start by saying, welcome home, Lady Serafina DarkwoodsAzar.'

The moment the last word slips from the King's mouth, I catch the hint of movement out of the corner of my eye.

My entire world stills.

My father.

The Lord of the Darkwoods steps forward, flanked by my brothers and a wing of Drengar. Yet, it isn't the sight of them that makes the colour drain from my body and seep into the stone floor. It's the male beside them. The face that haunts my dreams and waking life. Medir Leon. The male who took my autonomy and disregarded consent for years. Who tormented me and kept me locked in my nightmares.

Chapter Twenty Three

Three things happen next that I fear will be etched into my brain for the remainder of my days.

Firstly, my father and I make eye contact. The power of it has me quickly look away. I can't take the emotion looking back at me. I expected the anger and the fury but not the creases of sadness around his eyes or the hint of fear that flicks over his features.

He steps forward and says, 'My King, I had heard of my daughter's return from my son,' he indicates to Emmet. The poor male is holding himself so tightly that he must be uncomfortable. The way he is eying Wilder makes me worried.

To his credit, Wilder doesn't seem to give a shit, and one of the new males beside me growls low in his chest. Clearly, he doesn't appreciate what my brother is doing.

'It was very upsetting to hear that my daughter was not handed over to her family the moment she returned. We have lived the last ten years believing her dead. I want her returned to me now! Wilder BlazeAzar has no right to call my daughter mate. He disrespects me and my name by implying he does.'

'What the actual fuck?' I murmur, not able to help it. Father looks over at me sharply. I swear, the way my lip pulls back from my teeth is involuntary. Wilder grips my arm in warning. This male hasn't seen me in ten years and the first thing he says is this. Staking some claim over me.

Wilder shows-off his power by speaking to everyone in the room again, I can tell by the way each word sounds. *'If the Lord of the Darkwoods would like to challenge me, my King. He need only declare it.'*

The hall erupts in murmurs. Wilder spoke to everyone.

My father growls. So does Emmet and Luka.

Sun Gods, Luka is so different to how I remember him. The same eyes as Emmet. The same build. His hair is cut too close to his head and the way he stares has me feeling judged and raw. He isn't happy.

Well, fuck him. I'm not happy being here either.

The king raises his massive hand, stopping my father from speaking further.

King Oswald nods slowly. There are some murmurs from the tables around the room. 'I understand what you are saying, Lord Darkwoods. The return of the Lady of the Darkwoods is quite a shock and frankly has raised numerous questions.'

Far out, I'm fucked. I'm only standing right now because Wilder is still holding me.

'I have heard a few stories. Interesting stories,' the King announces to the room. I swear my father pales. 'I believe it is now time that we hear these stories from the source. Lady Serafina, would you step forward please. Lord DarkwoodsAzar, you may find your seat at your table.'

Wilder and Alistair follow close as I step before the king. My heart pounds in my ears making it hard for me to hear anything.

The second thing that I fear will change me forever is when the King says calmly, 'Medir Leon of the Darkwoods. You stay where you are.'

Frantic, I look over to see the tall, lean male frown and then stop. My father throws a worried glance my way but stays quiet. He wouldn't go against the king. King Oswald waits for the Darkwoods family to be seated.

'Medir Leon, step forward.'

I watch in horror as he does, his feet light on the floor and look over when a group of robed Medir step to the left of the podium. Their hooded faces are barely visible and I suddenly feel very hot.

Wilder and Alistair stand like silent statues, not showing any hint of surprise over what is happening.

'Lady Serafina before we get to other matters, I have had claims brought to my attention of the misconduct of Medir Leon towards you for the majority of your youth and that he was instrumental in you deciding to run from our lands. Is this correct?'

Gaping, I can only blink as my mind tries to protest at what I'm hearing.

Two male voices shout a, 'what?' at the same time from where my family sits in the hall.

I think I stand there for way too long, unspeaking because the king and Wilder share a look. The king nods and then Wilder is gripping my shoulders, drawing my full attention.

Wilder sets those dark obsidian eyes on me and says, *'is that the Medir who forced you to sleep, against your will, as a youngling, Astgeer?'*

Mouth dry, I can only nod.

'Then tell our king, my love. It's important that this is handled.'

'Handled how? I don't want them to know about the dreams.'

'No one will know unless you want them to. You know the king is aware and that is all, I promise. You have to allow me to do this today.'

'*Do what?*' I demand in my head.

Wilder doesn't move. He doesn't react or say a single thing more.

'Lady Serafina, I understand that this is hard. Please answer.'

Knowing that everyone in this hall is watching, I turn back to the male on his throne and answer with, 'yes.'

The murmurs start back up again. Medir Leon starts shouting in a horrible, high-pitched tone that has me flinch. His voice would get that high when he was angry with me for fighting against his control.

I can hear my father yelling something that has King Oswald rage and shut everyone up with a single aggressive warning from his beast. 'Enough! Lord Darkwoods, I will address you and your sons soon. For now, I suggest you stay quiet,' he roars. 'I have reports of the abuse this male conducted against a female of our kind. You all know the punishment for such crimes. Our females are sacred and should be cherished. What say you?'

Every hair on my body stands on end at the command in King Oswald's tone. I have no idea what is going on but I have a really horrible feeling.

The room erupts in shouts calling for the male's head. No one calls their support for the Medir whimpering on the floor.

The group beside the podium moves forward slightly and catches my attention. The leader pulls back his hood to reveal a male so ancient in appearance that it kinda gives me the creeps. Snow-white hair. Skin like paper but eyes so sharp and clear that I'm not sure if they have any colour take me in before flowing back to the King.

'Your Majesty, we accept the claims and are happy to deal with this matter at the Medir academy.'

Holy fucking shit. I know that voice. The scent of sand fills my nose and my small gasp draws Wilder's attention.

'What is it?' Wilder asks, full of concern.

'I know...I...' but I can't reply because Alistair has started laughing, catching my attention. It isn't really a laughing matter.

'Master Medir Tamor, this will not be handled by anyone but my wing and I.'

'Actually, Prince Alistair and my wing are not needed here. This is my duty,' Wilder states, his voice scarier than any other in this room right now. It echoes, meaning everyone can hear him. *'My King, I challenge Medir Leon of the Darkwoods for his crimes and abuse against my future mate, Lady Serafina Darkwoods.'*

The hall erupts in murmurs while I watch, my jaw hitting the floor as Drengar Wilder BlazeAzar Medir removes the weapon on his back and throws it to the floor, at the foot of the podium. The power that vibrates through the hall has me look to my future mate with a newfound sense of awe and trepidation.

A challenge in Azanir is a serious matter. It's a fight to the death.

What happens next out of the three things that will change me forever is when the King nods once in agreement and Medir Leon roars and jumps up. He runs towards me with a look of pure rage.

Chapter Twenty Four

The world has a way of slowing down when I'm in these situations.

Turning, I watch Medir Leon race at me, his teeth half shifted to fangs, his eyes frenzied hearing Wilder declare the battle between them. Someone shouts something in the distance.

My focus moves from the Medir to the male near the podium who walks calmly towards me, seemingly unfazed by the imminent attack.

'Close your eyes Astgeer, if you don't want to watch what is going to happen next,' Wilder says, every word slow and drawn out now that I've stepped into this slow motion existence.

'Why would I want to do that?' I say aloud. 'You are going to kill him, aren't you?' My gaze collides with black obsidian and I feel a deep sense of calm.

Wilder smiles that arrogant, half smile that he does. It sets me on fire and the beast under my skin shivers so violently that I shudder. She wants this as much as I do. Medir Leon appears to be trying to shift into his dragon and I can't help but smile because Wilder is almost upon him. The fool could have accepted the challenge and faced Wilder, now because he has made a move to attack me, Wilder is free to do what he wants. I am his future mate. Technically even my father and brothers could step over to protect me.

The thought has me look over at the table of Darkwoods warriors. Emmet and Luka are up, swords in hand as if their intention is to come to my aide.

Not that they're needed.

I don't know what I expected to happen next, maybe some kind of Azanite battle. A fight with swords or teeth and claws. Not for the world to speed up and just before Medir Leon gets to me he stops abruptly, his arms spread wide and his eyes bugging out of their sockets.

There is a beat of silence the moment he stopped and then an ear-shattering scream comes from his lips. Pain washes over his face and he falls heavily to his knees before me. Arms still stretched. Sweat falls down his face as he wails in agony.

I can see him struggle to fight against whatever is happening. It's horrifying and satisfying at the same time. My beast growls a weird sound in my head and my skin heats. She's been quiet since the moment we had together in the ocean. She is clearly loving what is happening right now though.

I can't look away. This is a male who haunted my waking and dreaming world for so long. Even when I ran away, I still feared his power over me. I read about trauma and abuse with Laney's help. I know what I've been through and I tried to heal over the years with my found family.

Now, here he is. The male who took away my autonomy. Used me. Locked me in my nightmares. On his knees, screeching like he's being ripped apart from the inside out.

There is not a single sound in the hall beside his screams and Wilder's boots calmly stopping behind the weaker Medir.

It takes me way too long to realise that Wilder is doing this to him.

Wilder sets those black eyes back on me. *'The power of the Medir is a complex one. I can heal but...'* He indicates to the male between us. It's probably a weird time for a lesson in Medir magic, but it fascinates me. His power goes beyond anything I thought capable. It's intimidating and turns me on at the same time—very confusing.

'You can also kill,' I finish his sentence. *'He is a Medir though.'*

Wilder's laugher fills my head, it's all beast. *'No one is as powerful as me, love.'*

Wow. The arrogance is next level, and I fucking love it.

'Drengar Medir Wilder, enough of this, end it already,' Master Medir Tamor states. He doesn't sound angry, maybe like he has better things to do right now.

Bending down as if to whisper in Medir Leon's ear, Wilder's eyes don't leave my face as he says, projecting his voice to every Azanite in this room, *'anyone who threatens or hurts my mate will not die a peaceful death.'*

Medir Leon's next scream has blood bubble in his mouth and spill over the edges. I'm transfixed by the sight.

'If anyone touches her, they will face the same fate. She is mine. I will have no mercy.'

His words seem to settle over the room. A warning and a promise to everyone watching.

My abuser makes a final choking sound and falls heavily on his side. Then there is silence.

I stand staring at the dead body. Emotion after emotion floods my system.

Wilder waits, watching, giving me space to process.

'He's dead,' I say weakly.

'I will kill anyone who harms you.'

It's Wilder's tone that has me look away from the lifeless sack of shit that terrorised me for years and over at him. The skin under my arm ripples painfully. My beast wants out. She wants to touch and seal our mating. She wants to rip his clothes off and...I have to mentally slap myself out of the dangerous thought process.

Wilder knows exactly what I'm struggling with because he throws me that side-smile.

I want to throw my arms around him but keep control over my body when he steps to my side and brings me close. The King is barking orders to the Master Medir and I know this isn't over yet.

'What now?' I ask Wilder softly.

'Now, the meeting begins.'

Chapter Twenty Five

I'm exhausted.

I have answered countless questions. Alistair and Wilder have answered just as many.

The leaders of each family sit with their Drengar behind them, taking turns at asking for clarity or further information at points along the way. The Lord of the Riverways and his family are made up of very hairy males. Their Drengar crest is an intricate pattern of lines, representing the rivers that flow through their lands. It is the lands where my 'step' mother came from. She is the daughter of the Lord, a stern-faced male who is said to be very strict on the way his Drengar train and upholds tradition like it's his role in life.

He is the only lord who hasn't looked at me.

The Lord of the Cavelands is probably the biggest male I've ever seen, in terms of shoulder width. He takes up two spots on his table and the axe on his back peeks over his shoulders. Every time I look over there the thing winks under the light. I don't know much about the Cavelands. They live high up in the mountains and the males all wear the same hard-ness on their faces.

I'm sitting with the BlazeAzar's, their lands are not defined by where they are in the kingdom but by the family that rule over the most dangerous lands within Azanir. The Lands of the Blaze sits at the end of a cliff, their mighty house at the pointed edge, guarding Azanir from the wraiths that constantly attack. It is said the rift between our world and the world of the night-demons must be over the waters close to the Blazelands.

It's also home to the Drengar academy, where all males are trained to become the mighty warriors.

That's why the BlazeAzar are so powerful in the kingdom and why no one mentioned the fact that it is improper for me to be sitting beside Wilder at the end of the table amongst his family. I think maybe him killing the Medir without lifting a finger could have something to do with it.

I wasn't even able to fully acknowledge the group of intimidating males who rose as I approached, there are so many of them. I knew that Wilder had brothers, four of them but seeing them in the flesh is another thing entirely.

They're all just as big as him. His father has the same dark eyes and they all wore the same expression, like they are constantly waiting for a wraith attack. The Lord of the Blazelands is a male who sits, back straight with black eyes scanning the room for threats constantly. He hasn't asked a single question of Alistair or me.

Every time I speak, it appears like Wilder's family makes eye-contact with every person in the hall, as if challenging them to disbelieve me.

It's kinda weird, especially when across from us is the table of Darkwoods males. My father in the middle. Luka and Emmet seem like they'd rather be stabbing something than sitting in here listening to the recount of how Alistair and his wing found me in the human world. They seemed extra grouchy when he got to the part about how they took me with them on their road-trip to retrieve the sacred text of our people.

Thankfully, I haven't had to discuss my human family with any of them yet. I made a point of keeping Laney and my true family from the conversation. All these Drengar are going to know is that I offered to help and that's it. Not that I bargained my life away to save Van.

Hearing the last few weeks of my life spoken and pulled apart is strange. Every moment replays in my mind.

Every word. Every emotion. The wraith attacks and my dreams. The way I fell in love with Wilder unexpectedly.

But these are the parts of the story I left out. They belong to me and my Drengar family.

The Lord of the Riverways is the most vocal in his need to have more information, he doesn't seem too happy, especially when he hears of the ending of the story.

That is when the hall goes completely quiet.

'Can you repeat what you just said, my Prince?' The Lord of the Riverways says diplomatically.

Everyone tenses. Even the males at our table.

Alistair nods, throws me a sympathetic look and proceeds to end the story again. I know what is about to happen. 'The Lady Serafina was taken by the rebel humans. She was tortured and drew the wraiths to her in an attempt to escape.'

I feel every eye on me. The weight of them makes it hard to breath. Wilder's hand slips under the table and rests on my knee. I grip it tightly.

'I see,' is all the Riverways male says. The male I thought was my grandfather is assessing me from across the room and I hate it. 'And then you say she grabbed the book and then…' he waits for it to be repeated.

To his credit, Alistair is being very patient. 'Our sacred text opened for her.'

More silence.

'The text hasn't opened in over a thousand years,' the Lord of the Cavelands says slowly, as if picking his words carefully. 'I do not mean to insult the Lady of the Darkwoods, but how are we supposed to believe that?'

It's a valid question, and one that I don't have an answer for. Wilder goes ridged and I see the unease flash over the Cavelands Lord's face.

Gripping his hand harder under the table, I hope he understands the warning.

'Did you read what was in the pages?' the male at the table of Riverways asks me directly.

'No,' I say softly, probably too softly because everyone looks to each other. I see the scepticism. I see their unconscious sexism. 'It showed me instead.'

Again, the silence in the room is weighted. My words seem to sink in. My father looks like I have just told the room that I'm half human and giving away his biggest secret. A secret that would decimate the house of the Darkwoods.

It's Wilder's father who speaks first, his dark eyes bore into mine. He looks like his sons so much. They are all so similar. The six males of the house of the BlazeAzar are not males that you'd want to mess with. Like Wilder, they share the same bulky build. Looking closely, I can tell that they all have dark brown eyes, that Wilder is the only one with the obsidian co lour.

'Are you saying, Lady Serafina, that our sacred text gave you a vision?'

I clear my throat and remember the promises I made to myself when I was pulled from the water. I promised myself that I'd stop running. That I would learn who I am and find myself.

Steeling my spine, I nod once. 'Yes.'

'And what did it show you?' my father asks, his voice drawing my attention to him. I can't decipher his tone or the expression on his face. I know he believes me though. He knows so much already. His weird abomination of a daughter who has dreams of the future.

'It showed me the past,' I tell him. 'It showed me an Azanir where younglings of our kind ran freely in the streets. So many younglings.' The vision replays in my mind. 'It showed me a mated pair.'

It is the King who speaks next. 'And what exactly about the pair was important?' I know he knows. Alistair and the others kept nothing from him, well, everything about me was left out.

'It was a male Azanite and...' I don't know how to finish my sentence. I don't know how it will be received.

'Go on, Astgeer.'

Staring up at Wilder, I finish my sentence, 'and a human woman with their Azanite youngling.'

Chaos descends in the hall.

Chapter Twenty Six

I sit in the same spot for what feels like hours listening to the back-and-forth comments of the ruling families. After some shouting and debating, there are two sides to the conversation. The side that thinks what I speak is total nonsense and that believes humans are nothing more than our inferiors. This school is the Darkwoods and the Riverways. I know I wasn't the only one that saw my father waiting to see what his father-in-law said before agreeing with him.

Spineless prick.

The other side took pause and decided to argue that it's a concept that can be discussed further.

'How can you be considering this?' my 'grandfather' asks the Lord of the Cavelands.

The big hairy male doesn't seem too happy with the tone. Lord Britus rises to his feet dramatically. 'I have a land full of Drengar. Of males who live their lives knowing that they will never find their mate. Never have a family. The Cavelands are struggling. Wraith attacks are increasing, and as we have discussed in these meetings numerous times before, it seems like the demons have now focused their attention on the remaining females of our kind. We haven't had a birth in the Cavelands for nearly ten years.'

Hearing that is truly alarming. Ten years without a birth. The situation is worse than I thought. It has me look around the hall with new eyes. I'm the only female here and I thought that was just some sexist shit, not that females are a dying breed.

Yet, there is a push against the idea that humans are the answer to the problem. How ignorant and arrogant can you be?

'So what Britus, you're going to start looking to humans? Send your males off to the human realm to try and find their mates?'

Sun Gods, my grandfather is a douche bag. I want to stand up and shout that there's nothing wrong with humans. Humans took me in for ten years. That what I found in the human realm was incredible. That humans aren't our enemy.

'Humans are corrupt and obsessed with power. Look at what they took from us. Look at what Prince Alistair just said they did to one of our females! My own kin!'

Kin! Kin! *I've never spoken to that male in my entire life and now he wants to call me kin!* I can't help but sound a little petulant. Wilder's hand squeezes mine briefly.

'He is trying to make a point and justify his prejudice.'

That has me take pause. Every male in this room has been raised to believe that they are the superior, apex predator of this world. I've told Wilder, Alistair, Viktor and Felix what I saw in that vision. I left out a key part, but I told them. I never asked what they thought though. Would they vote in favour of changing the way the world of the Azanite work? Or do they agree with my 'grandfather'?

It makes me deeply uncomfortable.

It dawns on me how afraid I am of Wilder's answer to that question. I probably should have asked him already. Staring at the way my hand is lost within his, I can't help but fall into the rabbit hole of questions swirling around in my head.

He says that I am his. He killed a male for me without blinking. Saved me. Cares for me. Feeds me. Would all that change if he found out that I was half-human? Would he find my deception too hard to forgive?

'Can an Azanite even mate with a human?' one of Wilder's brothers contemplates. It's not said with any kind of hatred. It has everyone go silent again and draws me from my mind.

'Only a female Azanite can birth a beast of our kind. Humans are not compatible.' My father lies.

I want to stand on my chair and tell them that I think there's more to this conversation and that the vision showed me something else. Something that I'm struggling to make sense of but keep quiet. If they heard that I saw the human woman in my vision shift to dragon form, I'm not sure how these males would react. The ones sitting and standing in the Cavelands corner are already looking as if they may fly to the human realm today to see if they can find themselves a mate. It feels like a disaster waiting to happen. The human realm is not ready to know the existence of our kind and no girl out there deserves to be made a spectacle of, even if she does find her mate in the process.

I couldn't imagine what it would be like to have one of those hairy, massive males walk up to me on the street and get whisked away to this damn place.

'We need to think this matter through a great deal more before we make any decisions,' King Oswald states. He has been quietly listening the entire time, emphasising how great a leader he actually is. Not once did he reprimand any of the inappropriate comments or get angry when someone said something about his rule. He just listened, gave space and time for debate. I can see why Alistair is the male that he is.

Back and forth, it just keeps going. No one has any answers. Just lots and lots of words.

That is until the back door is opened and a group of robe-cladded males walk in, the leader holding a book made of gold.

Chapter Twenty Seven

The Priests of the Sun Gods are a group of lean, tall males who live secluded lives on an island near the capital. Everything I know about them filters through my mind.

It's a short list. They're weird.

Are all extremely old, like the Master Medir. They don't really talk, unless it is to give advice. They wear the same golden robes wherever they go and I have heard that they only speak through their beasts as they believe their true form is the dragon and our human side is nothing more than a 'show'.

I can only imagine what they'd say in the debate about the 'Azanite extinction'. Probably that the Sun Gods will provide us with the answer and that discussing humans would go against our beliefs.

'My King,' the elder says in a raspy voice. He has a striking, frightening kind of face. He's practically skin and bone, which is definitely not what you see around Azanir. It freaks me out and makes me feel like a bitch because I shouldn't judge someone by how they look. So when the priest starts to give his two cents on how they were hearing the conversation and feel that we need to think carefully about giving humans any power, I decide to judge them on that. Typical.

'I understand your concern, Priest Hughburt. However, it's a conversation we need to have.' I like that the King sounds a little frustrated. 'I have asked you here today so that we might discover if what the Lady Serafina saw could be understood. It is said she had a vision, given to her when she touched the golden book of our people.'

Priest Hughburt's face seems to suck in harder against the bones. 'We do not want to offend anyone, My King, but we have concerns with what we have heard. This text has been given to us by the Sun Gods themselves. It has not opened in a thousand years or more. We at the Temple of the Sun have devoted our lives to the teaching of the Gods. If it was to open, would it not open for one of their devoted servants.'

Ah. I see. These wankers don't believe me out of some kind of ego issue. Or maybe it's jealousy that their book would open for me and not them. I'd love to shout that I'd be happy never touch that book again and leave it to tell them weird-cryptic shit that messes with their brains.

I feel that the King is having a similar reaction to me because the right side of his lip pulls back a little before he catches it.

Wilder's soft cuss words in my head makes me smile to myself and I like that he doesn't seem to like these priests either. Alistair grins and I'm sure he heard Wilder to.

'Be that as it may, we have to test this theory. If the Sun Gods will speak to one of us, then we must listen. Lady Serafina, would you please step forward?'

It's a rhetorical question because there is no way that I can say no to King Oswald as he indicates me over with a firm gesture.

Fuck me.

'You don't have to go if you don't want to,' Wilder reassures me as I rise on shaking legs. His father and brothers are watching me closely. Actually every male in the damn hall is watching me closely.

'I gotta do this, Wilder. We spoke about this being a possibility this morning. I'm back to face this mess, not continue to run away from it.' Feeling very mature, I remind myself that I am not that scared little adolescent anymore. That I'm not going to let all these males make me feel small and powerless.

Wilder goes to follow and I make a point of stopping him. This feels like something I have to do on my own. I need to know that I can handle myself. That I am capable.

'I think I should go up,' he grumbles and it has me smiling up at him.

'You just showed everyone that you can kill them without being close or lifting a finger. I think I will be perfectly safe and protected with you back here.'

His growl is all beast. *'I will burn this entire lair to the ground for you.'* Reluctantly, he sits back down and I regret my decision the moment I step away from the BlazeAzar table and walk alone to stand before the podium.

The priest practically recoils from me. He's holding the book so tightly as if I might grow four heads and eat him *and* the book.

Side-eying the weird, robed male, I wait for instructions and have to pick my stomach up off the floor when King Oswald says, 'give the text to Lady Serafina.'

The priest bristles and his mouth snaps open and shut like a fish out of water. All the while, the churning in my stomach gets worse. I have no idea what is going to happen. Once I gave the book over to Alistair, I haven't had any desire to go near the damn thing.

Also, I'm not some kind of poor circus animal that they can use for a show. I don't know if I should vomit all over the stone floor with nerves or start yelling my fury.

'Is this a good idea?' the Lord of the Cavelands says and I'm genuinely surprised with the concern I hear in his tone.

'I agree, my son's mate should not be placed into a risky situation. We don't know what will happen.'

Damn, do my cheeks go all red hearing Wilder's father voice his concerns.

The next voice to speak actually has me look over my shoulder. 'I don't like this.' My brother doesn't sound too impressed. Emmet is eyeballing our father like he is waiting for him to also speak up. Both my brothers don't look very happy about what they are asking me to do. Which has my stomach rolling around even more. I didn't think they cared. Dad sure doesn't. He's sitting back in his seat, watching me. I'm guessing he's working out some kind of scheme in his mind. He already knows that the king is going to speak to him later about Medir Leon and I'm sure the questions he's going to have to answer aren't going to paint him as the loving, protective father. I've embarrassed him by running away, maybe he is hoping that I'll touch the book and just disappear again.

With a bit of luck, I'll disappear and find myself back in the human realm so I can go back to my true family.

'I said give Lady Serafina the book!' the King roars the end of the sentence and even I jump to take it from the poor priest who looks like he might have a heart attack.

The moment the weight of the book hits my arms, I find myself falling.

Slowly, I drop. My mind knowing that I am but my body no longer my own. There is nothing I can do about it.

The hall evaporates.

I fall into a deep nothingness.

Chapter Twenty Eight

Face flaming, I turn my back on the scene I've just stepped into. Hands pressed against the stone wall I'm now facing, I try to understand what is happening.

Nothing makes sense.

It's a dream that isn't really a dream.

The pair on the bed have clearly just had an amazing time with each other.

I shouldn't be here and instantly look for a door, which isn't on this wall and I'm too afraid to turn around and draw attention to myself.

No one is shouting at me for being here. I'm not being threatened by an Azanite warrior or being burnt to a crisp. From what I just saw, the male is definitely a warrior, I got a glimpse of his naked body and holy Sun Gods, he is massive.

I don't want to watch some kind of weird porno and pray that they have finished. However, when I hear the male speak, I can't help but look over my shoulder. The pair are covered so I don't see anything I don't want to see, thankfully. The warrior is above the female, speaking words so heartwarming that I instantly think of Wilder. It is clear he cherishes her and he appears to be upset to hurt her. He tells her that part of the mating is for him to bite her, to claim and mark her as his.

Confused, I have no idea why he seems upset or what he is talking about. I feel like I know what this is. That I've seen these two before. Yet, I can't seem to make the connections in my brain. I don't know much about mating and biting was never in the minimal information that I got. She should be okay though, she is an Azanite. At least I think she is.

Actually…

The male tells her that she is his forever, and then I notice that she is human just before he bites her.

Instinctively, I step forward with the intent to protest. He is going to kill her…

Transfixed by the scene before me, I watch the teeth bite into her shoulder and hear her gasp. His hips move, leaving no argument to why the woman looks to be stuck in a state of ecstasy. His teeth are locked onto her shoulder and he is doing something else under that sheet that has me blushing, hard.

Eventually, he pulls back, the male apologises and licks at the wound. She doesn't seem at all disturbed by it, or in pain. The wound looks a bit raw but not life-threatening, I guess.

Waiting, I stare, unable to look away, thinking it's all a bit anticlimactic as she smiles up at him.

Until a wave of emotions flicks over her face and then a blood-curdling scream comes from her lips. I clap my hands over my ears and whimper, afraid for her. She screams and screams while he holds her, his face covered in tears as if her pain is his.

When her body starts convulsing, I try to rush forward to help and trip. Falling, face first, the ground disappears just as I'm about to hit the stone…

I'm shouting for someone to help, my hands flaying around. That poor woman. She was going to die. The way she screamed is a haunting sound I can still hear.

He bit her.

Why would he do that?

He is an Azanite male, he should've known better. He spoke about loving her and being her mate and still, he did that to her.

So many things were wrong with that situation that I don't know what to focus on first.

A strong, calloused grip has my arms securely and gently coaxed beside my body. The touch forcing me from the turmoil within my mind. Words of pure comfort and affection seep into my hysterical thoughts, soothing me

'That is it, my love. You are safe. Now, breath. In and out. Slow and deep.'

Blinking up at the male hovering above me, I stop and comply, taking deep breathes. In and out like he instructs. I'm unable not to. My beast and I would do whatever Wilder instructs. There is no doubt in my mind that he is always protecting me and keeping me safe.

Slowly coming down from the haze and adrenaline, I try to piece together what just happened. I touched that damn golden text and passed out. No, I had another vision. A vision of a mating pair. First it was a straight up porno that I had no business seeing and then he...

'She was in so much pain, Widler. I don't know why he hurt her. He said he loved her.'

A deep crease forms between Wilder's brow, emphasising all his masculine features. Those black eyes search my face and he brushes the hair from my eyes. *'Who Astgeer?'*

'I don't know, but I felt the pain like it was my own. I don't know who they are but I should, I think,' I whisper, not sure why I feel the need to be quiet. Only he can hear me. The vision replays over and over. *'I don't understand why I saw that. She was dying and he loved her.'*

Wilder seems really concerned as I prattle on and on. He doesn't say anything, just keeps stroking my face, allowing me to process.

There is too much energy under my skin.

'What happened?' I ask, trying to sit up and realising instantly that I'm not in the hall anymore. I'm in Wilder's bed. What the fuck?

Wilder helps me to sit up and I blink away the stars in my vision. Viktor and Felix are sitting around the bed, both looking just as unimpressed as Wilder.

Rubbing the ache at the back of my head, I wince.

'The priest gave you the book and you collapsed.' Wilder's hand covers the one I have on the back of my head and in a heartbeat his Medir power seeps through my body, chasing away the pain.

'Better?'

'Yes, thank you. How did I end up in bed?'

'Well—' Felix begins, clapping his hands, eager to tell me the story— 'Poor Viktor and I were sitting around, waiting for you all to return. Both of us annoyed to be left out of the meeting. And just as we were about to eat our evening meal, Wilder storms through the doors with you all passed out in his arms. Lifeless. Scared the life out of us, hey Vik?'

The older Drengar grunts a noise, he's watching me closely and there is no secret that he isn't impressed about everything that has happened.

'This didn't happen the last time you touched the text, did it?' Felix asks.

'No, it didn't.' So, why did that vision hit so hard this time? 'It all sounds a bit dramatic,' I try to make light of the situation but it falls flat when the voices from outside the door filter through the room.

Allistair has guests and he doesn't seem too impressed. I can hear the king and…my brother…and my father. It kinda makes me wish to be back in my vision.

Chapter Twenty Nine

Gaze flying to the grim faced male beside me, I now know the look on his face isn't because of what happened. Well, maybe it is, because he is hovering close, but I'm sure he isn't impressed with some of the conversation happening outside this room.

Felix and Viktor share a look when my father starts demanding that the Prince and Wilder stop acting like they have some kind of authority over my health and wellbeing.

'She convulsed on the floor. My sister needs help. She will not be used in this debate about our extinction!' Emmet sounds like he's ready to beast-out and kill someone.

Alistair tries to defend me and reminds them all that what happened with Medir Leon can't be ignored. He implores his father to remember that. 'As if Lord Darkwoods wasn't aware of what was going on in his lair!'

'Do not accuse me of abusing my daughter! I had no idea what that sick Medir did and I will have to go to my grave knowing that she ran from me because she didn't feel safe enough to ask for help.'

What the actual fuck! My father is an expert liar.

Felix mumbles the word bullshit under his breath and I can't help but agree.

There is a moment of silence and even through the door I feel the tension. I rub at my arms and look up at Wilder knowing that this is going to get worse.

'We are returning to the Darkwoods tomorrow and my daughter will be coming with us! You don't want to start a war over this My King but be aware that the Darkwoods will not tolerate disrespect against our rights. She is my daughter. I haven't accepted any mating with the BlazeAzar's nor have any of them approached me. There are laws in our lands for a reason and I will have you all remember that.' My father too sounds like he is over this conversation. 'That starts now! When she is awake and ready, she will be escorted to my rooms. It is inappropriate for her to be staying here in the Princes quarters with a male who isn't her mate yet.'

My heart thuds painfully and all I can do is look up at Wilder in fear. I don't even know what to stress about first. The part about starting a war or the part where I will be going back to the Darkwoods. Or that my father is blocking my mating. Or...fuck there is too much.

War?

Wilder's expression is enough to have me swallow the lump that has just creeped up my throat. He's going to kill someone. I know it. I go to jump out of bed when he turns and starts heading to the door.

Clearly Viktor knew exactly what I had worked out because he springs into action first. 'Take it easy Wilder,' he states, his arms on my future mate's shoulders stopping him. Viktor is not as large as the angry Medir but he has the authority to stop him and have him think through what he is doing.

I remember Viktor from my youth. He was always spoken about with such respect. He was set to be the commander of my father's Drengar. Yet, here he is, working with the prince. He told me that he left the Darkwoods not long after I ran away.

'Serafina doesn't need you walking out there making this situation worse.'

There is a beat of silence before the stern-faced Drengar nods. 'I know, Wilder. However, it is the world we live in.'

I don't know what Wilder must have said or what Viktor clearly communicates back to the Medir that has Wilder change direction and head over to the monstrous fireplace. He leans on the mantle, deep in thought.

'I won't have anyone go to war for me,' I state just as Alistair and the King walk into the room. They both look exceptionally tired.

'There will be no war,' he states and every male in the room steps back and gives the King some space. He's clearly unhappy and I don't blame him. His pale eyes land on me and I know what is coming. There is a part of me that accepts this as my fate and another that wants to beg and cry and ask Wilder to hold me. 'Lady Serafina, tell me what happened just now in the hall.'

Instinctively, I go to lie. To tell them all that I didn't see anything. It's a habit I have to teach myself to stop.

'I saw a mating pair. It was a male Azanite and a human woman.'

It takes a moment for my words to sink in. 'Is that all?' the king questions like he knows that there is.

'It didn't seem to go very well,' I offer, unsure what was the actual point of the vision. 'He hurt her.'

That clearly isn't what they want to hear because the King makes a disgruntled sound in his throat.

'It's clear that there's a great deal surrounding you, Lady. Hearing your story, listening to what happened when you helped retrieve our sacred text, watching you just now as you touched that book. I am no fool. I believe the Sun Gods have favoured you, even if right now you do not see it as a gift. I am concerned for my people and I feel you have been given the answer to our problem. I don't like doing this but I feel I have to. I'm tasking this wing with finding the answers to what the Sun Gods are trying to tell us and how it can help our people survive.'

Shocked at what King Oswald is saying, I can't look away from the male.

'My King, you are asking us to find out what Serafina's visions mean and how to save our race from extinction?' It seems like I'm not the only one that is stunned by what we've just been told because Viktor speaks slowly, as if thinking through each word.

Poor Felix appears to be having some kind of episode as he stares at the male telling us that we have a mission.

I've never been on a mission. I'm not technically part of this wing, am I ?

'Yes and I think it best we keep this one quiet. I have spoken with the priests of the Sun Gods. They are researching our past further, though I do not trust their judgement on such matters,' King Oswald states simply, seemingly unaware of the affect his words have had on everyone.

'Father, I think—'

Raising his hand to stop Alistair saying whatever it is he was about to say, King Oswald explains that he knows what he is asking. 'There is a small group of influential Azanites that have been discussing the matters spoken about today. I have had word of groups meeting up from my spies and I want to know what they believe. This matter has the potential to cause a great stir in our lands. One that could break us forever.'

The mood sobers. 'This mission is important and I trust you all to see it through. There are laws in our lands that cannot be changed. This will take time. I don't want any of the families to know I am thinking this through before I am ready to make an announcement which I can't, and won't do, without facts. For now, Lady Serafina, you must return to the Darkwoods for a time, while your mating to Wilder is made official and the correct procedures are put in place. There is too much going on and this tension with the Darkwoods has to be squashed. We must do things properly so that we can focus on the bigger issue here, the extinction of our race.'

I expect the room to erupt. I expect Wilder to flip-out and start burning things down. There is only silence. A deep, heavy, sad silence.

Felix sits forward in his chair and rubs at his face like he is tired or worried, or both.

Wilder hasn't turned from the mantle.

'Also, there is an exceptional library in the lair of the Darkwoods that might have some information. There is a book within the library that is said to document our history. My advisors and spies tell me that this book holds key information that we need. I have tried over the years to get my hands on it, as subtly as I can, however it's the properly of the Darkwoods.'

'You would like me to get that book?' I stammer, shocked at what I'm hearing.

Another damn book.

All the pieces of the King's mission fall into place.

Eying Wilder, I study the coiled muscles along his back. I guess now that we are on a mission, there is really nothing that we can say. The king has just made it very clear that we are discussing matters of life and death.

'I understand that being apart from Wilder will be challenging and we will organise the details including opportunities for Wilder to visit you in order to ensure your health and safety. These things are already standard practice when situations like surprise matings occur. I will be speaking with the Lord of the Darkwoods. I think it best we do not provoke your father and grandfather and you follow his instructions to return to his care.'

Hanging my head, I breath through my fear.

The King goes to leave and then stops. Turning he says, 'I know I am asking for a great deal but it is imperative that we find these answers and for you to get that book. The longer you can drag out the mating, the better.'

Drag out the mating? Is the king asking us to not...have sex?

That has Wilder turn around finally. This is no longer about me but about an entire race of Azanites.

Chapter Thirty

I NEED A DRINK. A strong, stiff drink.

A large one.

The conversation in the sitting room has been going back and further. Every aspect of the mission has been pulled apart and my anxiety levels are through the roof.

On and on, the four Drengar go about the new mission. They examine every detail, every possible plan and theory. Roles. Complications. Dangers.

They've discussed my visions, multiple times. We've relived the entire road-trip back in the human realm and have analysed the debate in the kings hall, over and over. The biggest question is who is meeting up in groups to discuss the matter of our extinction and what do they believe.

They've decided that Viktor and Felix will go with me tomorrow to the Darkwoods and that Wilder and Alistair will head to the Cavelands. After hearing of their struggles, it seems like the best place to start. Wilder has given us seven days to get the book and call on him to come and get me. He doesn't think we can be apart any longer than that before it will impact our health.

I've had to recount my visions and answered a myriad of questions that I've already answered. All the while I try not to throw-up everywhere because despite the seriousness of the conversation and what we've been tasked to do, I still keep certain details of what I've seen to myself.

I don't tell them that I saw the human woman shift to a dragon in the first vision and I don't say anything about the male biting that lady while they were mating.

I do try though. About a hundred times I open my mouth to tell them that I haven't been completely honest and get all tongue-tied. How do I confess that I've been keeping things, important things, from them all? This mission could probably be solved by me confessing that I'm half human.

That's a lie. I don't have any answers. I can't even connect with my beast and shift, so I'm not going to be the key to our race extinction.

Sun Gods, what am I doing! I should've stayed in the human realm and continued to be the lost lady of the Darkwoods. When they find out that I've been lying, I'm fucked. They'll hate me.

I hate me!

Curled up in the armchair in the sitting room, I pick at the food on the plate balanced on my knee and try not to hyperventilate.

Now the conversation has moved to the fact that I have to go and retrieve a damned book from my father's lair that we have no information about.

Do we know what it looks like—no.

Do we know if it has a title and what that might be—no.

Am I beginning to form a serious dislike of books—yes.

The only topic they keep skirting around is the fact that the king has told Wilder and I that we are to *hold off* on completing our mating bond and that my father has requested I come to his rooms tonight.

Now officially too queasy to eat, I plonk my plate down on the table and sit back in the chair, hating my life right now. I don't want to go back to the Darkwoods and I definitely don't want to go anywhere without Wilder. The beast under my skin always seems to be looking for him and I know how it felt when I was taken by the humans. Being away from him hurt. Physically and emotionally.

I can't help but regret not completing the bond. The only reason I haven't is because I'm harbouring this massive, life-changing secret.

I should tell Wilder.

The Medir is sitting across from me. His large frame takes up most of the couch he and Felix are on. We haven't said a word to each other. He hasn't even looked my way. It's starting to worry me. I know that me passing out in the hall scared him. I'm not a fool. I can see the worry lines on his face and am very aware that the King's words didn't just affect me.

I don't want to go but I will and only because I'll not be the reason for a war between the BlazeAzar and the Darkwoods. I didn't come back to cause problems. I came back to find answers. To understand myself better and to not feel so…isolated and alone.

Deep down I know that the answers I need are only going to be found in the Darkwoods. That means leaving Wilder for a time and stepping outside of my comfort zone. At the end of the day, how can I give myself to him when I don't know who I am. That's not fair on him, or me. It wouldn't be right to start a life with someone, maybe even have a family, without being comfortable in my own skin. I feel like there's enough generational trauma in my bloodline to not add to the fucking chain. I won't do that to Wilder. I can't do that to the children I hope to have one day.

'Astgeer.'

Looking up from playing with the blanket resting over my lap, I get caught in eyes of obsidian. The force of the gaze has all the worry and tension building in my body float away. The conversation has heated up around us and the noise of it fades until there is just Wilder and I, staring.

'Yes?'

'*You are thinking too loud,*' he states and I see the corners of his mouth kick up a little.

Nodding, I know I am. I'm scared and worried and a little lonely. '*I don't want to leave you but I have to. I just don't want...I don't want anything to come between us and the king said...*' I can't finish the sentence. I don't want Wilder to hate me. I don't want to not be his mate.

Widler's features soften as if he can read every one of my thoughts and emotions. He uncrosses his ankles and opens his arms. '*Come here, my heart.*'

Sun Gods, he is just perfection.

Uncurling myself from the chair, I don't think twice. I step around the table, knowing that the others are watching us as they keep talking and I fall into Wilder's lap. His massive arms cage me instantly and I pull my legs up and lay against his chest, my head fitting snuggly under his chin.

Breathing him in, I still can't believe that he killed a male for me today and no one has said a single word about it.

His hand begins to brush through my unbound hair, the feel of his fingers has me shiver.

'*Nothing can come between us. You are mine, forever. You don't have to go to the Darkwoods if you don't want to. I'll take you away from this, if that's what you want. However, I see that you need to do this. I understand that you have your own questions you need answered and that you need to go home to find them. I want you happy.'*

There's a deep part of me that wants to take up his offer to take me away. Running would be great right now.

'I won't lie, I'm scared to go back but I need to do this for myself, Wilder. I need to prove to myself that I'm not that scared little female anymore. I battled wraiths and human rebels. I can face my family and the Darkwoods. I can find this book. I can help our people.'

Wilder doesn't stop touching me. He listens without interrupting and when I go silent, he waits to see if there is more I need to say.

I just sit on his lap, with his hands on my body and the others discussing matters of life and death.

'Of course you can. You, my dear mate, can do anything. I agree with the King that the Sun Gods favour you. You are a gift, Serafina and I thank the Gods every day that you are mine.'

Snuggling in closer, I can only hear the sound of Wilder's heartbeat and try to lock the sound into my memory because tomorrow I will leave him for the Darkwoods.

Chapter Thirty One

Dozing against Wilder's warmth, I have no desire to move or go pack my things.

'My Prince, the Lord Darkwoods is here to see you,' Alistair's butler states, waking me up fully.

Wilder squeezes me gently as Alistair grumbles and informs his servant that he can let the Lord in.

I practically jump from Wilder's lap. 'My father is here! What the hell?' I practically shout, watching the butler walk away.

Pacing, I fuss over my clothes and then stop and contemplate running to the room and jumping from the balcony. Closing my eyes, I try to connect with the beast under my skin, the quiet bitch who I know is there. *Help me. I'll jump and you fly us from here!* I shout the words over and over again in my head. Nothing.

Damn useless dragon! I heard her in the ocean, she told me that I just had to let her take over. To give her control.

Face scrunched, I focus on giving her everything. Nothing. My plans to run off the balcony and get out of here slip away into the silence in my head.

'Uhm, Raff. You need some help? Are you going to be sick?'

'No! I'm concentrating,' I grumble, trying desperately to ignore Felix. I can do this. I'm not useless.

'You are? It looks like you need to use the bathroom,' he laughs and then shuts up when I open my eyes and glare at him.

'I don't need to go to the bathroom,' I pout and wrap my arms around my middle feeling useless.

'I think it best if we all stay calm,' Viktor says. The words 'stay calm' become a mantra in my head until Viktor states, 'I'm speaking to you, Serafina. You need to calm down.'

Wilder is behind me in an instant, holding me close.

'What?' I thought I was.

'Your energy is making it hard for us to stay level-headed,' Alistair chimes in as he pops a grape in his mouth and rises. He indicates in my general direction and I look up at Wilder with his red-eyes and his deep scowl. Shit.

We can hear voices coming closer.

'Okay. Okay, I can do this,' I pep-talk myself out loud. 'And, you need to remember what the King said.' I poke Wilder in the chest and get the full force of his dragon as he stares down at me. 'Both of you,' I warn. I lose a bit of my bravado and whisper, *'I need to know that you are okay with me making this decision to go back, Wilder. That you and I are solid because it's the only thing keeping me together right now.'*

Red turns to black and my future mate frowns down at me as if realising that he wasn't in control. *'You have my full support. Just be patient, it's not easy for me or my beast knowing that we have to let you go.'*

'I know,' I say, rising on the tips of my toes so I can place a soft kiss on his lips.

I feel the moment the Lord Darkwoods walks into the room and know instantly that it's not my father. Wilder tenses and I turn around to see Luka standing at the doorway, staring at me like he still can't believe that I am here. Alive.

Drawing his green eyes from me, my brother nods his head to Alistair in respect while the butler gets the hell out of the room. I envy him.

Where Emmet looks like my father, Luka is the image of his mother. Lush, dirty-blonde hair that falls to his shoulders. A straight nose and a subtle boy-ish look about his eyes and cheeks, Luka has the typical tanned complexion of an Azanite and a roundness to his eyes that has the green stand out. I don't have much of a memory of the last time I saw my youngest brother. Just like with Emmet, he and I never had much in common. He was off learning the skills to become a Drengar and going on missions, while I was at the lair, being kept separate from the world.

I have fuzzy memories of him bringing me home sweets from his travels but that could've been Emmet. I don't really remember.

'My Prince, thank you for letting me enter. I honestly didn't think that you would.' Luka grins and it drips with mischief.

'Why wouldn't we, Luka?' Alistair sighs as if he is very aware of my brother's nature.

'Because the last time we saw this asshole, he caused me to fall from the sky,' Felix grumbles but there is no hatred or anger in his tone. Actually, it's full of affection and he gets off the couch and strides over to the Darkwoods Lord and they clasp hands. There's males back slapping and genuine display of friendship and I vaguely remember Felix speaking of Luka back in the human realm.

'You two know each other?'

Felix nods and then steps back so that once again, Luka and I are staring. 'We were in the Drengar academy together. Learnt under the same Commander.'

It's my turn to nod and the awkwardness in the room is definitely coming from me.

'Serafina,' Luka greets, still looking at me as if I'm an apparition.

'Hi Luka, it's been a long time,' my voice shakes as I speak. Luka takes in the way Wilder is standing at my back, his arm now around my waist.

'It's been eleven years, two and a half months since I last saw you. I thought you dead for ten years and one month this coming full moon.'

The colour drains from my face and seeps into the stone under my bare feet.

'Right,' I choke out. There is no anger in his tone. No reproach or condemnation. He speaks as if he is just giving me facts. 'I...I...'

'I heard why in the meeting,' he says for me.

Silence fills the space.

'Let's sit, you've obviously come here for a reason,' Alistair announces and indicates to the armchair I like to use.

Felix claps his friend once more on the back before taking his own seat and Luka lowers himself slowly into the chair, his focus on me. Or maybe it's Wilder. I've learnt pretty fast that there isn't much love between the BlazeAzar and the Darkwoods.

Wilder pulls me with him and I end up squashed between his oversized frame and Viktor's on the couch. Alistair takes one of the single chairs.

I'm getting really sick of these awkward tense moments, my nerves can't take much more. Wilder's hand falls on the ones I didn't realise I was wringing together on my lap.

Luka watches the entire exchange and after a time I realise that he is openly ignoring the grumpy male beside me, and I'm not talking about Wilder. Realising that Viktor hasn't said a single word, I sneak a little peak up at the scary Drengar. The expression on his face could curdle milk. My family is clearly not on everyone's Christmas card list.

'So, what can we help you with?' Alistair inquires, crossing his legs in that ankle-over knee way that men do.

'My father has sent me to bring my sister back to our rooms. She won't be staying here tonight, and tomorrow she will be returning to the Darkwoods with us.'

Chapter Thirty Two

I sit, stunned by the swagger and genuine blasé attitude. With not a hint of worry about facing off four Drengar, one of which is a very powerful Medir and another is our prince, he waits with a calm smile on his face for someone to respond.

Alistair chuckles and it doesn't calm the tension in the space, it actually increases it. 'You can see why we'd hesitate to comply with your father's request.'

'I can but I also know that our king has told you to comply. So, you don't really have a choice. And neither do I. We all do what we are told. We are the Drengar.' Luka asks if he can have a piece of fruit and Alistair just nods, eyeing the male like he's trying to work him out.

No one speaks.

It's as if no one can argue with what he is saying. Luka isn't here to cause problems. He is here to deliver a message. I'm kinda waiting for him to start yelling at me or something.

'Your sister is part of my wing, she has every right to stay in our quarters.'

Alistair claiming me as part of his wing has me sit straighter and stop fidgeting.

I'm part of his wing? I guess I am. I've been included in this mission to the Darkwoods.

A swell of emotion forms in my chest and then dies when Luka laughs. 'You can claim her in whatever way you want. She is an unmated female of my house, she is coming back to the Darkwoods. My father is already furious and I honestly don't think that anyone wants to unleash his rage. Not at the moment.'

I should never have come back here.

'Your father can blow smoke around as much as he wants, Luka Darkwoods, it won't change what your sister is and who she is mating to,' Viktor states each word so calmly that it's kinda creepy. I'm dying to know what happened to him. He seems to hate the Darkwoods and my family more than Wilder and his.

Wilder, to his credit hasn't made a noise. He is actually pretty calm.

'Come on, Luka, you know that there's so much going on here,' Felix interjects. His easy-going attitude turned on to the max.

'I know. What can I do?' Luka pops a grape into his mouth and shrugs. 'You come back from the dead Serafina and have attached yourself to a BlazeAzar and this wing without a single word to your family. Our father is angry and I think he has a right to be.' Luka seems to realise the mistake he's made when Wilder is no longer quiet. Every Drengar in the room tenses and Felix sighs heavily, shaking his head at my brother in reprimand.

Quickly, I place a hand on Wilder's arm. *'We decided that I would go. Fighting won't make this any easier.'*

'They have a right to their feelings,' Felix says in my head and I'm a little taken aback realising that I may have projected my words to them all.

'They can feel whatever they want but he doesn't have to be a bastard about it,' Viktor grumbles.

'He is the messenger. We can't condemn him for doing his father's bidding,' Felix states.

Felix is defending Luka but he should be on my side. I thought he was my friend.

Wilder squeezes the hand I still have on his arm. *'He is my heart.'*

'Shit, did I say that out loud?' Gaze flicking to the Drengar sitting across from me, I see the hurt on Felix's face and feel my heart sink. *'Sorry, I'm new to this whole beast talking thing.'*

'It's okay, Raff. I get it. I just want you all to remember that your family grieved you. They thought you were dead and built a stone in their woods for you to mark your leaving of this world.'

They did? I shiver at the thought that I have a gravestone erected in the Darkwoods. That's fucking creepy.

'I ran because of what my father did...what...what I...' I block the thought, my secret on the tip of my tongue. Stop talking. Stop talking.

'We decided on this mission and Serafina needs to help us get that book. She is right, we need to play nice. For now,' Alistair chimes.

Luka sits at the end of the seat, watching us all. I can't help but think he knows we're speaking to each other.

'I will go with you,' I say, mustering up all my courage.

'And Viktor and Felix will be returning to the Darkwoods with the Lady Serafina, Luka Darkwoods. That is my command and if your father wants to blow smoke, we can see who's will be hotter if you anger me, my wing and your sisters future mate.'

Damn, Alistair is a bad-ass and I'm here for it.

Chapter Thirty Three

'*Do you have everything?*'

'Yes.' I shove another shirt into the travel bag I've been given and consider if I want to change from the loose fitting pant and off-white tunic I'm wearing to one of the many dresses that had been delivered to the rooms today. My father will probably hate that I'm wearing such mundane clothes. I was raised to believe that a female should wear dresses. Long, flowing ones that emphasised my girl-ish-ness.

I look at the pile of clothes that Wilder places down beside my bag and I look up at the imposing male for the first time since I told Luka I would go with him. I bite my bottom lip to stop it from wobbling.

Wilder's eyes flash from black to red to black again.

'Those are your shirts,' I release my lip to say and then clamp it down again. My words come out quietly and shaking.

'I know. My scent is all over them. It might help while we are apart.'

Sun Gods, my heart stutters and I pick one up and shove my face into it and breath in his intoxicating, calming scent. 'It will. It won't be you though.'

If this is hard for me, it must be killing Wilder. Male Azanites are possessive, loyal and extremely protective of their females. It's still hard to believe that I'm Wilder's mate and equally as hard to think that he will be in just as much, if not more, pain because of our separation. Yet, he is still thinking of how to make me comfortable. Putting my needs first.

Diving back in my bag, I remove one or two of my own clothes and quickly shove it under his pillows and then throw myself down on the sheets and begin to roll around.

Wilder watches quietly, his expression unreadable.

'Will this help?' I ask, probably being a little dramatic as I squish my face in every pillow.

'Yes, Astgeer. It will help.'

I stop rolling around and look up at him. I probably look a mess, my hair is all over the place.

'Will this be really hard for you? I don't know a lot about males but if you're feeling this,' I rub the aching space between my breasts and watch as he tracks the move, 'then I'm really sorry. I'm sorry I'm not ready to…take this further yet. If I was and we had already had…you know…then we wouldn't be in this position. I just don't know…I don't know who I am, Wilder. I have so many…' Secrets. Fears. I could end my sentence on either word, they'd both be true.

His face softens and the bed dips as he kneels on it and slowly crawls over my body until I'm on my back. Breathing becomes difficult as I stare up at the gorgeous male who owns my heart completely.

His dark hair falls around his shoulders and I trace the scar that runs across his throat with the tip of my finger. All my worries and fears evaporate being surrounded by him. His energy settles mine and nothing in this world seems scary. I know that all I have to do is trust Wilder and he will keep me happy and safe for the rest of my life.

'You never have to say sorry to me, Serafina. You are mine, no matter what we do or how far apart we are.'

'And you are mine,' I state feeling a little feral. My skin is becoming all scratchy and I look down at my arm and watch as it ripples. I tense under the pain of it and then release a sigh when Wilder lowers himself down and buries his head into my neck.

'Your beast wants to connect with me. She knows that we will be separated. She just needs a little attention.' Wilder growls and the vibrations of his body against mine has my back arching off the bed and my panties instantly wet. My moan is deep as his tongue flicks out and licks along my throat and ends at the underside of my ear. A spot that has me quiver in need.

'Wilder,' I beg and hear his chuckle in my mind. It has me nearly lose control.

Gripping his face, I pull his attention from my neck to my mouth. Slamming my lips onto his, I try to take the lead and am quickly overwhelmed by the passion of the male now devouring me.

Our tongues dance and I let go to his assault.

Needing his weight, I wrap my legs and arms around his body and try to pull him down. It seems to take him a while to realise what I want and then he is no longer holding himself up on his arms. His weight feels amazing and I'm pushed into the mattress, my future mate still holding himself off a little so that I can breathe.

His warmth is next level. It heats me from the inside out.

'I'm going to miss you. Thank you for letting me do this,' I whimper, afraid to say the words out loud. I might just start begging him to take over and find us a cave to live in somewhere. I've heard of mated pairs who do that. It was a story I listened to growing up. It never made sense but now

it does. All I need is Wilder. I don't need the rest of the world. A cave is looking mighty enticing right now.

'I won't be too far, Astgeer. Alistair and I will go the Cavelands and start our search for answers. I know you need to do this. It's hard to let you go but I would never stand in the way of you doing what you need. I'm your mate. Your partner in every way. I refuse to keep you caged like you were as a youngling. I want to see you spread your wings and be happy. It is my job to make that happen and if watching you go will do that, then my pain is my own to bare.'

Could he be any more perfect.

Chapter Thirty Four

I'm on my own with Luka, walking the halls of the King's lair feeling as if every step is ripping my heart out. Wilder was acting all calm and even-tempered when I gave my bag to Luka but deep down I know his dragon was raging.

Felix and Viktor promised that they'd be in the courtyard ready to come with me tomorrow. I was a little shocked that they weren't coming with me now but realised pretty quickly that they wouldn't be able to go to the rooms of my father. The houses of Azanir follow strict rules. They wouldn't be welcomed, despite the fact this is the lair of the king. Everyone has their own section to claim while they are here. It is the law.

Luka doesn't say a word as he leads me through the maze of a place. The darkness outside has me rubbing my arms. We pass a few open doors and despite the mass of Drengar on watch, I still want to run and find a place to nest. No, not a place. I want Wilder's bed. My nest should be there, with him inside it.

Finally, we get to a big wall of double doors and Luka holds them open so that I can step inside. He barely looks at me as I do.

The room I step into is very similar to Alistair's, maybe less furniture. It has the same light stone as the rest of the lair and the floors are covered in richly-patterned rugs. A sitting space is set up across from the massive fireplace taking up most of the side wall. It casts the only light in the open space.

I stop moving at the sight of the males in the sitting area though. Instinctively, I look for the exists. To my left is a wall of thick curtains that I'm guessing leads to a balcony. We are on the fourth floor of the lair but I will jump off that damn balcony if I need to. There are an array of other closed doors and a walkway through the middle of the space. I spy a handful of Darkwoods human servants, each one has stopped what they're doing to stare at me.

They don't have my attention though, my focus is on my father and Emmet and the Lord of the Riverways who rises along with the others. There are a handful of Drengar along the walls from both houses. They too are watching me and right now, I wish I had refused the request to come here.

The need to run pounds heavily in my chest.

Luka is at my back in an instant as if he knows what I'm thinking. His hand rests between my shoulders and before I can protest, he is pushing me forward. Further into the room and closer to the males openly staring, my anxiety gets worse.

My father is still the stern-faced male who ruined my life. Emmet is the spitting image standing beside him, looking at me in the same way, like I am somehow the bad-person here. Not them. Not this place.

The Lord of Riverways is the first one to break the silence by telling my father that he will see him soon. Then the horrible male eyeballs me, clicks to his Drengar like they are animals and walks out of the room. He practically huffs his displeasure as he passes.

Luka makes a grumbling noise in his throat and I'm pushed to the sitting room, my feet moving of their own accord.

Dad stares and stares. The furniture isn't as decorated as the ones in Alistair's rooms. The small table is covered in plates of fancy looking food and decorated pots full of sweet smelling teas. At least that's the same as the princes. Azanites eat a lot.

Emmet bends to fill a delicate looking cup with more tea from the teapot before he sits down. The sight of him crossing his legs at the ankle and drinking has me bite the inside of my cheek.

'Sit down, Serafina,' my father snaps and indicates for Luka to take a seat too.

Looking around, I quickly plonk down in an armchair so that I don't have to sit beside any of them.

'The rest of you can leave us,' the lord states, walking to the fireplace and leaning on the mantel like one of those villains in Van and my favourite television show.

Sun Gods, I feel like I've stepped into the principal's office, which was not uncommon in my adolescent years. Van was the reason for most of our trips to that old arsehole's office. He liked to shout and pace around the room and honestly thinking of all the trouble I used to get in with my foster brother has me not feeling so anxious. I've had an entire ten years without these shifters in my life and it's been amazing.

The Darkwoods Drengar disappear, some through the heavy curtain and the others down the long hallway.

Luka starts popping bits of cheese and bread into his mouth while we all wait for the room to be cleared out.

The moment the last Drengar leaves is the moment my dad turns around and I get the full force of his attention.

The same pale grey eyes that I look at every morning narrows in my direction. 'Serafina, do you have something you'd like to say?'

I open and close my mouth a few times. I glance at Luka and Emmet before trying to answer again and then clap my teeth together when Dad starts talking for me.

'Why don't we start with where you have been for the last ten years or why you ran away? You might start by explaining what you thought you were doing and what possessed you to leave your home, my lair, on your own in the middle of the night! Or telling us what happened back there in the hall when you touched our sacred text!'

'She could probably start with an apology,' Emmet interjects, sipping at his fine porcelain teacup.

'Yes, that might be a great place to start,' Dad agrees, his teeth all clenched and his eyes flashing red. Which is funny, because that's the colour I'm seeing right now. How fucking dare they!

'Apologise?' I say slowly, making sure that I've heard them correctly.

'Yes, Serafina! Apologise. We thought you were dead! We mourned you. We buried you and now we hear that you've been living, illegally, in the human realm, while we've been here thinking that we lost you forever!' Emmet is on his feet emitting such heat that I begin to sweat. I'm lost for words. His emotions confuse and shock me. 'Then you appear out of nowhere without anything to say to us, under the arm of Wilder BlazeAzar!'

No longer stunned, I glare up at the male yelling at me like *he* has the right. 'Don't,' is all I say and he shuts his mouth. He will not speak about Wilder with that tone.

'What do you expect, Serafina?' Luka questions, drawing my attention. A log cracks in the fireplace.

'Leave us,' Father says and my stomach drops into my butt at his tone.

Emmet gladly jumps up and storms down the hall while Luka takes his time eyeing our father before he sighs and walks after our brother. I'm left alone with the male that I ran from all those years ago. A male that lied to me and caused me so much pain.

'Serafina—'

'I know!' I half-shout, jumping to my feet. 'I know what you did and I know what I am.' Everything comes up. My anger and betrayal. All the trauma of my life as a youngling under his 'care'. 'I know everything, *Father*,' I snap, not allowing him control over me any longer. Yes, he scares the shit out me and yes, here in Azanir he owns me, but he doesn't get to intimidate and push me around.

The noise he makes has my insides liquify and slowly those pale eyes staring at me turn red. 'You don't know anything, *Daughter*.'

Chapter Thirty Five

'I KNOW ENOUGH,' I counter, clutching my shaking hands into fists. 'I heard you speaking with Medir Leon and the other males in that room a few days before I left. You were talking about me. About my future! And then later about who I am and who my—' I'm cut off by a growl, a warning not to speak the words I was about to say out loud.

Furious, I cross my arms over my chest and huff.

How dare he!

'We will not have this conversation here.'

'Where should we have it?' I bite out, this is unbelievable. The worst thing is that I'm standing here enraged, looking at my father, knowing this was how he was going to behave and yet, I wanted something more. Deep down I wanted him to show some emotion other than anger and tell me that he is happy to see me, maybe even ask for a hug.

How silly I am.

'Not here,' is all he replies.

There is a short pause where I refuse to speak and he refuses to look at me.

Eventually, he states, 'you will stay with us, where you belong. You will come back to the Darkwoods and from there we will work out the next steps on how to deal with this situation.'

I want to shout, 'am I the situation or is my mating', but I keep my mouth shut. It doesn't matter. All that matters is that I am here for a reason. A reason he has no idea about and maybe it makes me a child but the satisfaction knowing that I'm on a mission from the king to steal from him has me feel a little less homicidal.

'I will comply but I need answers to my questions, Lord Darkwoods. I didn't come back for you and I didn't come back to be thrown back under your roof to be used and abused—'

'I never—'

'Just stop!' I shout, unable to keep calm. 'Just stop lying! What you and that arsehole fucking Medir did to me was fucking child abuse. I will not be used. Never again. I will play the nice daughter while I am with you but it won't be for long. You won't keep me away from my mate longer than is necessary and you will not force me to do anything that I don't want to do. Or I will tell everyone the truth of what you did. I don't know why you wanted me back under your care. I left for a reason.'

Sun Gods that felt good and I'm on a small high until he says calmly, 'I see you've forgotten your place and your manners in the human realm. Don't worry, Serafina, I will remind you. Hear me when I say that you can threaten me as much as you like, Daughter. At the end of the day, my secret is your secret and I know for a fact that it will jeopardise your mating if it comes out. So, you can shout it to the world but it will bring you down as well. No one wants someone like you, an Azanite who can't shift, in their family, especially those arrogant males of the BlazeAzar.'

He steps forward, his eyes blazing the colour of the fire within the fireplace. 'And you will do what I say and be quiet about it or I will rage a war with your future mate and his family until there is nothing left of them. Mark my words, you will regret the day you embarrassed our family by running away.' He is standing so close now, his large frame bending over me. Intimidating.

I refuse to bend.

'Play by my rules Serafina, or I will make this very hard for you.'

Breathing hard, I'm shaking with fear and rage. My father on the other hand looks cool and calm like throwing out threats is an everyday occurrence. He snaps his fingers and shouts a name and slowly I become aware that there was a group of human servants along the far wall, quietly waiting.

My father turns and I quickly wipe the tears that escaped. They slipped out under the energy needed to keep my emotions in check.

Turning my face away, I take a proper breath when my father steps away. The Lord of the Darkwoods barks a few orders in Zaric to an elderly man who steps forward and I barely hear them. His words are spinning around in my head, replaying over and over.

My father's servant bows. The elderly man speaks to two younger women who step forward and I'm too lost in my own head to understand what is going on.

'It's up to you how this plays out, Serafina.' He gives me one more glare before he walks down the hallway, leaving me with my stomach churning and my palms all sweaty.

Sitting is the only thing I can manage. I don't know how I get into the armchair without passing out or falling over. I'm numb but can also feel a sharp pain through my chest that seems to throb with the pounding of my heart. My father just highlighted my biggest fear. When everyone finds out that I'm half human, everything is going to change. I thought I had power here. That things would be different. What a fool I am. Nothing has changed. It's gotten worse.

I just want to go home.

'My Lady?'

Blinking up at the elderly man hovering nervously on the other side of the sitting room, I frown, not sure what he wants. He speaks in perfect Zaric, meaning he is high up in my father's lair. 'I will show you to your rooms now. Otwin and Clarice will help you get comfortable.'

The two younger women from before bow. They clearly have no idea what he's said and the man snaps in the human tongue for them to do everything they can to make sure that I am comfortable.

Comfortable. I will never be comfortable. Not while I'm here.

Chapter Thirty Six

I'M FALLING.

My back lands on a plush mattress, covered in the most exquisite fur blankets just as a hard body collapses with me. I've been in this dream before and I moan when his warmth and scent surround me. This time, I know who it is. I feel every groove of Wilder's muscles as his bare chest presses against my exposed breasts.

The only sound in the oversized, sunlight-filled room is our heavy panting. Our passion. I cry in ecstasy as he pushes deeper into me, changing the tempo. I lift my hand to his back and smile at the rough, animalistic noise he growls in pleasure. That sound will be my undoing.

He will be my undoing.

Wilder nudges my neck to the side, trailing kisses down to my nipple. His beast is rubbing against my skin. His sharp teeth graze the side of my breast and I shudder. Grabbing his face, unable to not touch him, I lift his mouth up to mine...

I'm falling.

Running through the thick woods, I dodge trees and shriek at the sounds that fill the world. Trees fall beside me and I know they are getting closer.

My feet stop and I look down to see...

Agony. I'm being ripped apart and nothing will ever be the same. Someone is shouting. Someone is touching me but nothing is stopping the way my body feels as if it's being ripped apart.

I wake with a sound-less scream on my lips.

Panting and sweaty, my palms are shaking as I push the hair from my sticky brow.

The remnants of the dream cling to my emotions as I try to remember where I am. The room is cold. The bed is colder and the heavy curtains hanging over the windows are blocking the morning sun. My body pulses with my need to seek out Wilder.

Jumping out of bed, I hurry to the curtains and pull them open. The sun is hot and I take a moment just to soak up the healing heat of it.

Everything that happened last night comes back in waves. I'm going back to the Darkwoods with my father this morning. Last night he showed me that I have no control or power. Everything that I feared about being back here in Azanir has come true.

Taking a moment to find my feet, I take in a few deep breaths and focus on what is important. I need to get the book that the King needs and make sure my father accepts Wilder as my mate, all of this while keeping the secret of my parentage and survive this shitty place. I want to go home and after last night, that need is stronger than ever.

Right now, all I want to be is back in my room at Laney's and hide under the covers with my foster brother. As an adolescent, every time I had a bad day or a bad dream, I'd jump into Van's bed and we'd pull the covers over our head and pretend that the world didn't exist. Sometimes even Scott and Brent would slide under the blanket and chat with us. We'd talk about dumb shit and laugh at even dumber jokes.

I want that now. I want a bed and a doona and my brothers. And I'm not talking about the brothers that I can hear talking outside the room that I was forced into last night. Not them.

I want to go home.

Turning when the door is opened, I study the two human woman who come into the room with their heads bowed and try not to cringe. They wear loose fitting brown pants and a matching oversized tunic. I remember the uniform from my childhood and am swiftly pulled back into my past.

The long days playing music with Meryl or watching her work. Eating all my meals with her and the handful of Drengar that were tasked to guard me. Meryl was the only one that spoke with me and she was the only one I mourned on those frightening days when I lived on the streets in the human realm. I wonder if she stayed in the Darkwoods once I left. I don't know what I'd say if I saw her again or what she'd say as well. Meryl helped me to escape the Darkwoods. It was her connections that got me a spot on the ship heading to the human realm. She knew everything. Saw everything. I can't help but to think how much she *did* know.

The women fuss around the room, both unsure what to do. They probably weren't expecting me to be out of bed yet. Females, especially those with the title of Azar, live a life of 'luxury' or so that is what we are raised to think. Our role in Azanir is to find our mates and produce offspring. Females, if we can manage. Definitely different to the life I lived back with humans. I had to work very hard to pay the bills and to help Laney with her 'strays'. Life was not easy and I loved it.

'Why isn't she sitting in the chair?' the blonde one says, now making my bed.

'I don't know,' the shorter one whispers from across the room. She is pulling a baby blue empire waisted dress from the wardrobe. I can see all the embellished jewels around the bust and I hate it already. 'How are we supposed to ask her to sit down so we can get her ready? She wont understand us. They always know to wake up and sit down.'

I move to the chair sitting before the vanity along the left wall and plonk my butt into the seat only because they both sound so panicked and I'm starting to get a headache. I could probably tell them to leave me to get ready on my own or tell them that I understand but I don't feel like socialising or answering questions or having them look at me like I'm a freak. Which is exactly what they will think if I start speaking in the human tongue.

'Thank the Gods,' one of them sighs and before I know it they're behind me trying to work some kind of magic over my puffy eyes and my un-loved hair.

'So, do you know who she is?' the blonde one asks the other over my head. I catch her eye and she quickly smiles politely and averts her gaze. 'No, but the way the lord spoke to her yesterday, he sure wasn't happy.'

I snort and cover it with a cough. I don't care what they think or what they say, I will smile and I will get the book for the King and then I want to go home.

Chapter Thirty Seven

The moment I step out into the courtyard my gaze lands on the male standing like a statue of a Sun God. His focus is on me and only me.

Without thought and having all forms of propriety and decorum smashed out of me in the ten years I've been attached to Van's hip, I run toward Wilder with my heart pounding in my chest.

I know I'm giving everything away by being this vulnerable and only just manage to keep my tears in check when I crush my body against his and hold on for dear life.

Wilder holds me, his arms like steel clamps around my body, keeping me safe and secure.

'Tell me what happened! Are you okay?' Wilder is calm and yet I feel the tension radiating off him and rightfully so because I refuse to let go and have buried my face into his rock-hard chest.

I'm so tired. I could fall asleep right here, standing in Wilder's embrace.

I know that I can't tell him what has happened between my father and I. No matter how much I want to share my fears and worries, my dad's words are still ringing in my ears. My secrets will change everything, and selfishly, I don't want that to happen, not yet. I'm not ready to lose Wilder or the three Drengar that have become so important to me.

As they step up around us, I feel their energy.

'Raff, I think you'll need to tell Wilder if you're good or he might just burn your father to a crisp,' Felix states seriously and I push off the deliciously smelling chest to squint up at Wilder.

He doesn't look like he's ready to burn anyone. That's when I realise that Felix is looking mighty smug and throw him a glare.

'I'm fine,' I tell them.

Viktor doesn't look too persuaded, actually he looks down-right enraged and when I follow his gaze, I realise he is staring daggers at my father.

Wilder waits patiently for me to refocus on him, his arms are still around me. 'I just missed you,' I say, wishing I was brave enough to say more. Do more. Be more.

'Ahhh…Raff, what are you wearing?'

Looking down at myself, I try to understand why Felix sounds so confused. 'What? I'm wearing a dress.'

'I don't think I've seen you wear a dress before and your hair is *brushed*.'

Shocked, all my worries and fears leave my mind. Patting my head, I become all self-conscious. 'I brush my hair!' At least, I try to, when I can remember. Granted, back on our weird 'road trip', I didn't have much care or motivation to look presentable, I probably did look like a mess all the time. I still found Wilder though and Sun Gods, it makes me fall for him harder and instead of being offended by Felix, I stare up at my future mate assuming that there must be little red hearts in my eyes.

Wilder strokes my newly-brushed hair. *'You always look beautiful to me.'*

My smile fades as I realise that Wilder didn't challenge what Felix said but told me that to him I look good, I frown.

Felix chuckles. Damn fool.

'Stop being a youngling,' Viktor grumbles much to Felix's amusement.

'Well, it made her happy, didn't it?' the big oaf says with a shrug.

I could kiss the big goof, which would be inappropriate and he's too tall for me to reach his cheek, so I hug him instead. 'It did.'

'Now we can have a pleasant trip to the Darkwoods,' he says casually and I swear I have no idea where the growl comes from but it rumbles through my chest.

Swatting at him, I step away until my back is against Wilder's chest. I have no idea if I meant to do it or if it was an accident, all I know is that every nerve in my body feels better being against him.

'Pleasant is not a word we use when describing the Darkwoods or any journey towards it,' Viktor interjects.

I can't hold it back any longer, I need to know. 'What happened to you at the Darkwoods?' I ask and get told that it's a long story for another day.

'Come on, we need to get moving,' Alistair states, giving me one last look as if assessing for himself if I am truly all right. *'This is about our mission from the King even if this will be uncomfortable for us all.'* Alistair's voice filters through my mind, reminding me that I am part of this wing now and that no matter what, I have to keep focused.

Taken over to where my father and his Drengar are waiting, I try not to act like a petulant adolescent. It's really hard to not pout or glare at the arseholes I share DNA with. Emmet and Luka are watching me closely.

Actually, I think they're eying Wilder who has a hand curled around my hip.

Slowing down when we get a little closer, it turns into a stand-off between us and the Darkwoods. Until King Oswald appears out of nowhere with his own Drengar, then it's a huge gathering of males. I know that there are some issues with females in our race but honestly, I could use some female energy, just to calm down these masculine vibes.

Cursing my stupidity, I finally realise that we have a massive audience out here in the courtyard. Even Wilder's father and brothers are at the back of the open space, watching everything closely.

The sight has my stomach hit my feet. Everything happened so fast yesterday that I didn't get to meet them properly and I can only imagine what they think of me. I passed out yesterday after touching a damn book. They probably think I'm the most dramatic female alive.

This entire situation is dramatic.

Chapter Thirty Eight

My father is at the front staring at me with a mixture of disapproval and warning as if I have forgotten what we spoke about yesterday.

'So, I believe we all understand what is to happen over the coming weeks.' King Oswald takes the lead, eyeing the males around me with a stink-eye I admire. 'The Lady Serafina will be heading back to the Darkwoods with her family were she will have time to reconnect with them and the logistics of her mating with Drengar Wilder BlazeAzar Medir can be finalised. To ensure that she is healthy and safe, Drengar Wilder will be allowed permission to enter the lair of the Darkwoods when he or Serafina request it. This will happen after the first seven days of Serafina's return, as requested by the Lord of the Darkwoods so that their family can reconnect.'

My lip pulls back in a snarl as the king goes on and on and everyone nods stiffly as if they've heard these terms before. It's obvious that these males have organised and worked out all these details without me. Probably when I was asleep and they had a 'dicks only' chat about my future. I see red. This is why I never wanted to return to this place.

'Seems like you all have this under control. Should I just stand here quietly and let you and my father run my life?' Each word I snap over at

Wilder drips with aggression and the poor male shuffles a little on his feet, a gesture I have never seen from him before. It makes me angrier. He is focused on what the king is saying and eye-balling my father and Emmet like he is ready for a fight.

'Astgeer—'

'*Don't* Astgeer *me Wilder! You're in the doghouse.*'

Black eyes flick down at me and I can see the confusion on his face over what I've just said. My eye roll is the only explanation I'm going to give. He fucked up and he knows it. They all did. Felix glances my way and I fight the need to flip him off. He gets my glare instead and hangs his head, looking somewhat ashamed. I will deal with him later.

'If at any time lady Serafina wishes to leave the Darkwoods, then she is to be allowed to return here to my lair. She is under the protection of my family until her mating into the house of the BlazeAzar,' King Oswald finishes just as my dad bristles loudly. After what we spoke about yesterday, there is no way he would let me just leave the Darkwoods if I wanted to. I have 'embarrassed' the family enough, apparently.

'She is my daughter, she is under my protection!' he barks.

'*A daughter you let be abused in your lair!*' Wilder's voice has that echoey, creepy quality that lets me know everyone can hear his little jab at my dad. The older Lord goes red and not because he is enraged or embarrassed. It's the colour of his dragon's skin.

'Remember your place, Wilder BlazeAzar!' Emmet threatens and the tension in the courtyard goes from an eight to a million with those simple words. The Darkwood Drengar step forward slightly. The watching BlazeAzar's are now behind us. I swear the King sighs. Alistair tells my brother to remember *his* place, which honestly is so unhelpful at this moment.

Fuck, this situation has taken a dramatic turn, very quickly. There is a lot of growling and cussing. Wilder's father is now telling mine that after everything that happened yesterday at the meeting, he's lucky that I've agreed to go back to the Darkwoods. 'When Lady Serafina is my son's mate and my daughter, you will never have anything to do with her again,' Lord BlazeAzar states and honestly I think I have some kind of episode. My brain short-circuits to the point where I just end up standing like a fool, gaping up at the male who looks so much like Wilder.

'How dare you!' my father snaps.

'How dare you not protect her from that Medir! He abused your daughter. A female Azanite!' one of Wilder's brothers hisses back. I really should know his name. What does it say about me that I haven't asked? I've been so selfish.

'You have no idea what you are talking about. We had no idea!' Luka retorts.

'And you have no idea the impact this information has had on you and your family's reputation,' another BlazeAzar brother counters aggressively. 'Let's just say that the Darkwoods relationship with the Riverways is serving you well right now.'

Holy shit. Those are heavily multi-layered words. I'm standing here right now to prevent a war, yet, it appears as if these predators are itching for one and are using me to have their pissing contest.

The entire thing is absolutely absurd. Peeking around everyone's too-large forms, I spy the groups now in the courtyard. The Lord of the Cavelands and his Drengar are watching the exchange between our families, the big, hairy males look extra-warrior-like this morning. It appears that they're here to support the BlazeAzar, which is crazy.

It hits pretty hard to think that my story incited so much anger and not anger aimed at me for running away. I was so worried about what would happen when I returned to Azanir that I didn't entertain the idea that my actions would be pitied and understood.

I formed this image of Azanir, and the males who call it home, based off my childhood experience. The fact that over the years that idea could've became more and more inflated until hatred and fear clouded my understanding of my homelands, is not lost on me.

Sun Gods, it's not the first time I wonder if running was the wrong thing to do. Wilder, Alistair, Viktor and Felix challenged my views when I met them. I didn't think that would extend to all Azanites. They have always been the villains in my story. So why am I standing here being fought over and protected? By both sides.

Chapter Thirty Nine

My skin heats dramatically and it takes way too long to realise it's not because of my emotions, it's because the warriors sizing each other up are emitting dangerous heat levels.

The king begins to try and placate everyone. Wilder has pushed me further behind him after Luka attempted to use his own body to cover me, which confuses me more.

I swear, my blood runs hot and cold at the same time.

My father tells everyone that negotiations have been made and if Wilder and his family don't respect the terms for my return to the Darkwoods then he will not be permitted to visit. Obviously that sets my future mate off and his echoey voice filters through the growing crowd, threatening my entire family.

King Oswald counters with a very firm demand for everyone to stand-down after Wilder takes a very threatening step forward and I can only imagine what he has said to the king to have the male rise to his full, intimidating height. King Oswald glares at my future mate and Wilder just glares right on back. It's kinda hot but also, kinda fucking scary how much danger Wilder is placing himself in.

Damn these males and their fucking egos.

Quickly stepping in front of Wilder when his face darkens, I rest a hand on his chest. I like him alive and breathing and while I'm so fucking mad right now, I don't want this to keep going.

Everyone stops shouting now that I'm in the centre of the group and I feel every eye on me.

Taking a deep breath, I find my courage and try to channel Van or my foster brothers and what they'd do and say in a situation like this. Which is why I spurt out, 'I have made my decision to go the Darkwoods. There is no need to get the measuring tape, whip them out, and see whose is the biggest.'

You can hear the shout of a distance dragon, that's how quiet the courtyard goes and I swear a hundred confused brows scrunch down at me. Rolling my eyes is involuntary. 'Trust me, that joke would've slayed in the human realm.'

Felix is the only one who reacts by grinning wide. I can always rely on that guy.

Wilder grips my shoulder and even though I'm still being assessed like they think I may be a little loopy, the tension in the courtyard has softened.

Turning my attention on Wilder, I forget for a moment that I'm angry or that we're about to be separated because under my hand his chest feels rock-hard and mesmerising. 'Wilder, I'll be okay,' I whisper, lying through my teeth. I'm fucking shaking and he knows it. Those dark eyes flick to me and I swear they devour me whole. 'I'm okay.' What I want to say is, 'I don't want you to be eaten alive by the scary King,' but keep my mouth closed.

'He can't threaten the deal we've made.'

'Everyone is threatening everyone!' I counter, unimpressed by the expression on his face. *'I'm not a child and I don't want this to continue. We've been given a mission. We decided this is what we'd do. Now, stop.'* Throwing him what I hope is a stern look, I try to remind myself why I'm here and that I'm no longer that young, frightened girl. 'All of you, please stop. I don't want this.'

I seem to have shocked the males into silence.

It's time.

After I told them all to stop, the groups of Drengar went back to their respective sections of the courtyard and the King gained control over the males. The negotiations were not threatened and everyone agreed to follow the rules.

Now, I'm with Wilder, both of us taking some time alone to say our goodbyes. Not that we don't have an audience. I can feel my father watching.

'At any time, you just say the word and Viktor and Felix will bring you back here.'

Nodding, I'm too nervous to say anything. My stomach is in knots and my heart keeps skipping every second beat. Wilder is fussing with the coat I'm wearing. His large frame hovering over me, crowding me in the best possible way. The buckle isn't closing around my shoulders and he's seems just as nervous as I am to let this happen. He keeps mumbling how the flight will be cold and that if I get sick, he won't be around to heal me.

It has all the anger I felt towards him a moment ago evaporate.

'Viktor and Felix will look after you. Stay close to them at all times and I will be there on the seventh day. Find the book quickly because when I come on that day we are never being parted again.'

Sun Gods, I don't want to do this. Wilder makes a deep noise in his chest and then he is removing his own coat and throws it over my shoulders. The weight and smell of it is divine and all the tension evaporates from my body. It's as if Wilder is hugging me.

I cocoon it around myself, listening to him give instruction after instruction about being safe. His hand runs through my unbound hair and I lean into it. Savouring him touching me. Afraid what it will mean when I leave. It will hurt, I know it will. My beast always wants to touch him. To be close to him. We are doing this for something bigger than ourselves.

'I will miss you, my heart.'

I nearly lose the control I have over my emotions and I fall into his chest and wrap my arms around his middle. Wilder rests his chin on my head and I hear him breath in my scent. I understand because I do the same to him. I draw it in, like a drug, needing as much as I can before I go.

'This is torture,' I confess.

'Just get the book, find your answers and we can finish this. Then you and I will bind ourselves together officially and no one will take you from me again.'

I pull back and stare up at my future mate with words I want to say stuck in my throat. I want that. I wish we had already done it.

I just nod, the tears too close to the surface to speak. He knows it because he lowers his lips to mine in a quick chaste kiss that does nothing to satisfy the beast in my blood.

The moment he pulls away, I grip his face and pull him down and crush my lips against his once more.

He gives me exactly what I need. Devouring me with his passion, consuming my thoughts and taking away all my fear and apprehension. His tongue dances with mine in a perfect performance that should have everyone around us clapping.

Breaking away from him is the hardest thing I've done in a very long time.

Forehead to forehead, he tells me that he loves me and I choke out that I am his, forever.

My father snaps some arsehole words from across the courtyard that has Viktor step over and tell me it's time to go.

Wilder shares a look with the two males now behind me and they both nod grimly.

Walking away from Wilder is like ripping my heart out and leaving it on the ground. I force both legs to walk, each step painful as my beast starts to protest what I'm doing, like she just worked it out.

Wilder stands with Alistair and his father across the courtyard and I'm glad that he has them to help because I can only imagine how hard this is for him. A male Azanite is devoted to his mate. The bond is all about the beast and we dragons don't share or like to be separated from what we want.

I try to stay strong so that he doesn't get upset and throw him what I hope is a confident smile as Viktor and Felix shift beside me. Their dragons stretching into their bodies. My father and brothers are already in dragon form and when Emmet's deep burgundy dragon steps over to me as if he is going to pick me up, Viktor snaps his large fangs at the younger male's throat.

Emmet pulls back and growls furiously. Felix's mighty leg keeps me safe and secure why the two bare their teeth at each other and then Viktor is before me and I'm gently taken into his paw.

Heart in my throat and not able to get enough air into my lungs, I turn just as Viktor bends to take off and I catch my future mate's eyes turn red as he watches me go.

I want to scream and shout and ask to go back.

Instead, I cry silent tears as I wrap Wilder's coat over my body and curl up against Viktor's claws.

Chapter Forty

The Darkwoods.

I'm back in my father's lair.

In my rooms, standing on the balcony, leaning against the dark stone. Even on top of a hill, looking down at the kingdom everything seems so much...smaller.

I remember my rooms being gigantic. Yes, the bedroom is the size of Laney's house nearly. The bed in the centre is massive and the fireplace across from it takes up the entire wall. Azanite's love fire, even when they don't feel the cold. They just love to be around it. I feel the weather though so I always had it blazing as a youngling. I have a modest sitting room with three rooms off it, two now taken by Viktor and Felix and yet, everything seems tiny.

We've only been back a handful of hours and I already feel so unsettled. This place is all dark stone floors and walls. All the corridors are wide and every door along the three storeys are always closed. The only open section is the front entranceway which is used as the courtyard for Azanites to land and can be transformed into an entertainment space. There is a massive, split staircase that you can watch everything from. It is from those stairs that I witnessed my first dream come to life.

Sighing, I wish like crazy to have Wilder here with me.

The moment we landed, my father barked at everyone to go back to their duties and dumped me with the same butler that I met briefly back in the capital. He was the one to lead us up here to the third floor. My stomach was in knots the entire walk. I don't think I could've done it without Viktor and Felix beside me despite how uncomfortable Viktor seemed the entire time.

I didn't miss the way some of the Darkwoods Drengar stopped in their tracks at our appearance and I know that it wasn't because of me. I doubt any of them know I'm back yet. It's not like they have phones here. They have the ability to speak via their beasts but I can't see my father announcing my return to the world.

The Darkwoods. Standing here with the light breeze blowing through my hair under the falling sun, I take in the beauty of this place.

This place is the ultimate contradiction.

Beauty and danger, in equal measures.

From my balcony, high above the world, the woods surround the lair on all sides and is like a dark ocean. The tops of the trees are thick, rich green, almost black in colour. I can see the cleared spaces where the city lies in the distance and the other pretentious lairs owned by the nobles of the Darkwoods. It's a stunning vista that I have dreamt about for the past ten years.

The smell of this place.

The nature.

I grew up running in these woods. I'd have lessons with grumpy tutors amongst the trees, learning of the dangers of my homelands.

It's from this balcony that I would cry as a youngling, wishing that I could join the beasts flying under the hot sun.

There are countless dragons in the sky right now in the distance. Each one clearly going about their business.

Turning as I hear the door being opened in my rooms, I make my way back inside when I spy the humans fussing around the place.

'My Lady, I have decided to allow Otwin and Clarice to continue on as your maids, if it pleases you?' The butler bows, presenting the women who assisted me yesterday. The ones that had no idea who I was.

'That's fine, I don't need maids. I can get myself ready.' I've lived ten years without help, I think I can dress myself.

The butler bristles, frowns, opens his mouth about three times before he clears his throat and says, 'Lady, I was given instructions to provide you with your maids and see to your comfort. I don't think that…I don't want you to not…'

The poor guy looks like he is going to have a meltdown. Then I remember my father and the mood he is in and take pity on the man. 'Fine, it's okay.'

The two women watch our exchange closely, their arms full of stuff. There's just so much stuff. Looking toward the bed, I take in the round mattress, the fresh white bedding and the piles of blankets and pillows to the side of it. All waiting for me to create my safe space each night.

There isn't enough soft items in the world to make this place feel safe for me. So much happened in this room. The pain. The trauma. The loneliness. It all comes back.

My silence must have been taken as a dismissal because the butler bows again and then snaps at the young women to do their jobs and begins to walk out.

'Actually, Mr...' I start and frown because I don't know his name. He definitely wasn't here when I was young.

He turns and watches me closely as I wait for him to properly introduce himself, which he does after a painful amount of time. 'Wakely, my lady, you can just call me Wakely, if it pleases you.'

It would please me to be far from this place, but I don't say that, instead I ask him the one thing I really need to know. 'I had a maid when I was growing up. Her name was Meryl, I would like to see her. Do you know where she is?'

Wakely hesitates. Fuck, he looks upset. 'There was a change a few years back. An incident that had most of the workers of the lair either be dismissed or...' his words trail off and I grip my stomach to keep from losing it's contents.

'Or?'

Wakely's lined face softens at whatever he sees on my face and with a deep sigh, his brown eyes turn sad. 'Some did not survive the incident.'

'Was it a wraith attack?' I ask, panic lacing each word. Wakely seems to contemplate if he should tell me. 'Please, I need to know.'

'It wasn't a wraith attack, lady. It was an incident involving the Lord of the Darkwoods and the humans in the lair.'

My insides liquify. What does that even mean?

Wakely tries to leave again.

'When did this happen?' I half-shout as he is about to walk out of the room.

Looking at me from over his shoulder, Wakely's brown eyes take me in and I see countless emotions and a hint of pity maybe. Or maybe it's curiosity. I can't tell because my mind is reeling and I think I'm about to have a panic attack. Could Meryl be dead? She was like a mother to me. She raised me and I left her here with my father. I left her in the damn place.

'About ten years ago.'

My gasp is audible and I'm finding it hard to stand up.

Leaning over so that I can grip the edge of the bed to keep from falling, I battle with the burning hot anger and guilt that begins to boil in my chest.

'Please leave,' I shout, my tears thick and choking as they begin to slide down my face. I don't need an audience for my breakdown. The gossip mill is probably in full swing at the moment without me adding to this.

'Out!' A deep masculine voice demands from somewhere, the power and authority in it has me look through the tears to see Viktor and Felix standing in the doorway, assessing the scene.

'They died because of me. I know it. He killed them because I ran away,' I cry out and the humans dart out of the room, leaving me to collapse against the cold stone.

Felix is on the floor beside me in a heartbeat, his warmth enveloping me. His hand guiding my head to his shoulder.

Side by side, shoulder to shoulder, we sit against the bed while I cry ugly tears. 'Who died, Raff?'

'It was me. I left and my father killed the humans of the lair. It can't be a coincidence.' My words come out as broken as I feel.

Viktor sits on my other side, pulling his knees up, he rests his forearms on them and sighs. He looks younger like this, more open. 'It's why I left the Darkwoods.'

I stop crying for a moment just to understand if I heard him correctly. Studying the rage and grief on his face, it's like finding the puzzle piece that

I was missing to understand Viktor better. He saw what happened and he left.

'You were going to be the next commander of the Darkwoods, you left because the Lord killed some humans?' Felix questions slowly as if he is trying to fully understand what Viktor has just said.

'Yes,' is all the grumpy male replies with and I push off Felix's shoulder to study him. 'We don't kill innocents. Females. Humans. It is our oath as Drengar.'

Sun Gods, I find my heart swelling and my love for Viktor growing. This big grump has firmly lodged himself inside my heart.

'He did this because I ran away.'

'Yes, he thought that something had happened to you and that it was one of the humans that hurt you or something. He thought you were killed. Never did he think that you ran away. They were all questioned to see if they were human rebels. When I got word that he was killing them, one by one, without cause, I stepped in. Your father and I fought. The commander at the time didn't stop him and I was banished. I helped as many as I could.'

'And...no one told him what happened to me?' I sniffle, my heart in pieces.

'Did the humans know?' Felix questions softly as if building his own idea of what he's stepped into.

'Some of them. It was the humans of this lair that helped me escape. Meryl and a handful of other men. They got me to a ship and hid me.' Oh gods, the pain in my chest in unbearable. My tears are back and this time I fall against Viktor's shoulder, in need of comfort. 'Thank you for trying. I will never forgive myself for what I've done.'

'They knew the risks by helping you, Serafina.'

'I didn't,' I wail and fall apart. 'I want Wilder.'

'We will be out of here soon, Raff. We will get the book. Get your dad to stop being an arsehole and then we will get the fuck out of here.'

'I want to go home.' I feel vulnerable and powerless. My beast is whining in my head and I want to curl up with her and forget about the world.

Chapter Forty One

I'M FALLING AND THE *world is on fire.*

A large figure blocks out the night sky and I watch in horror as it falls against the stone wall of the lair jutting out before me. My heart breaks. It shatters into a million pieces and it hurts.

Someone grabs me and I'm spinning.

Standing in a room with wood-slatted walls, I scream in rage. It's hot. I'm burning. Moving. Why am I tilting left and right? Why is there no door. My heart is hurting. My rage is boiling. I need to be somewhere. I need to go back.

There is a noise and I turn and then fall backwards just as a section on the far wall opens and a figure steps through. Just before I can see who it is, the world goes black and I know nothing will ever be the same again.

My groan is loud and painful. I feel like I've been hit by a truck. My head is pounding from crying myself to sleep and the morning sun blazing through the open balcony door isn't healing me. It's making my eyes water and my brain feel as if it's trying to exit out of my skull.

Whispered voices and shuffling feet has me peek through my little nest to the women moving around chatting quietly as they lay out an ugly dress and fix up the already cleaned room. The blonde one, I think her name is Clarice, moves in and out of the bathroom that's attached to the left wall.

I can hear the water running in the bathtub and smell the aromas of citrus and fruits from the bath salts. They're such familiar smells that I roll over onto my back and fight with the fresh wave of tears that threaten to pull me back into grief.

I spent hours crying last night, feeling guilty and horrible about myself over the information I discovered. Viktor and Felix stayed with me until I crawled into bed and got myself comfortable. They made sure that I ate from the simple meal that was brought to our rooms by Wakely and must have waited until I passed-out from exhaustion.

My father left me alone yesterday, probably to let me get settled before he starts his torture. Which is probably why the bath is being run and my clothes selected. Sun Gods knows what he has planned as a punishment.

I haven't allowed myself to consider what I'm going to do when I'm faced with the rest of the Darkwoods. The Azar. My wicked stepmother. It's just all too much. Throw on the fact that we have to find a library I have no memory of and steal a book that no one here wants to part with is making my head pound harder.

Blinking over at the women whispering, I pay attention to what they're saying and sigh heavily knowing I have to get up.

'Do you think she will get up soon? She should be down at breakfast with the lord.'

'Wakely is going to send us back to the kitchens if we screw this up, Clar. I don't want to go back down there. Not after what happened with Robby. I want to keep my distance.'

'I don't know what you saw in that loser.'

'I saw a man,' Otwin snaps. 'It's not like I'm some gorgeous Azanir female like the one in the bed with two hunky males waiting for me in my sitting room.'

Two hunky males. That makes me smile. Viktor and Felix must be starving and ready for breakfast, we didn't eat much last night. It's the only reason why I roll out of bed and stretch. They had to deal with my tears last night, I owe it to them to get them a decent breakfast, even if it means sitting at a table with my fucking father.

Two sets of eyes fly to me, relief written on both of their faces when I roll from under the covers.

'How do we tell her to get into the bath?' Clarice asks Otwin under her breath and I can't help but laugh softly.

I'm being childish by not telling them that I understand what they're saying. I only keep quiet because I'm sure I'll be able to learn more if they don't think they have to watch what they say around me.

Sitting in front of my old vanity with Clarice pinning my hair, I finger the small engravings on the wood table remembering how they got there.

I would sit in this exact same chair as a youngling, on my knees because I was too small, and chatting away with Meryl as she brushed my hair. Sitting still was never something I could do easily and so I'd end up scratching words into the wood in my boredom. Every time I'd get in trouble and yet, I'd continue to do it.

One engravement has my attention, the one that has mine and Meryl's name with the word family written underneath. Despite how much she smiled when she saw it, I did get in trouble for this one too.

'What do you think she is thinking about?' Otwin says from across the room.

I keep my focus on the words before me.

'I don't know. She seems sad though and she was so upset yesterday. Wakely wouldn't tell me what happened or what he said. He just told me to be the best maid I could be and look after her. Who do you think she is anyway? And who are the new Drengar out there?'

'Your guess is as good as mine. I asked my grandma yesterday if she knew who she might be and she just told me to take care in looking after her. I don't think she knows but I could tell that she may have an idea.'

'Your grandma used to work here, no?' Clarice stabs me with a pin and her big wide blue eyes frantically look at me through the mirror. We stare for a moment as she waits to see what I will do. There is so much worry and fear that she will get in trouble, it makes me mad and I offer her a small smile which she returns and goes back to her work.

'Yeah she did, a long time ago.' Otwin is on her knees filling the fireplace with more wood so her reply is a bit muffled.

'Well, get all the gossip for me. The girls in the kitchen are dying to know.'

'Did you hear what they were saying last night in the servant hall about the bigger Drengar out there?' Otwin stops what she is doing to excitedly look over her shoulder at the woman doing my hair.

Clarice's eyes light up and I can tell she is a real gossip. Perfect for me getting information but also something to be mindful of. 'The attractive one with the blue eyes and that cut jawline or the one with the weird honey-lined eyes that looks like sex on legs?'

I snort-cough at that and pretend to use some of the smelling oils on the table to keep from losing it and ruining my little plan. I will never tell Felix and Viktor how these two have described them, they definitely don't need anyone telling them how attractive they are. They won't be able to fly every again under the weight of their swollen egos.

'Sex on legs,' Otwin states and Clarice is loving this. So am I, if I'm being honest.

'What are they saying?'

'That he was a Drengar here years ago. That he left after having some kind of altercation with the Lord of the Darkwoods.'

'Wow,' Clarice breathes the word out like she is stunned by that information. 'That's huge.'

'And did you notice the crest on their uniform?'

'I know it's different to the ones here,' Clarice replies, finishing up my hair.

'It's the crest of the King. Rumour is that they are part of Prince Alistair's wing. The one everyone talks about with that scary Medir.'

Clarice shivers and I fight the need to snarl at her. I get it. Wilder is freakin' scary. He is mine and I love him but when I first met him, I was petrified. Now I know he is a total softie. At least to me.

Rising when I can't sit any longer, I go over to the dress that has been draped over the bed. Now thinking of Wilder and the way my skin crawls not being near him, I grab my travel bag and pull out the clothes that I stuffed in there. Finding one of Wilder's tunics, I decide that my father can go to hell.

Chapter Forty Two

AWKWARD.

That is what the tension around the table is. I have no idea why I came down here or what I should do with my hands right now.

The shit part about this is that I've only ever sat around this table a handful of times to eat with my 'family'. I was never invited. My father and the wicked bitch I called mother were always off doing their own thing and my brothers only came back every few months. When they did, I still ate with Meryl and the Drengar who wouldn't speak with me. If Meryl was off work, I'd be kept company by a younger maid who didn't know how to speak Zaric. So, she'd sit at the small table in my sitting room and watch me eat.

I busy myself moving the meats and fruits around my plate, reliving the pain of my youth.

Emmet sits across from me looking like he was forced to be here as well. Luka is to my left and keeps glancing over at the double doors. My father is at the head of the table, looking like the angry warlord from mine and Van's favourite television show and my wicked stepmother sits to his right. The damn bitch hasn't stopped glaring from the moment I entered the hall. She hasn't spoken a single word.

Viktor and Felix are at the table, eating quietly, knowing that their presence was not asked for or welcomed. I gave my father no choice when we walked into this hall with its extremely high ceiling and it's typical dark stone walls and he told us that it was a family gathering. My response was that my Drengar are family and should be treated like guests in his kingdom, it didn't go down well. Actually, the arsehole looks like he's still trying to swallow my words. The only thing he has said since is that next time I come to his table it better not be wearing male clothes was. That was actually pretty funny and he didn't seem too impressed when I couldn't catch my smirk in time.

I wasn't going to wear the damn dress laid out for me. I'm wearing fitted beige pants with a thick brown belt and Wilder's white tunic that I've tucked in so it doesn't swim on me. The top was way too big so I threw on a short, leather jacket that buttons in the front.

Five of my father's advisors sit at the long wood table with us. The Tymber tree with a colour that matches Viktor's honey-lined eyes makes beautiful, grand furniture.

They are the only ones talking right now, all about me and how to handle my return in a way that will give power back to the Darkwoods.

'We have to show that we are happy for the Lady Serafina's return,' advisor one says.

Rolling my eyes at the choice of words, I try not to take it to heart.

'I suggest the family go into the city, together. Maybe we host a dinner or some kind celebration.' Advisor two is probably the oldest male I've ever seen.

'We should invite the king,' another one says. 'Make it a big celebration of how our lady has been found.'

'I cannot be expected to create some kind of event with such short notice!' Wicked Bitch shrieks.

She's a horrible female. Not in looks but personality.

Her blonde, perfect hair falls down her body. It shines like she does that brushing it a hundred times a day thing that I read about in a magazine at an appointment with Laney once. Actually, she wouldn't lower herself enough to brush her own hair, who am I kidding. Her green eyes are full of outrage that she is expected to do anything at all. I can't help but compare her to Laney and how she conducts herself. My foster mother is no lady. She barely finished school and works multiple jobs to support her family. She swears like a sailor on leave and has the worst table manners but she is perfect. Full of honour and loyalty, Laney is everything Lady Celina of the Darkwoods is not.

It just shows that riches and titles mean nothing.

'Of course, we would ensure that everything is organised by the servants,' advisor three grovels.

My father just eyes me like I'm a bug he wished stayed in the shadows and believe me, I wish I had stayed away. 'Fine. Do whatever must be done to repair the reputation of the Darkwoods.'

Felix and I share a look that has me cover my smirk with my mug of juice. There is nothing that could repair this reputation.

'We will begin to make preparations,' the elderly male says.

Everyone focuses on their meals. Human servants move quietly around the table, refilling drinks and plates.

'Papa!' a little voice shouts, drawing my attention to the doors as they fling open.

Luka rises quickly and I watch in stunned silence at what happens next. A female Azanite walks into the room carrying a small babe in her arms while a little boy, around five years old, comes running towards my brother who bends down and scoops up the youngling who just called him papa.

The female behind the boy is gorgeous. Her hair also has that shiny brushed look but it's not annoying me like how it does on Wicked Bitch. It's the colour of chocolate, her skin is a gorgeous cream and I'm instantly jealous. In the best way. Her smile is wide and genuine as she looks to the table of males who have risen at her appearance. Viktor and Felix bow and I have to do a double take when I see Emmet smiling. I didn't think he could. I've never seen it.

'Papa. Papa, Mumma said that I can spend the day with her and not have to go to my morning studies.'

'Really? Have you finished your work from yesterday? Tutor Barth told me that you didn't.'

The little boy's features darken in a way I'm way too familiar with. He looks exactly like Luka, just a little mini version. His mop of bone-blonde hair is adorable and the curve of his features is just like the facial structure of all the Darkwoods males.

It takes my mind a ridiculous amount of time to process this new piece of information. I have a nephew. Two it seems as the female steps over to Luka and plants a kiss on his cheek. The open affection between them has my soul weep for Wilder. I know instantly what these two mean to each other. Luka kisses the top of the baby's head. It looks to be only a handful of weeks old. Not that I have much experience with babies.

'Papa, who is that?'

'That is your aunt, Lady Serafina. Now, go and say hello to your grandfather and grandmother before you sit down with Uncle Emmet for some food.' The boy practically leaps from Luka's hold to rush over to my father, who *kisses* the boy affectionately and then drops him beside Wicked Bitch for another greeting.

Wicked bitch is grinning and my throat clenches. Emmet has already made room for my nephew as he finally finds his chair and everyone gets to work adding food onto his plate.

I watch all of this with a mixture of emotions.

'Eat all your eggs Deklan before you have the pastry,' Emmet says and honestly I don't think I can take anymore. Deklan. He is so sweet and happy.

I'm so lost in my own head that I don't notice the female until she starts speaking. 'Lady Serafina, it is a pleasure to meet you. I'm your brother's mate, Penelope. And this is your other nephew, Rehan.' She shows me the baby and his cheeks are so chubby and his little fingers have a grip on her lush hair. 'I hope that we can be friends. There aren't too many females around here,' Penelope states with a huge smile on her face and all I can give her is a rude head nod that must make me look like a complete and utter bitch.

The hurt on her face isn't missed by anyone. I don't mean to be impolite. I just…I can't manage this. The awkwardness around the table is gone and everyone is putting on an amazing, peaceful and loving show. They're acting like a…family. Something I dreamt of living in this lair. Deklan chats on and on and everyone is listening so intently and the beast under my skin loves his little voice already. It's her nature to recognise kin.

'Would you like to hold, Rehan?'

'I don't think that is a good idea,' Wicked Bitch states like a real arsehole and everyone around the table stops moving.

'Oh.' Penelope hesitates just as she was about to hand me the baby. No one seems to care that I didn't agree to take him. Penelope wildly looks over my head at Luka, clearly unsure what to do.

Luka says nothing.

Emmet. Father. They're all silent.

'I am not sure why you'd say something like that. I can't see why—'

Raising my hand to stop Viktor from continuing. He and Felix are on their feet. I appreciate them so much but this is my fight.

'I really don't need to be part of this. Excuse us. Send for me when you want me to pretend that I'm here because I want to be.'

Chapter Forty Three

'I HATE THIS PLACE! Why am I surprised? I shouldn't have even gone to breakfast.' I shout to the sky to release some of the energy under my skin.

It does nothing to help.

'And Luka has a mate and they have younglings. Everyone was acting...did you see how they were acting!' I'm furious at myself more than anything and stop in a familiar garden on the far side of the lair. The area around the lair is all flat land before it starts to dip down. The path leading into the woods takes you from the front entrance all the way into the forest and then will eventually lead to the city where the humans and Thal's live.

Only the family and the few that live here in the lair use the gardens and spaces around the structure. The Drengar training areas are a small fly east and that is where the majority of them live. That hasn't seemed to change as I find myself back in a small, enclosed garden that dominated my time as a youngling here.

Standing in the centre of the space, I turn in a small circle, sad over what I see and what this unkept place represents. Weeds and bushes have overtaken the once beautiful flower shrubs and fruit trees. Meryl and the human gardener maintained this garden so that we always had somewhere to enjoy the outdoors. I guess with Meryl and me gone, it wasn't a priority anymore.

Gaze falling on the once well-crafted and inviting bench, I take in the way vines and leaves litter it's surface, making it a spot you'd never be able to sit and enjoy the sun. My poor heart squeezes.

'That female is a piece of work!' Viktor growls low and it makes me chuckle.

'She's always been a massive bitch.' I have to switch to the human tongue to say the last few words. There isn't a word for 'bitch' in Zaric.

Felix finds that hilarious. It helps to ease the rage.

'I understand why you're angry at that horrible female but the other stuff. Raff, you've been gone for ten years. What did you expect to happen?'

I know Felix isn't trying to be unkind, it's just how these males are.

'I don't know what I expected. To be honest, I hardly thought about this place. When I did, it wasn't remembering anything nice.'

'Why does it upset you so much?'

'Because I never had this,' I blurt out and hate the words and my vulnerability. After the way I behaved last night, I feel raw. This place is messing with my head. Being back here is bringing up things I wish would stay buried. 'I wasn't ever allowed to eat at the table. I was very rarely invited to sit at their table and eat with them.'

'What!' Viktor and Felix demand at the same time a deep masculine voice at the entrance to the garden says, 'that isn't true.'

Lips pulling back from my teeth in a snarl, I have no power over the rise of anger that assaults me.

'Wasn't true?' I bite out, glaring at the bastard who is glaring right on back. 'I wouldn't Emmet. After what just happened, I'm really not in the mood to pretend with you right now.'

'It isn't true though. You always had your meals earlier than when we did. You weren't purposely left out.' Emmet speaks with such conviction that I have no idea if he's being serious.

'You have no idea what you're talking about. You are so ignorant of what my youth was like, Emmet.'

I've never seen Viktor so angry when he takes a threatening step toward my brother. 'The reputation of the Darkwoods is never going to get any better. The way you've treated your own flesh and blood will taint the Darkwoods for a very long time. Inviting your sister to your table now will do nothing to correct the injustice. I see what is happening here, you will use Serafina to repair what the other families think of yours. It's disgusting. and when the King finds out, he will think so too.'

Emmet takes a moment to digest what has just been thrown at him and I have to give the male some credit, being threatened and yelled at by someone like Drengar Viktor Longwing is intimidating. Yes, my brother is an Azar and a Drengar but Viktor is...Viktor. The stories of his conquests and the way he fought the wraiths were famous when I was young. The nobles and Drengar of our lands spoke about our luck in having him as part of our kingdom. It's why he found himself in the Prince's wing, working for the King.

'I don't think you remember things correctly Sera—'

'Oh for fuck's sake,' I retort in the human tongue again, not knowing the cuss words in Zaric to really emphasis my rage. 'Do speak to your mother! Ask her what my life was like here and how she would tell me every so often that I wasn't good enough to eat with you all. How she taunted me because I couldn't fly. She'd tell me I was defective. That I was dramatic and cried too much for attention. She sees me as deficient and clearly contagious if she won't let me even touch one of you.'

Felix shuffles beside me and I quickly look over to understand why my skin ripples with energy. His stunning blue eyes are no longer blue. They are as red as the poor rose peeking out of all the shrubs behind us. I'm making him angry and his beast is responding.

'Our mother,' Emmet states, drawing my attention back on him.

'What?'

'You said, go ask your mother. I'm saying that she is *our* mother.'

Is he serious? After everything I have said, he focuses on that. 'I left my mother in the human realm. Laney was everything to me. Took me in. Loved me. Fed me. Allowed me to grow.'

Shaking his head, Emmet doesn't react like I expect him to. I thought he'd rage-out and get all angry that I spoke about a human and my time away from here. 'Is that why you left? Because Mother didn't love you enough?'

Done with this conversation and the stupid question he has just asked, I turn my back. 'I'm here to play nice and help fix the reputation of the Darkwoods like Father wanted. The moment I can, I will be leaving this place with my mate and my wing. I won't be staying here any longer than is necessary. You can believe what you want about me or what I did. Frankly, I don't care.'

I do care. I care a lot. That is the problem.

'Well, you can start by heading into the city with us shortly for the damn walk through. You will come and *play nice*.' He all but spits the last words and leaves.

'You okay?'

Nodding, I fall against Felix's chest when he pulls me in for a hug.

'Let's just focus on our mission,' Viktor states. 'I'll start making some enquires about the library and the book we seek. Hopefully we will have our mission complete and be ready to leave with Alistair and Wilder.'

I couldn't agree more.

Chapter Forty Four

The city of the Darkwoods is exactly what you'd expect for a place surrounded in thick forest. Trees everywhere. It's exactly what I need after the drama of this morning.

Viktor and Felix are hovering like mother hens. I asked if we could walk to the city, even though it would take us a while and they instantly agreed despite the fact that they could've just flown the few minutes to get there.

I was told to be in the market centre by the time my father gets there. Viktor reassured me that he'd detect if any of their beasts started flying past so we took our time.

To be honest, the walk was exactly what I needed. We passed so many humans and Thals going about their business. The stone path leads all the way to the city with the thick Darkwoods on either side. Carts were being pulled along the road, most going to my father's lair for their deliveries. We got a number of funny looks but mostly everyone was too busy to care that three Azanites were walking toward the town.

Now that we're here, I feel better and it could be because I can't see my family yet.

Every shade of green you could ever imagine and some I didn't see in the human realm fills the landscape.

The sight has me pause, thinking of the vision the golden text gave me. It was so different in the vision and yet, still so familiar. The streets weren't as crowded and the buildings not so big but it was still the Darkwoods. There were less dwellings on the hills too. They were smaller as well.

Walking along the stone streets, we pass storefronts, some permanent structures and market tents that can be taken down and put back up in the morning. Not many Azanites or humans live within the city itself. Some shop owners and craft persons have apartments on the top floors of their buildings but they are few. The city is divided in sections depending on your needs. Food stalls and shops are mostly located in the middle of the town. There are woodworkers and craftspeople on the right of the city. That's where you can find ironworkers working over massive firepits and sword makers bending their pieces into wraith killing weapons. There are a small group of human run businesses on the furthest point of the city where their own healers and apothecaries and clothes makers work. It's not really a section an Azanite would go. That is also the side of the Darkwoods where humans live. Their dwellings are tightly packed together, like the townhouses I saw in the human realm. Humans prefer to stay together as a community here in Azanir, I think it has something to do with being more comfortable in larger numbers. They do have dragons flying around all day and night and the threat of wraith demons haunting the night. Now that I know that wraiths eat humans too, I understand why.

Thals and humans fill the streets and it's busy, in the best kind of way.

'It is really beautiful here,' Felix exclaims and I can't help but agree with him.

'It's beauty is not the problem,' Viktor replies soberly just as multiple dragons begin to drop from the sky. The need to stomp my way back the way we came is almost debilitating. I have no desire to play these games with my father and am only doing it to get this mission done. There are a great many Azar's amongst the landing party, meaning that the Lord of the Darkwoods is going to be joined by various nobles.

'Where are you from originally, Viktor?' I ask him, pointing to the lairs on the rolling hills around the main city centre. I'm dragging my feet on purpose because the group is growing and they're now all on two legs and I don't want to do this.

'The Cavelands.' Damn no wonder he is so intimidating. I don't know what they eat over there in the Cavelands but after seeing those males at the King's meeting, I wouldn't want to piss one of them off.

'And you, Felix?'

'Riverways.'

The way my face scrunches up at that piece of information has Felix chuckle. I hate thinking of him coming from a kingdom run by my 'grandfather'.

'Come on, I know what you're doing. Let's just get this day over.'

Felix wraps an arm around my shoulders and begins to lead me over to the crowd of Azar. 'The sooner we start this pompous Azar walk, the quicker it will go.'

Chapter Forty Five

FELIX IS A LIAR.

There is nothing fast about this Gods forsaken walk around the city with the twenty or so Azar's who haven't stopped throwing me weird, questioning glances. I had a few of the older males of the group eye me like I was the worst individual imaginable. I didn't have much to do with the nobles of the kingdom when I was younger. I remember some.

The biggest kick in the gut was that one stern-faced male even made a point of moving his daughter away from me. As if my rebellious nature is somehow catching. I wanted to reassure him that the female with the pretty pink dress and rosy cheeks was safe. She appeared around my age and is the only other female in our group beside my brother's mate.

Lady Penelope is at the front of the procession, between Luka and the female that I'm not allowed to corrupt. Their son runs around everyone's feet and the horde of Drengar warriors have formed a circle around the group. It's funny how Father's advisers told him that this would help, but not a single Thal or human can get anywhere near us. I have watched numerous workers having to stop what they're doing and move away, interrupting their business so that we can all walk past.

Not one of them looked too impressed or excited to see their Lord. It's disgusting really. A true example of the division between the classes of this world.

The only plus is that Wicked Bitch isn't here and that my own Drengar are with me, right at the back of the group. Father didn't say a word when we first came over. The elderly advisor from this morning was the one to introduce me to the Azar as the 'lady who has been found'.

If I could turn into a beast and fly away, I would've already. Fate is too cruel to give me a break.

Ignoring the way the Lady Penelope and the other female keep looking over their shoulder at me, I'm about ready to ask Felix and Viktor to take me back when we turn a corner and the entire vibe of the city changes.

I know instantly that this is the human quarter. There is music coming from a tavern down the road, children run and play up the alley-ways. The energy and life around me is electric. Men and women stand in groups while others move in and out of the open shops.

Well, it *was* electric because the moment we start walking into the area, heads snap up and conversations stop. Every child that was happily playing, halts their game and stands gaping at our group.

Father doesn't acknowledge anyone. He doesn't do anything but speak to the other Azar's. Emmet is the only one that seems uncomfortable as he moves around the outside of the group, monitoring everything with the other Drengar. A few times he walked past, looked at me as if to speak and then continued on. It could also be that every time any of the males get too close, Viktor or Felix growls a small noise that has them either look away or scurry off.

We're at the very back of the group which is why I spy the little bakery nestled between two fresh produce stores. All I see is cake and my legs just stop moving. My father has stopped up ahead to speak to a group of priests so I slip away to see what goodies they make here in Azanir.

I remember a pastry, custard tart-like thing from my youth but haven't been able to picture it. Van and I tried to recreate it once. He got so frustrated and didn't understand why he couldn't just search it to find the recipe. We ended up making a huge mess and burning the custard. Brent stopped down at the shop and got us just plain-old tarts because we had promised everyone dessert. It was hilarious.

Trying to slip away to have a look in the shop window, I'm blocked instantly by a monstrous body of one of the stone-face Drengar. The big, hairy dude gets checked pretty quickly by Viktor with a warning growl.

'Don't do that again,' Viktor warns and I'm swiftly moved away from the situation and led over to the shop with Felix.

'This is an absolute nightmare,' I whisper up at him, getting really over the drama. How many times can I wish that I wasn't here before I accept it?

'Tell me about it. If I have to cop a glare from another Darkwoods Drengar, I might just beast-out and kill one of them.'

Frowning up at the gorgeous male, I sigh, feeling a little selfish that I'm only thinking of myself in this situation. It mustn't be easy for him and Viktor. I can see the looks they're receiving too.

'We need to get out of here,' I say under my breath and walk up to the window and try desperately to not look threatening. The humans around us are standing close together, no one has moved since we've stopped, as if they don't want to draw attention to themselves and I don't blame them.

Offering what I hope is a kind smile, I step onto the stone curb and have a look at the bakery's display. The poor woman behind the glass pales, her eyes flicking between me and Felix. I don't look at her or anyone else so that they don't feel any more uncomfortable.

The problem is Felix is well, Felix. He is a Drengar. His very aura is dominance and power. I nudge him in the side when he makes an aggressive noise just as a man steps from the doors of the shop next door and I sigh. The poor guy clearly had no idea we were out here because he stops dead and visibly starts shaking.

'Don't be a dick,' I tell my friend who apologises. My attention snags on the human who rushes off. Unsure if I imagined the white tattoo peeking from under the cuff of his shirt, I get distracted by the sweets in the bakery window.

I point to a few cakes and slices that I remember and when I finally find what I was thinking of before, I practically squeal. 'That's them!'

'What?'

'The pastry things I would try and make back home. Meryl used to feed me them all the time. What are they called?' I'm like a small child, bouncing around, pointing.

The human woman behind the glass watches me intently and cocking her head she studies me before moving slowly towards the display. Eagerly I watch as she indicates to what I am pointing at and I nod enthusiastically.

'They're called honey delights,' Emmet states in Zaric coming up behind me.

'Honey,' I murmur, a light bulb going off in my mind. 'I totally forgot that it tasted like honey. I forgot we ate honey here. I hated the stuff in the human realm.' I definitely didn't put honey in the custard when I tried to make them with Van. Not that it would've helped the not so delightful pastries we attempted.

'I think you will find that a number of items from the human realm are used here,' Emmet replies. He's being nice and I look from the window to him suspiciously.

Felix, obviously satisfied that I am with my brother, pats me on the back before disappearing into the shop. I watch through the glass as the frightened shopkeeper quickly packs a few honey delights and a few other things I start pointing at into a bag. I laugh softly to myself when Felix gets in on the action and starts buying half the shop.

We're going to be so sick later.

Viktor appears at my back and sighs when he notices what Felix is doing and it brightens my shitty day.

'I remember that you had a sweet tooth as a youngling. I would bring you back treats from the Blazelands when I visited from the Drengar academy,' Emmet says, ignoring the Drengar who has just joined us.

'I couldn't remember if it was you or Luka.' Now I do. He'd bring me things and Wicked Bitch would take them once he left so that I wouldn't over-indulge.

'Listen Serafina, I think we need to sit down and talk. We have to—'

'Raffy!'

Turning from my very serious brother to the familiar voice that calls my name from the crowd, I spin just in time to see a little girl with the most gorgeous orange curls sprint towards me and the Drengar who pulls his weapon and goes to intercept her.

Chapter Forty Six

'No!' My shout is full of rage. My beast waking under my anger to make a sound that I've never made before. I move without much thought, my body no longer my own. Everything becomes a blur and then I'm standing before the Drengar who dared threaten a little girl.

The male is on his back before I realise what I've done and I grab Roxy and lift her in my arms the moment she reaches us.

'Raffy! You're here. Daddy said we'd find you in this place! That's why we decided to come there even though someone told us to stay in the other place but I told Daddy that I wanted to find you.'

Hugging the innocent child against my shoulder, I try to control my breathing. I'm shaking and disorientated and everyone is gaping at me like I have three heads. Humans and Azanites.

All except the Drengar on his arse before me, glaring up at me like I'm going to be his next meal.

Roxy is thankfully oblivious and Viktor, Felix and even Emmet are there in an instant, positioning themselves around me.

I have no idea what I just did or how. I only wanted to make sure that Roxy was safe. The crowd watching us is big now.

'Raffy, did you see this, Daddy's friend got me this,' Roxy states proudly as she pulls back and shows me the bracelet on her wrist.

Planting a smile on my face so that she doesn't know that anything is wrong, I make a big fuss over the piece. 'That is beautiful Roxy. I love it.'

Emmet is staring daggers at me and I couldn't care less.

A few gasps go out in the human crowd, I vaguely hear them whispering about how I can speak the human tongue. I don't have the energy to care.

Placing Roxy down, I recognise the man who runs from the group of onlookers instantly. James, Roxy's father, comes to a screeching halt at the sight of me. He smiles and then it drops seeing the amount of Drengar around his daughter right now.

'Felix, look at my bracelet,' Roxy squeals seeing her favourite and the massive predatory male picks up the human girl much to everyone's horror and places her on his hip.

I love Felix so much in this moment. He doesn't seem to care and I could kiss him. This nonsense is so absurd. I've been gone for ten years. I will not play a part in the class division here.

James tentatively steps forward, my brother only keeps from stopping him from coming close when Roxy starts calling to her dad to see who she found.

'It's her father Emmet, and my friend,' I inform him and move toward the man now looking at me like I'm some kind of god.

Confused, I realise why he has that dopey look on his face when he drops to one knee before me and says, 'Lady Serafina, you saved my daughter's life. I came to the Darkwoods to find you. To pledge my loyalty to you.'

Stopping dead, it's my turn to gape. There are a few humans I remember from the ship who stand a little closer now. They bow low to me.

'Please, don't,' I quickly say, bending to grip his arm so that he will stand. 'James, please. You don't have to pledge anything. I saved Roxy because I wanted to.' Pulling, he doesn't budge. Sun Gods, I don't like all this attention and ignoring Emmet, I look to Felix to help.

'Get up James, pledges in this world are very serious. You should understand them before you say one,' Felix states now beside me and my heart plummets into my butt. He is right. A pledge of loyalty would mean that James would become a member of my house. Meaning I am now able to create my *own* house. It's unheard of. Absurd. I'm a female. James would become a servant or my champion or whatever I want him to be. Legally, it would mean I would have power over my own life, no longer under my father's rule.

'I know what I'm doing, I've spoken with the leaders here and they told me, I just have to say, that I pledge my life to Lady Serafina DarkwoodsAzar and pledge my service to her and her house until the day I die.' And then he pulls a knife that has Viktor and Emmet grab me and cuts his palm.

I don't hear any sound. I only see the blood that falls from his palm to smash against the stone walkway. The energy under my skin increases as my beast stirs within my body. My entire body ripples and I suck in a breath under the pressure of feeling like my insides are too big to be contained.

'Holy shit,' Felix states, staring at me intently and I look down to see that my skin has a faint golden hue before it disappears.

Blinking is all I can manage. I can't move. I don't know what to say which is the exact moment my father steps over and demands to know what is going on.

His presence has the crowd cower back.

'What is the meaning of this?' His pale grey eyes fall to Felix and the child in his arms to the man on the floor, bleeding from the palm.

'It seems Serafina has gained herself a pledge,' Emmet replies and while he sounds calm, I can hear the tension in his voice. The King and Alistair told me to not stir anything up.

Well, fuck. I was never very good at doing what I was told.

'Excuse me!'

I know for a fact that Father heard what Emmet just said. He turns, ignoring James. I see the control he is managing with such an audience, he can't reprimand me just yet. It's impressive actually. He wants to lose his shit, I can tell. I have a pledge. I legally can leave his lair. He has just lost control of this situation. 'Let's return to the lair, it is getting late.'

Chapter Forty Seven

'What is the meaning of this!'

Sun Gods, his shout shakes the walls of the lair. Emmet indicates to the leather seat beside the blazing fire and I take it with a sigh. Here we go again.

'It sounds like Serafina saved that man's daughter when they journeyed here,' Emmet replies for me, sitting on the heavily patterned three-seater lounge with a straight back and those little buttons pressed within the material. It's a bit fancier than I expected from my father's working space.

There is a massive desk and the high-backed, throne-like black seat behind it. I'm not too surprised about the ancient looking books lining the shelves behind the desk either.

The comfortable sitting area is definitely not what I expected. The table between the furniture and the fur rug below my feet confuses the hell out of me. It's so warm and inviting and fills a great deal of the space. The double doors have been shut on my Drengar and the new man who has just pledged himself to me holding his daughter. He has no idea what he has just done. I know I don't fully understand either.

Felix and Wilder were not impressed to be locked out of the room. It took me ten minutes to convince them that I was fine. I'm not sure if they listened when I told them they could go back to their rooms, even

James hesitated and honestly the idea of having another over-bearing male hanging around all the time is making my head pound.

I really need to speak to Wilder. He would know what to do and how to calm me and the situation down. It's only been twenty four hours away from him and I feel as if I've lost the reason to breath. Logically, I know that he will be here the day after tomorrow but it's getting too hard to control the way my mind constantly drifts towards thinking of him. I want to know what he is doing and if he's okay. I want to speak to him and feel his arms around my body.

'Would you like to explain this to us, Serafina?' My father wraps his thick arms around his chest, the action drawing me from the pit forming in my mind. I'm too tired for this.

Knowing that I won't get out of here if I don't share, I take a deep breath and explain the events on the ship, minus a few details. I don't share any of my dreams or that I thought I accepted that I was going to die or that I was able to speak to my beast when I was in the water for the first time.

By the time I'm finished, I have been asked to explain my time in the human realm and how I came to being with the Prince and his Drengar. Again, I leave out a fair bit of information.

'And when you touched the book, you had a vision?' Emmet asks me to clarify for the hundredth time.

'Yes.'

'What did you see?'

My father sees me hesitate and narrows his eyes at me. Trying hard to bury my trepidation, I clear my throat and repeat exactly what I've told everyone else, leaving out the fact that I saw the human woman shift into her own beast.

'What happened when you touched it at the King's meeting?'

I swear, I don't know why I'm replying. I don't owe these two anything. 'I saw an Azanite male hurt a human woman.' I'm not sharing that I saw them have sex. That's weird. It's my brother and Dad.

'This entire thing is a mess. Humans and Azanites, it's absurd.'

Emmet rubs at his face while my dad and I share a look. The need to expose his secret hurts. Too bad his secrets are my secrets. 'Yeah, it's really absurd. Yet, that is what I saw.'

Dad turns away. 'You need to be careful the nonsense you spill, Serafina.'

Emmet frowns deeply at our dad's back.

'It's not nonsense. It's what the book showed me. What if that is the answer to our race extinction?' I probably shouldn't say this but I need them to understand that I didn't come back to cause problems or create more division between humans and Azanites.

'Just because you're a human-lover now doesn't mean—'

'That's disgusting. Don't speak to me like that,' I bark and get the full force of Dad's gaze. Wrapping my arms around my middle, I huff. 'Humans are not lesser!' For fuck's sake, he made me with a damn human, why is he being such a bigot? 'I lived with humans for ten years, they are my family too.'

Dad makes a deep noise in his chest and walks over to his desk. I watch him go until something metallic catches my eye on the shelf behind him. A book made of copper. Weird.

'I needed you to come back here to help with our reputation, Serafina, not cause more problems. I've already spent the day telling the Azar of my kingdom what happened to you.'

He doesn't ask about my family or for more details of my life in the human realm. It hurts my heart. You'd think that he'd show some kind of interest in my life and where I've been. His daughter was gone for ten years. A father should be curious, worried even. He has no idea if I was safe or if my life was full of happiness or grief.

'Now there will be more questions and rumours around this human man pledging himself to you. I don't care what he has done, you and I have an agreement. You will not do anything about this pledge, not yet. Don't forgot our understanding or I will draw out this mating between you and that damn Medir.'

'Father,' Emmet reprimands.

'I will play the dutiful daughter, Father. Don't worry about that, but not for much longer. You know, I left this lair of my own free will.' I stand slowly. Emmet tracks every one of my movements. 'I wasn't stolen or hurt. The humans you killed after I left will haunt me for the rest of my days. Instead of looking at the reasons why I'd leave, reasons that you know, Father, you blamed defenceless humans.'

Emmet's brow furrows. 'What do you mean?'

Studying my brother, I have no idea if he's being serious or acting. 'Father killed my maid and a number of humans in the lair when I ran away.'

'You did? You told me you couldn't trust anyone and let them go.' Emmet's words are emotion-less like he's trying to work out what the truth is.

'Who told you that nonsense?' Father snaps.

'So it's a lie?' I question, praying to every Sun God that it is. 'Do you know where Meryl is?'

'How am I to know? It's been ten years, she is probably at her dwelling in the human section. Why are we talking about her? You mustn't have cared that much if you left her as well.' Every word gets louder and louder. Hope swells within my chest despite the harsh words. I know I left her, she knows why I did. The only thing that matters is that Meryl could be alive.

Feeling Emmet staring, I turn. His green eyes seem curious. Not sure what his deal is, I don't say another word and leave the room.

There is so much going on and so much to think about.

James. The mission and finding the book. My mating. Finding out who I am.

All I know is that I need to work this shit out.

Chapter Forty Eight

Too deep in thought and with my beast needing me to hurry and find my nest, I don't see the female up ahead until it's too late for me to get the hell out of here.

I come to a screeching halt the moment I sense her. The colours of the setting sun paint reds and yellows on the floors and walls of the stone lair. The large, round glass windows to my left aren't covered and I'm becoming increasingly aware of the time. It will be dark very soon.

'So, you've decided to come back.'

It's not a question but the wicked bitch pauses as if waiting for me to answer. I have no idea why her words hurt me so much still. The pure hatred in her green eyes breaks something deep within me, something I thought was healed when I found Laney and my foster brothers.

Now, without them here and fearing that they hate me too after I left so abruptly, I feel it crack and shatter again. It's hard to fight against the small youngling in my soul that just wanted to be loved and included.

I stare at the Lady of the Darkwoods, with her perfect golden hair and her lean, tall body that I'm completely envious of and wonder what I did to make her despise me so much.

'I didn't choose to come back,' I say and thank every Sun God that every word comes out confidently and unaffected. I'm a good liar. I've had to keep secrets and deal with the messed up situations I've been dealt by fate on my own for a very long time.

'No, you left. You should've stayed away, Serafina. We don't need someone like you here, causing trouble. You shouldn't even exist.' Hatred laces each word.

It takes every ounce of strength to keep my emotions in check. 'Why do you hate me so much?' I ask, genuinely confused. 'I have done nothing to you. It is not my fault that your mate did what he did.'

Wicked Bitch scoffs and wraps her thin arms over her chest. Her green eyes are narrowed still. 'So you know.'

'Yes, I know.'

'Well then, I don't understand why you'd be stupid enough to risk being discovered. I hear you are planning to mate with a BlazeAzar.' She cackles like a witch in the human fairytales that Van and I secretly watched. 'You are absurd. Why would he want to mate with something like you?'

Her laughter grates on my nerves. 'He is my mate, neither of us made the choice. It is fated.'

'Sun Gods, you are pathetic. Must be the human in you. Mates is all nonsense, we females just go where our fathers tell us. Mates.' She laughs again and it's genuinely wicked.

Her words bounce around in my head until they settle. 'Father is not your mate, is he?' Every muscle in my body is tense. I feel sick.

Wicked Bitch throws me the best 'don't be dumb' look. 'Mates. If we all sat around waiting for that to happen there wouldn't be any pairing, no younglings. Mating is an ancient custom. No one finds their mate anymore.'

An ancient custom. What if mates aren't being found because Azanite males are looking in the wrong place for one?

'I've found my mate,' I declare and feel truly sorry for her.

She huffs. 'How? With your parentage, you shouldn't even exist. To think that a human produced a *female* Azanite is abhorrent. I guess it makes sense why you can't shift.'

Gods, that hurt. It was like she knew exactly where to jab that fucking knife but the sting of her words don't stop me from trying to decipher why she said female like that. Is she...jealous that a human, my birth mother, produced a female when she couldn't? Is that a thing to be jealous of? Are female Azanites blamed for not having girls?

'Do you hate me for being who I am or for representing something that you can't accept?'

I see the mask of disgust slip from her face for a second like I shocked her.

'How dare you!' She steps forward aggressively and I ready myself for whatever she is about to do.

'Mother?'

I startle and it appears that Wicked Bitch does too. Emmet comes striding up the corridor, clearly leaving Father's office and stopping whatever was about to happen. He takes in his mother's stance and probably the look of utter shock on my face and frowns deeply. For a moment I fear that he may have heard what we were talking about but if he did he gives no indication.

'What are you both doing out, the sun is almost down. You should be in your rooms.'

Emmet stops right beside me and I don't think I ever really paid attention to how tall and big he is. He is almost the size of Wilder and he has massive shoulders.

'Serafina and I were just having a conversation about her return and how excited I am to meet her future mate.'

It's my turn to glare over at the bitch. She lies like a pro.

'Right,' Emmet states, not missing a beat. 'Well Mother, I think you should find your rooms. I'll escort Serafina to hers, we need to discuss a few things.' Emmet grips my elbow and I'm kinda glad for his appearance.

'Of course,' she replies sweetly and smiles wide at us both like she is genuinely happy to have her young in front of her. 'I will see you both when the sun rises, be safe.'

We both watch her go.

'What was that about?'

'Just welcoming me home,' I say tightly and pulling my elbow from his grasp, I storm down the corridor feeling beaten and bruised.

'I'm not stupid you know,' Emmet calls after me.

'I never said you were,' I shout back as calmly as I can, not slowing. If he heard anything that Wicked Bitch just said then I'm screwed. I don't even know what lies I could tell to explain anything, she basically told my entire life story out loud.

I'm already getting a headache recounting everything that she just said.

I practically run to my rooms.

Chapter Forty Nine

'I KNEW WE SHOULDN'T have left you!'

'Viktor, stop. I'm fine.'

Viktor stomps back and forth, wearing a track in the patterned rug in my sitting room. The sitting room is surrounded by walls and doors, no windows so that females can eat and rest without our beasts flipping out about being outside. It's the bedrooms that can be a bit tricky. Azanites need air, we need the sun and sky and so we love big windows and balcony's to take-off from. Unfortunately that means that there's always the danger of wraiths getting to us. This lair is fortified with a glass not known about in the human realm. It is practically un-breakable. That's why I can sleep without fear. Covering them with a thick curtain placates our beasts.

'So your mother cornered you? What is her problem anyway? You're her daughter,' Felix muses in the human tongue, stuffing his face with meat and breads. The small table to the side of the room is covered in our evening meal. The exact spot that I would've eaten with Meryl or one of the servants as a youngling. Now, James, Roxy and Felix are there, eating and listening to Viktor grumble about not keeping me safe.

'I have no idea what her problem is. I guess she is mad that I ran away.'

It's James who looks over at me and I see the scrutiny in his gaze as if he knows that I'm lying. I have my lower lip between my teeth, maybe he knows about the lip thing.

It makes me uncomfortable to think I'm so easily read, especially with the amount of secrets I'm keeping to myself right now.

I quickly grab at the plate piled high with food and stuff something into my mouth. Viktor filled it the moment I sat down and practically threw it at me. I don't know what they saw on my face when I first walked in but my Drengar nearly lost it. They were furious and demanded I tell them what has upset me.

I don't think they were expecting me to say that it was my 'mother'. My mind is reeling from the conversations I just had. Wicked Bitch tried to make me feel like a piece of worthless shit but that isn't what has me dizzy. She highlighted a fear that I never considered. A human and an Azanite male made me, a female, something that is growing increasingly more and more uncommon in our race.

Could that be the key here? If in ancient times, humans mated with Azanites and our people were thriving, could the class division and the issues between the two races have caused us to slowly die out?

It's all speculation at this point and there are so many questions that need answers but it seems like a valid connection.

The vision the golden text gave me in the office showed me a human female shift into a dragon and I think that was the point of the vision. Not that she was human. It wanted me to see her change. Then it wanted me to see the same couple before their mating speaking of consummating their love. That is the part I don't understand. He hurt her badly. If that was the same couple though, I know she didn't die.

Rubbing my fingers over my scalp, I try to relieve the pressure with a quick massage. My head is throbbing.

'The sooner we leave the better. I can't wait for Wilder to hear that you have a pledge.' Felix chuckles in amusement and both James and I stare at him. Clearly he is wondering the same thing I am.

'What will Wilder say when he finds out about James?' I ask, unsure if I have the brainpower for his response.

Shrugging, Felix throws more food in his mouth. 'Just that he doesn't have to wait any longer to finish your mating.'

My core clenches at that thought and I find myself speechless.

'You legally have the power over your own life now. If you choose, you can leave your father's lair and establish your own. Your father is bound by our laws to give you gold. It's rather exciting to see what will happen. A female is never pledged to. You can create your own house,' Felix ends his little speech completely unaware of what his words have just done to me.

I honestly can't take in any more information.

'You all keep saying her own house, what does that mean? It's a very human word,' James enquires, adding more juice to Roxy's cup. She seems very comfortable being here and that makes my shitty night a little better. They both appear to be oblivious to the way Wakely and my two new maids went all bug-eyed when they saw them. I'm sure the gossip in the lair is going crazy. My poor Father's plan to have me come back here and fix the mess that *I've* made is backfiring—I love it.

I stop rubbing at my head because he is right, house is a very human word.

'Probably should've understood that before you did it,' Viktor snaps out. I throw him what I hope to be a reproachful stare. I must have gotten my point across because he huffs as he sits in the chair across from mine with a grimace.

'The word *house* is used to speak of a family name. Lady Serafina is now able to start her own life and *house* outside of her father's. She can have her own Drengar and live as an influential Azar in Azanir,' Felix explains and I push my food away and lay back on the couch, unable to stop the room from spinning. I can't do this. I'm drowning in information.

'How does she do that, financially? How do Azar's make gold? Is it a job?'

Felix wipes his mouth and shares a look with Viktor. The bigger Drengar shrugs. 'He is pledged to Serafina, he's going to have to know these things. He will be with her for life or forfeit it.'

I might be sick all over the rug.

'It's not something that happens very often. I know maybe four males who have had this power. Everyone else is given their lairs and stay within the rule of their father's. If they are Drengar, they enter their father's Drengar or the house that their father serves. If they are Medir or Thal, you do the job and get your gold from the Lord of the house you serve. The throne pays Lords, taxes paid by the Azanites and humans in the kingdom, it all goes to the house. The Blazelands have a few houses that rule the lands t ogether.'

'What about land though? Does Serafina's father have to give her lands here in the Darkwoods?'

'Yes, he does.'

'Wouldn't Lords hate to divide their lands?'

'No, we don't care about that sort of thing. The Lords of Azanir are responsible on a daily basis for the lives of thousands of Azanites and humans that live on their lands. Giving a portion of that responsibility is not an issue. Well, it shouldn't be. Some Lords from other lands even offer pieces of their own kingdoms to new pledged Lords if they have need of more support in their kingdom.'

There is a moment of silence while James sits gaping at Felix. 'You never said pledged to a Lady,' he muses and looks over at me quickly. 'I did something big didn't I?'

'Yep,' Felix pops the word and grins. I want to smack him.

'I'm sorry, Raff. I didn't realise. You saved Roxy, I owe you my life. I heard that is the best way to do it.' Poor James shuffles on his seat.

'Who told you to do it?' Viktor asks, his eyes flashing a little red and I think that's a great question.

'Um…a group of humans that I met. When I told them my story, they explained that the only way to repay a debt like that to an Azanite is to pledge your loyalty. Say the words and cut your palm,' he states like reciting what he was told.

I don't miss the way Felix and Viktor tense.

'What?' It's my turn to be grumpy.

'I don't know,' Viktor muses, he even scratches his chin. 'Every human in Azanir would know that it isn't done with females. It's strange they would advise that.'

Sick and tired of all this female, male, Lord not Lady bullshit, I jump off the couch. 'I can't take any more of the nonsense that is Azanir politics. I'm going to bed and we will keep all of this quiet until our mission is complete.' James goes to ask a question and I stop him with a small wave. 'The guys can tell you. I'm out. I need to sleep.'

Chapter Fifty

Sleep is not what I get.

Tossing and turning, I find it impossible to calm my mind enough to rest. Rolling out of bed, I stay clear of the curtained glass doors to my balcony and head to the sitting room. I didn't eat much before and filling my grumbling stomach seems like the only practical thing I can do right now. Things like saving the entire Azanir race, becoming a Lady with my own house and dealing with Wicked Bitch and her insecurities seems too big for one person.

My rooms are dark and quiet but the fire is still blazing in the fireplace and I find it instantly comforting. Wearing one of Wilder's tunics that I found in my bag, I curl up on the couch and spy the food that has been left out. It is common practice for fruits and non-perishable items to always be on the tables in sitting rooms. You never know when a Drengar is going to return from patrolling the night for wraiths or battling the demons.

Hugging Wilder's shirt, I make myself a plate and lean back against the cushiony chair and eat slowly. Nothing is going how I expected it to and whilst the scent of my mate does calm me a little, it doesn't stop the rolling turmoil of emotions keeping me from sleeping. If he was actually here, I know that I'd be able to snuggle against his chest and sleep soundly, even with all this shit happening in my head.

My mate. If what Wicked Bitch said was true, does anyone here truly find their mate or is it just a messed up world we live in where arrangements are made between fathers?

The conversation I heard between my father and Medir Leon all those years ago about them finding me a male that they can control makes a great deal of sense now. There aren't very many females left, it seems cruel to force them to mate without this feeling I have for Wilder. Are females missing out on finding their one true soulmate for the same reasons males are? Can females mate with human men?

'Raff?'

Realising that I was staring off into space, I startle and spill half my plate. 'Shit.'

'Damn, I'm so sorry,' James exclaims, grabbing at a new plate so that I can add my spilt food onto it.

'Thanks. It's okay, I was lost in my own head.' Damn, I think I may have ruined Wilder's shirts.

'You sure were,' he laughs and helps me to clean up the mess. He sits on the table, facing me and I give up trying to get the fruit stain off the tunic. Thankfully it's black. He might not even notice.

'So, it seems like a lot's going on,' he says sweetly, taking my plate when I go to place it down. 'Drengar Viktor and Drengar Felix told me a few things about your mission and how you haven't got the best relationship with your father and mother.'

Nodding, I sigh. 'Too much going on,' I agree.

'I'm sorry if I've added to that.' Studying the kind man, I take in his blonde, stylish hair. It sits at the top of his head in a funky curve. His brown eyes are always inviting and from the moment I met him on the docks back in the human realm, I felt instantly at ease with him.

'Do you realise that you are bound to me for the rest of your life James?' I ask, genuinely concerned that he doesn't realise the magnitude of what he has done. 'You're my servant now. Mine. No one else's. You get that, right?'

James smiles. 'I do, Raff. I've had a long chat with your Drengar and they outlined everything. I don't care what job you give me or what I have to do to prove myself. You saved my daughter's life, I will always be indebted to you.'

'I would've saved her no matter what.'

'I know,' he replies, fixing me a new plate. 'I'm doing this for my own selfish reasons too. The guilt I feel at letting her get away from me has kept me from sleep.'

Leaning over, I grip his knee, seeing the sheen of moisture building in his eyes.

'I just want you to know that I will be loyal to you for as long as I live Raff. I know you are keeping things from the others, I was an officer of the law back in the human realm,' he says as a way of explaining how he may have known. I don't know what to do with that information. 'You can tell me Raff. If you need an ear or a shoulder, I am here.'

'Thanks James.' I take the plate he's filled for me. 'I hope your room is okay. It's probably not ideal to share with Roxy but we aren't going to stay here for very long. Once we work out what the next steps are in my life, we'll find a more permanent place.'

'We will manage. It's all an adventure for her right now and Felix fed her about three of these custard pastry things and she is just in love.'

Laughing lightly, I stop when I realise he would've eaten all the sweets we bought today. Damn fool wouldn't have left me any. I totally forgot.

We converse for a while about our history and I learn a great deal about James' life before his wife died. He has lived such an amazing life. Travel. Dangers from his jobs. He is amazing and it becomes very clear that I'm very lucky to have him in my life.

Then I realise that he actually can help me with something. 'You know, I do have something for you to do. I need to find someone who may be in the human quarter of the city.'

'I can do that, no problem.' James seems just as eager as I am as we chat long into the night of what I need him to do.

Chapter Fifty One

'Why are we doing this Raff?' Roxy sings pulling a vine and falling on her butt.

I freeze, waiting to see how she will react and then laugh when she does. Me more in relief than humour. I don't know what to do if she hurts herself. I don't think telling her to rub some dirt in like Van and the boys would say would be the right thing.

Pulling off the garden gloves, I help her up and watch as she rushes to the other side of the garden unbothered and full of energy. It's why I took her with me. We were stuck in our rooms while Viktor and Felix were summoned by the Drengar Commander of the Darkwoods this morning. They weren't too impressed. I told them not to go but apparently they 'had' to.

Blah! After my day yesterday, I couldn't give a shit about 'have to's'. I've made it my mission to avoid my entire family today, which is why I am in the garden pulling these damn weeds.

The sun feels amazing today and I'm ignoring my problems like a real adult.

'Raffy, can I go over there where the trees are?'

Looking to where Roxy points, I ask her to stay close and watch her go the few metres to the tree line and look at the wildflowers.

'My grandmother says that we aren't allowed to speak to the servants.'

Turning to eye the youngling at the entrance to the garden, I have to force myself to not say the first thing that comes to me. Which would be something like, 'your grandmother is a brainwashed moron.' I don't think that that would go down well.

Instead, I remind myself that this kid is a product of his upbringing. He's a baby really. I can feel his uncertain energy. He doesn't know me but his eyes are twinkling and he keeps gazing over at Roxy like he wants to play. I remember living here and there never being any other children around to play with. It's a crappy life for an adventurous kid.

'Yeah, I was told that too when I was your age.' I go back to cleaning out the weeds but in a spot that I can still see Roxy. This place used to be so well loved.

I hear his little feet as he moves closer, still uncertain. 'Why did you not listen?'

'Because I don't like being told that I can't speak to people, especially when they could be my new friend.'

I don't look up when Deklan stops beside me. 'I don't have any friends except Mummy and Rehan. Daddy is too and so is Uncle Emmet but they are busy all the time.'

That breaks my heart.

'I can use another friend.' I blurt out without much thought. 'Some of my friends would like to meet you too, if you wanted. Roxy would love it if you played with her. She only just came to Azanir and she doesn't know anyone.'

His little eyes light up. 'Really?'

'Of course. Do you want me to introduce you?'

Deklan hesitates before his little head nods making his mop of blonde hair bounce.

'Roxy, come meet Deklan. He wants to play.'

'I don't know how to speak with her,' Deklan muses, watching his new friend run over excitedly.

'You'll figure it out.'

They do. Roxy and Deklan have been playing happily despite the fact they both speak two different languages. They laugh together. Pointing at things and stay within the zone I instructed them to keep to.

Sitting in the grass, taking a much needed break, I hear the female just as she steps close.

I have no idea how my brother's mate is going to react to seeing her son playing with a human girl.

A little shocked when she sits gracefully beside me on the grass, I stay focused on the children, ready to protect Roxy if I need to.

'I know I shouldn't be surprised to see you all out here together. Deklan loves this garden. Luka used to bring him here when he was very little.'

'He did?' That's news to me. I never saw Luka out here.

'Yes, he said this was where he'd remember his lost sister the most. That he could sit on his balcony and see you playing down here when you were younger.'

Staring up at the lair behind me, I spy Luka doing just that from the balcony high above us. Probably making sure that I be nice to his mate and kid.

Rolling my eyes, I don't let her see how much her words have affected me. 'I didn't know that he would care that much.'

'I can see why.'

Gaze moving to the female beside me, I study her to better understand her motive. She is like any other Azanite female. Calm. Pretty. Sweet. Soothing energy. Everything I am not.

I wonder, and not for the first time, if my brother really did find his mate or was this mating arranged.

'What do you mean?'

'The way Lady Celina spoke to you and the tension between you and your family, I don't know anything really but I'm not ignorant to the gossip in the lair. Or in the Darkwoods itself. You are the Lost Lady of the Darkwoods, everyone spoke about you like you were a myth. I guess you aren't lost anymore.'

'No, I'm definitely not.' Though I wish I was. I have returned to this place and I regret it...well, most of it. I don't regret Wilder or my Drengar.

'I was a Thal you know.'

That truly shocks me and it must be written over my face because Penelope laughs in a sing-song tone that does nothing for my self-esteem. 'You were a Thal! How did that horrible female take that news?'

She frowns for a moment and then grins wide as if she worked out who I meant. 'She wasn't very happy,' she giggles. 'Your mother certainly doesn't like surprises.'

It's my turn to laugh though I just sound bitter. 'Tell me about it.' I was the biggest surprise and I've been dealing with how much she doesn't like me my entire life.

'So this doesn't bother you?' I motion to the two children playing and my answer when she smiles at the way Roxy shrieks in joy at whatever Deklan has just shown her.

'No.' She pauses. 'Serafina, what I said yesterday about wanting to be friends was real. There aren't a lot of females here to talk to. I'm sorry for what happened, I never hesitated because I believed you were unfit to hold Rehan. I'd be honoured if my young knew their aunt, especially after I saw how amazing you were in the city, protecting the human. It was just your mother and our history.'

Waving her apology away, I forgive her. 'You're not to blame for the tension I have between my family.'

We sit in silence for a while before she asks in a cheeky whisper, 'did you actually run and live in the human realm for ten years?'

It's my turn to smile and I tell her all about it.

Chapter Fifty Two

Slowing just as I get close enough to the Drengar training fields, I squint up at the dragons diving and manoeuvring under the afternoon sun.

Viktor was right, the beauty here in the Darkwoods is not the problem. With the trees spanning as far as the eye can see and the mighty Azanite beasts filling the sky, it is a wonder to behold.

Attention snagging on the two males across the flat clearing reserved for hand-to-hand training, I get about five steps into the Drengar zone and am stopped by a big chest. 'Females are not supposed to be down here.'

Blinking up at the male I pushed yesterday in the city, I sigh loudly. He's dramatically bulky and has the weirdest tiny waist I have ever seen, like the action figure that Van swears he has no idea how it got into his room.

'Really,' I reply in mock horror. Frantically searching the area, I stop and snarl up at him. I remember the aggressive way that he went for Roxy. This male is a dick.

Trying to step past him, he blocks my way again. 'Did you not learn your lesson the last time you did this?' I ask sweetly, reminding him of how Viktor got all up in his face when he did this yesterday.

'Drengar Viktor Longwing doesn't have authority here. Not anymore.' Gods, what an arse hat.

'You want to tell him that?' I point behind him as if Viktor is there and watch as he quickly looks back in worry.

I nearly burst a blood vessel keeping in my laughter. I'm probably going to regret that but it was worth it.

Red eyes meet mine when dickhead turns back to face me.

'Drengar Groven, you should be in the sky!'

I get one last unimpressed snarl from the big guy before he stomps off and I'm left with the male who just saved me from an arse-kicking.

'Thanks for the save.' I salute Emmet and try to walk away. He doesn't let me go anywhere.

'What are you doing down here provoking the Drengar?'

'He provoked me!' I retort. Groven is still eyeing me from across the clearing and when he shifts, I swear he snaps his massive dragon mouth in my direction.

I flip him off and get growled at by Emmet.

'Sun Gods, you have no sense of self preservation, do you?' He pushes my arm down and runs his hand threw his hair.

'What is that supposed to mean?'

'It means that yesterday on our city walk, you showed no regard to protocol and tried to break ranks. You interacted with humans the way you did and you got yourself a pledge. Then I found out what happened with that young girl you've been with all day. I don't know how Wilder BlazeAzar puts up with you.'

Pulling my arm from his grip, I see red. 'You are half the male he is.' I'm panting in rage at how he is speaking to me. We both stare the other down, waiting to see who will break eye contact first.

I win and smirk.

'How did you learn to move like that?' he asks angrily and then mumbles how annoying I am under his breath when I don't answer. 'Yesterday, when Drengar Groven approached the human girl.'

'Roxy!' I correct him, he could at least use her name. Emmet gives me a look I've seen on my father's face one too many times. 'I don't know what you mean.'

'You moved so fast. Like a Drengar. Like an Azanite who has true discipline and control over their beast.'

My mouth hits the floor. I had no idea. 'I don't really…I didn't know…I just had to get to Roxy.'

His answering grumble shows me he doesn't believe a word I've said. 'Do you understand the target that is on your back after you announced that the golden text gave you visions? You spoke about dangerous topics, Serafina. You have to be mindful of that.'

Skin prickling, I have no idea what he is referring to.

He lowers his voice so it's only me who can hear. 'Humans and Azanites mating. You have no idea the box you've just opened saying what you did. I want to talk to you about this. I think we need to understand each other better.'

I can't help but wonder why he didn't say things to me like this when we were in Father's sitting room.

Viktor and Felix appear at my side the moment I go to ask and the expression on their faces when they tell me it's getting late has me not fight when they lead me back into the lair.

Chapter Fifty Three

'What happened?' I ask for what feels like the hundredth time and get the same response of 'nothing'. 'Felix!'

The blue eyed male gives in and explains that, 'it is not common for Drengar to spend this long in another kingdom. The Commander has let us know that we are to remember our place and that while we can train with them, we aren't to patrol or be out at night in case we get hurt.' He says the last part like it's the biggest insult he has ever received and I guess I can understand that.

Viktor just stomps ahead of us, clearly pissed.

'I'm sorry. We only have to stay a few more days. Did we learn anything about the book?'

'No, no one will speak with us.'

Damn. That has my shoulder slump.

Felix tenses just as Viktor stops walking. Then Emmet's voice calls for me to wait.

'I would like a word with you,' my brother states and I wave the pair on when they hesitate. My rooms are only around the corner and I think that's why they leave me. They'll probably listen from around the corner or something.

Emmet waits for them to disappear before demanding, 'I said we needed to talk. Tell me why you ran away. Tell me what Medir Leon did to you. The real reason.'

Taken aback, I hesitate. 'Do you really want to know?'

Watching as his face hardens as if he's preparing himself for whatever I'm about to say, I realise that I may have judged my brother too harshly too soon.

'Yes, I want to know. I'm your brother. I need to know.'

I don't know what makes me tell him. He has been such an ass. Maybe it's the look in his eye or the way he stands waiting, almost like a plea.

'Medir Leon and Father believed that I had dreams that told the future. That arsehole Medir would lock me in my nightmares. He would inject me with a sleep serum. Without my consent. No matter how hard I begged. Those dreams were frightening, Emmet.'

Emmet's jaw clenches as he studies me for the lie. I see every emotion flash over his face and land on rage. 'And father knew about this?'

'Yes. He was there every night I woke screaming. He did nothing. No one ever did, except Meryl. She was the only one that tried to protect me.' I didn't realise that I was crying until a tear drips onto my lips. I quickly wipe them away and avert my face. Being here, reliving all of this isn't healing. It's breaking me more.

Emmet seems to need a moment to process. He is studying a spot on the wall. 'Mother?'

'She knew.' I have no control over the hatred that drips from each word and he knows it because he is staring at me now.

'You had Drengar assigned to your safety, where were they?' his words are all beast and I fight the need to take a step back. Not because I'm afraid of him but the energy he is emitting right now is scolding.

I hesitate, unsure why retelling all this is helpful.

'I need to know, Serafina. I need to understand.'

'They were in the room, Emmet. Every time. They did nothing to protect me from that Medir or from father.'

His growl is menacing and he takes a few steps away from me as if he needs to put some distance between us. His glowing red eyes tell me enough about how he is feeling. He's mumbling something about a Drengar's role and protecting innocents, especially females.

'Do you remember their names?'

I shiver under the tone. My brother is a dominant predator who has just found out that his sister was abused.

'No. I don't. They never spoke to me. I only remember little details,' I offer, closing my eyes for a moment to see them. One was big around the middle as if his core was the only part of his body he worked on. He has deep brown eyes. Another was tall, like exceptionally tall, with these strange mahogany eyes.

His answering growl is not as aggressive, more like a promise. Emmet is pacing back and forth, making all sorts of noises.

'Do you still have these dreams? Is that why you were able to have the visions our sacred text showed you?' he asks the floor. I can practically see his head spinning.

'I do and I'm not sure. All I know is that the book opened when I opened it and I was pulled into the vision.'

'Of a mated male and human woman with a youngling?'

I clear my throat and answer with a quick, 'yep.'

His gaze flies over to me and his brow furrows. 'You're keeping secrets. I know you are. You do the same thing with your mouth that Luka does when you have something you want to say and can't. He's a terrible secret keeper.'

His words have me feeling a little sick. 'Good to know,' is all I say and I watch him roll his eyes. It's a familiar gesture that has me realise that maybe I'm a little like Emmet too. 'Why are you telling me this?'

'Your lip is doing that thing, Serafina.'

Cursing, I can't help but grab my bottom lip between my teeth.

'What else?' he asks and it's such a brotherly demand. I miss Van and Brent so much right now. Scott was more of a silently waiting kinda brother.

'I don't know—'

'Lip,' he says.

'Fuck.' Damn mouth. I just stay quiet, I don't want my lip giving away my secrets.

Eyes narrowed in the best glare I have seen in a very long time, Emmet grumbles his displeasure. 'You can trust me. I know I haven't shown that and I'm sorry.' He hesitates. 'I'm sorry I didn't protect you. I failed you.'

'Emmet—' I'm stopped with a simple hand gesture and know that there is nothing I can say right now that will fix how he's feeling.

Chapter Fifty Four

*M*Y BACK HITS THE *plush mattress and I can't help but rub my body against the furs. It's exquisite. The laughter above me has me stop and stare up at the male standing naked beside the bed watching me. His warmth and scent surround me.*

Wilder crawls over my body, keeping most of his weight on his strong, thick arms even when I pull him down against my chest so that I can feel all of the male-ness.

He enters me and I see stars.

Our panting is heavy in our passion. I cry in ecstasy as he pushes deeper, changing the tempo. I lift my hand to his back and smile at the rough, animalistic noise he growls in pleasure.

He nudges my neck to the side, trailing kisses down to my nipple and then back up. His teeth graze my neck and I fear his beast in my mind, telling me that I am his. Forever.

I'm on the floor, withering in a pain unlike anything I could comprehend.

The dream flashes. I'm on the stone, dying and then I'm on grass, surrounded by trees, feeling like my life is slipping away. Stone. Forest. Stone. Forest.

Until I'm clutching at my abdomen, feeling the blood pooling under my hand. The pain is so intense that I begin to drift.

Then smoke fills my vision and I shriek just as teeth clamp against my calf.

My eyes snap open. I'm screaming and I can't stop

'No. No.' I'm manic with no way to calm down.

My skin is on fire.

My body aching with the remnants of the dream. Such unbelievable pleasure that has me still feel the ache between my legs and such incredible pain. This dream lingers too long, emphasising what I just saw in my nightmare.

Another death. Another future where my life will come to an end because how can anyone survive the agony my dream just showed me.

There are multiple voices surrounding me. Speaking words of reassurance and comfort as I fight the hands that hold me securely against the mattress. They aren't the right hands I want on my body. The ones I need to be touching me right now. The scent that is able to pull me from this place of in-between nightmare and reality, is not the one surrounding me now.

I'm stuck, unable to find a way out of the fog clouding my mind.

'Wilder!' I shout, nothing is focused. Everything is a blur of bodies and movements and sounds. *'Wilder!'* I scream in my head.

I don't have the power to pull myself from my raging thoughts. Something is coming. Something that is going to change my life forever.

I'm not ready.

'Serafina, everything is well.'

'It's not,' I tell the voice, finding that if I focus on drawing in enough air with each breath the fog slowly starts to disperse. 'Something is coming, Felix.'

Piercing blue eyes hold my gaze and the room slowly comes into view. I want to melt into the blankets on the bed. Viktor is there, as is James and Emmet. My father is at the door, watching with a look of both anguish and apprehension. It's probably the most emotion I've seen from him. It's making the entire situation worse.

Sitting up, I try to scrub the dregs of the dream away by rubbing at my face.

'You okay?' Felix asks just as my father walks out of my room with a small shake of his head.

'I think so,' I whisper, embarrassed by my behaviour. The dream finally slips and I'm left a little raw and confused.

'Here.' Felix passes something over and I stare down at the piece of clothing trying to fight my tears.

Bringing a new shirt of Wilder's to my face, I bury my nose in it and try to find some kind of peace. His scent fills my lungs and my raging heart steadies. I miss him with every fibre of my being. Not having him here is starting to mess with my head.

'Is that Wilder's?' Emmet asks and gets snapped at by Viktor who demands that he consider what is to gain by keeping me away from my mate.

Peeking a little glance over at the big male now standing by the curtains, I feel a little bad for him. James has positioned himself on the other side of the bed and begins to fuss around pouring me some water and fixing up the blankets. He has no idea what anyone is talking about but he isn't looking at me like a freak so I guess that's a plus.

'Are you okay, Raff?' he enquires, handing me the water.

'Yes, thank you. I'm sorry I woke you. Did Roxy hear any of that?' My throat is raw from screaming.

'Nothing can wake that kid, she's like her mother. Head hits the pillow and she is out. I think you wore her out with all your adventures in the garden too.' The way he refers to his late wife makes me smile. The statement was full of love and affection. 'Do you want to talk about your nightmare? Maybe we can help understand it. I find that speaking about it can help.'

I hesitate and look over at Felix. 'I don't really remember now, all I know is that I was in so much pain,' I whisper.

They both lean forward and grip my arm. With them both holding me, I'm able to fight the terror sitting in the corner of my mind, as if waiting to fill me with more.

'Then why are you still here?' Emmet questions Viktor, drawing my attention. 'My sister has a pledge. We can talk to the King and get this all sorted. I'll make my father give her what is hers rightfully. I know she is a female but with Wilder BlazeAzar and the progressive ideas the King has, we can ensure the law is upheld. She doesn't have to be here anymore. I know that the Lord of the Darkwoods hasn't stopped going on about reputation but if it's hurting her so much, then why are you staying?' I can't tell if he is asking that question out of concern for me or curiosity.

Viktor and Felix share a look and honestly I can't help but roll my eyes. I swear these two think they're being subtle. Emmet isn't an idiot, he's actually pretty intelligent. After our conversation in the hall last night, I know he's suspicious about our motives.

'I think we can tell him,' I venture and get two very decent stares. 'Listen,' I throw my legs over the edge of the bed and wipe the sweat from my brow. I feel like I've been in the ring with cage fighters, and I lost. 'I think we need help finding it the book. I also think we can trust him with the mission the King has put us on.' At some point in my little speech, Emmet and I locked eyes and I pray to every Sun God who might be listening that I'm not making a huge mistake.

'You *can* trust me,' Emmet promises. 'You're here for a reason. I can help. I know that I haven't been very supportive but I'm not the male you think I am. I am not our father. I know what the King is trying to do.'

'And what is that?' Viktor challenges. He won't include Emmet into our mission without him saying the words.

Emmet's right brow lifts. 'I know he is looking into our history to find the answers to our race extinction. That is why he's so interested in what Serafina said about the book and her vision. That our answers might be in humans.'

Stunned doesn't fully explain what I feel right now.

My brother is part of the group the King was referring to.

I didn't see this coming at all.

He shrugs at whatever he sees on our face. 'There are a handful of Azanites who have been discussing this for some time. Not many. None here in the Darkwoods and you won't find any in the Riverways.'

'But in the Blazelands and Cavelands, there are others who are discussing this theory?' Viktor prompts. He turns and walks to the fireplace, deep in thought.

'Yes. That is why Serafina was believed by some so quickly.' Emmet is still staring and my stomach flips when he adds, 'we were waiting for answers or information and then you showed up with a vision from the Sun Gods. You have no idea what you have done. You have the answers it seems. You can help us to understand why we're dying out.'

There is a heartbeat of silence. Viktor and Felix share a look before Viktor says, 'we are here to find a book.' For the next few minutes, Emmet listens intently while we explain what the King wants us to do.

The conversation stops the moment my door is opened and Otwin and Clarice appear. The poor women pale and stop in their tracks at the crowd in my bedroom.

I don't know if it's the lingering dream or what we've been discussing but the pressure on my chest is unbearable.

'Why were you such an arsehole when I first came back?'

Emmet chuckles and I have to jog to keep up with his long strides. He left my rooms and I had to follow. I need some answers.

'I was hurt, Serafina. I mourned you. How did you expect me to react seeing you with Wilder BlazeAzar in that courtyard? You looked at me like I was your enemy. I know why now.' He visibly tenses.

'I never thought you were my enemy.' Did I? I guess I thought all Azanite males my enemy. 'Why do you hate the BlazeAzar's so much?'

'I don't hate them. I just don't like Drengar Wilder, he walks around like he is the biggest male in Azanir. He's arrogant.'

I can't help but laugh out loud. 'You're all fucking arrogant, what are you talking about?' Sun Gods, these males are going to be the death of me.

'Why does it matter if I like him or not?'

What a question. 'Because he is my mate and you're my brother.'

'So it matters to you that I like him? I didn't think you liked me very much.'

Smart arse is teasing me. 'I don't know you Emmet, and you don't know me.'

I practically run into his back when he stops abruptly. Emmet grips my shoulders to keep me steady and frowns down at the tunic I've decided to wear. This one of Wilder's is an off-white and I have paired it with butter-soft leather pants and a corset that goes over my clothing to pinch in the waist. It still swims on me but I think Clarice did an amazing job at quickly adjusting it so it doesn't hang off me. 'What did you dream?'

'I...it was more what I felt. I was dying. The pain was unimaginable.'

Stepping away from him, I fix my shirt, more to do something with my hands.

'I won't let anything happen to you, Serafina.'

Smiling, I believe him. 'I know. Right now we need to see the book, Emmet. The King wants to know what is in it and why Father won't share it.'

Emmet studies me closely. 'I told you I would look into it. I'm not sure what the King expects to find but I will start searching for some answers. You just have to sit tight and wait a bit. And I'm sending word to Wilder BlazeAzar. Keeping you separate while Father works out your mating is all nonsense. He is just being an arsehole and if you're having dreams like that then you will need your Medir close.'

My entire body lights up at his words. 'Really?' I'm about to cry.

'Yes. You've suffered enough.'

Throwing my arms around his monstrous frame, I hug my brother even though it takes him way too long to get over his shock and hug me back. 'Thank you.'

'You're welcome.'

Chapter Fifty Five

I'M RUNNING THROUGH THE dense forest, the sound of footsteps heavy behind me, I know I have to run. I need to get back.

I need to keep going.

Fear grips me as I stumble, falling heavily to the hard, forest littered floor. A cry of pain escapes my lips and I scream for help as a monster made of darkness jumps out and envelops me.

The next day, I'm lounging around my sitting room, bored, when James comes hurrying in with a broad smile on his face. 'I found her.'

'What?' I have no idea what he's talking about. I've been falling hard into a pit of misery as the last day and a half has worn on. I've had the worst dreams. I'm tired and Emmet hasn't found any answers about the book our father has. I don't know if word was sent to Wilder yet and Wicked Bitch has made it her life mission to exclude me from every family meal that they've had. Also it's raining and I haven't felt the sun on my skin all day. I've just been sitting here waiting for others to do all the work. Viktor and Felix are off with the Darkwoods Drengar doing only the Sun Gods know what. They made me promise that I'd stay here, which I did like a petulant youngling.

Father didn't want anyone to see me because he is trying to manage the damage of the nobles of the Darkwoods hearing that I have a pledge. It's like being a youngling again.

'Meryl,' James announces, stopping at the table for a drink of water. Roxy is with Clarice and Otwin in the gardens.

I jump up so fast that I knock the table and the water jug crashes to the rug. 'You found her?' Hope spark in my chest.

James is so excited he nods like crazy. 'I can take you to see her. Come, where are Felix and Viktor?'

'They went to train with the other Drengar.' I'm already grabbing my cloak and making sure it has a hood so that I'm kept hidden while we walk down there.

'Should we wait for them? I can go run down and let them know. It is late afternoon.'

Waving off his concern I make sure I have everything and tell him not to worry. 'We'll be down and back before they realise I've gone.'

'Okay, wait a sec, they gave me a few weapons to carry if I'm with you to keep you safe.'

Rolling my eyes, I wait impatiently and don't say a word when he comes back with a long sword strapped to his back like a Drengar. Trust Viktor and Felix to give him a sword.

I head to the door without waiting to see if he is following.

It takes us a while to get down to the city. Ensuring that my hood covers most of my face and thanks to my human-like size, no one notices me leaving. James is practically attached to my hip so there isn't an opportunity for anyone to get too close.

By the time we head into the residential section of the human zone, we are both drenched and shivering. James leads the way and moves with a confidence that shows he knows where we are going. I find it weird that there aren't any Drengar around protecting this part of the city. There were some in the city centre we had to avoid but none here.

'I have a family member here in the Darkwoods, she has been helping me find her.' He stops us at a door. The dwellings here are all lined up like townhouses with a single step up into the landing out the front.

He knocks while I wring my hands together and search the streets for what has my skin crawling. The rain is a constant sheet of water. The sun is hidden and there are only a handful of people out and about still having to do their jobs. The street is about twenty or so dwellings long before it stops for a new street and then identical townhouses start up again. On and on it goes. The one we are standing at is the fourth one along and is at the very start of the residential zone.

'James,' a friendly middle aged woman says when she opens the door to find us. Her cheeks are round and her brown eyes are very similar to James'. She is wearing an apron over her sensible, long sleeve brown dress. 'Come in out of the rain. We told you that you don't have to knock, just come on in,' she says with a smile, wiping her hands on her apron. She can't see my face and is trying to get a look at who James is with. It says a great deal about her that she let me in.

Stepping into the home, I'm instantly hit with warmth. The hall that leads into the place is lined with coats and shoes. The base of the staircase is the wall to my left and when the right wall ends it opens into a very cosy sitting area. It's all reds and patterns and black leather. The fireplace is lit.

The woman ushers us in and I let James take my coat while I absorb the energy around me. She continues past the sitting room until we get to the kitchen and another living space at the back of the home. She goes instantly to the ovens and starts to pull out trays of pastries and breads. My mouth waters realising that she has honey delights on her tray.

'We're sorry to come around unannounced, Katey.'

'Oh don't be silly, you're always welcome here. Where is Roxy? She isn't with...' her words trail off as she turns and realises who is standing beside her dining room table. Katey's mouth pops open. 'Oh.'

'I'm sorry, Katey. This is Raff...I mean, Lady Serafina DarkwoodsAzar,' he looks at me as if to see if he got my title correct.

I can't help but chuckle. Katey hasn't moved a muscle. She is still holding the tray over the table like she is in shock or scared to move. 'Raff is fine,' I tell them both, holding my smile to show her that she is safe. I can hear her heart pounding.

'You speak the human tongue,' Katey states in wonder. She drops the tray on the counter. 'I heard the rumour after your first trip to the city but I didn't believe it. They are talking about how you protected a human child and was pledged to. Wow!'

'Yeah, I lived with humans for ten years.' A little awkward, I shuffle on my feet. She watches every move I make.

'So they did get you out.'

My entire world tilts at her words. 'Who?'

'My aunt.'

Confused and a little lightheaded, I shake my head, not understanding.

Katey smiles sadly. 'Your lady's maid was my aunt, Meryl Darling.'

Chapter Fifty Six

'Was?' I whisper, afraid to hear what I know is coming.

James looks to me in anguish as if he realises what he's done. 'I didn't know...' he starts and I hold up my hand because I'm not mad.

'Can you tell me what happened, please.'

Nodding soberly, Katey indicates to the small four-seater chipped dining table.

James pulls out my chair and Katey fusses around in the kitchen for a while making plates of food and bringing them over. By the time I'm settled there's a mountain of treats on the wooden service.

It's obvious that she is nervous. James stops her from filling a plate with more breads and tells her to sit.

She does with a heavy sigh, wiping her hands on her apron in an anxious gesture.

'Please, I don't want to make you upset. I just need to know what happened. Meryl meant so much to me.'

'I know she did,' she says with a big smile. 'Meryl was obsessed with you. Growing up, I had no idea who she meant when she spoke about her lady. I remember the day I worked it out and I bragged about it to everyone in my school. My aunt was the maid to the Lady Serafina. I was very popular because of that.'

She speaks with such emotion that I find it hard to not look away. This lady is related to the person who raised me. I feel a sense of loyalty towards her.

'She was also always very sad about you. She never said what made her cry on her days off but it was obvious that she was worried to leave you. I think she would've lived in that lair if she was allowed. I assumed that it was because of the death of her own daughter that made her so attached to the relationship she had with her Lady. She got the job just after her daughter died so I think you gave her a purpose. My cousin was just a young adult when she passed. She was my best friend. A beautiful woman with a heart of gold. I miss her every day.'

My heart sinks. Oh Sun Gods, Meryl lost a daughter. That is heartbreaking. 'What happened?'

'She died in childbirth.'

James makes a sad sound and reaches out to grip Katey's hand that's resting on the table. 'That is devastating. I thought with all the human healers and Medir here in Azanir, things like that wouldn't happen.'

'It doesn't. We are lucky here in Azanir. Medir's are prohibited from saving humans but childbirth is always a little different. The dragons are tough predators who have a sweet spot for females in distress. I've seen a few rush to help when they hear a healer being called to a birth-bed. I think that's why we were so shocked when it happened. She was healthy and strong, probably the most stubborn and loyal woman you'd ever meet.'

I sit listening, my body numb for reasons I can't understand. Breathing is a little difficult right now and I have to clear my throat before I ask, 'who was the father?'

Katey shrugs, making me feel sick to the stomach. My reaction is odd. My beast is making a weird noise in my head that I've not heard before.

'We never knew who he was. She kept it tight lipped. The only clue we had was that he must've worked at the lair. That was where she worked. In the kitchens. She was only there for a handful of months before she fell pregnant.'

She worked at the lair. 'And Meryl only started working at the lair after I was born?'

'Yes, almost immediately. It was the strangest thing. She never had a desire to work with the Azar. She wasn't known for her love of them. Sorry,' she throws me an apologetic look that I wave off. I don't need that right now. I just need her to keep talking. 'We just assumed that she wanted to be around a new baby, even if it wasn't her daughters.'

'What happened to her daughters baby, did it survive?' James rises and begins to make a pot of tea.

'No, she didn't. Meryl told us that both her daughter and the baby died. We only got to bury my cousin.'

'I'm sorry Katey, what a horrible experience for you and your family.' James comes back over and starts to pour us all tea.

Katey dabs at her eyes and nods her thanks. Then those brown eyes lift to meet my gaze. For a moment we just stare as if both of us are battling our own internal struggle.

The thoughts rolling around in my head right now are absurd and silly and frightening.

'Meryl was devoted to you, my lady. She loved you dearly.'

'And I loved her,' I emphasis each word, happy to have a cup of tea to focus on for a moment. 'She raised me. She was the only one to show me any love.' She may have been my grandmother.

Oh Sun Gods, what if she was my grandmother.

'That makes me happy to hear that she meant so much to you.'

For a little while the only noise in the home is the clink of spoons hitting against porcelain.

'Actually, I have a few photos that you might like to see.' Katey doesn't wait for us to answer, she is up and out of her seat and then back in a flash with a small cardboard shoebox. She begins to pull out small square photos and hands them to James and I.

The one I get is of Meryl, a man I guess is her husband and the young woman...a woman with a heart shaped face, a small nose and brown wavy hair. My heart pounds painfully against my ribs. I'm shaking.

That's my face staring back at me. Yeah the eyes are different and the hair is shorter but it's the one I look at every day in the mirror.

James glances over my shoulder, makes a startled sound and then looks sharply at me.

He sees what I see, I know it.

Wide eyed, he just blinks as if trying to understand and I want to shout, 'me too buddy'.

Thankfully Katey is oblivious and I give James a threatening glare that has him nod and sit back. He does very well to control his emotions. Explaining this to him later is going to be tough. This little picture is my biggest secret laid out for anyone to discover.

I grip the photo. 'How did Meryl die?'

'When you went missing, the Darkwoods wasn't the safest place for lair workers for a long time. Meryl was questioned at length and it drained her. A number of humans lost their lives or were left out on the streets with nothing. Meryl grew weaker and weaker after that time and a wraith attack swept through the Darkwoods around six months after you left. The Lord was distracted, as were the Drengar. The human zones of the city were hit hard with no one to protect us. A number of people lost their life.'

Grief hits me so hard that I have to stand and walk over to the counter. I was told she was dead and yet, for a moment there I thought maybe Wakely had it wrong.

Hope is dangerous.

Hope hurts worse than anything else when it's shattered.

Chapter Fifty Seven

Standing before the monument, I stare at the engraved names on the copper plates lined up in perfect rows on the grassy mound. Bodies in Azanir are sent to fire. It's the Azanite way. Leaving me with only nameplates to say goodbye to. Meryl Darling. Hubert Darling and Quinn Darling.

I'm shaking and not because of the weather. The rain has stopped and the dark cloud set the mood just right. They reflect how I feel right now.

I want to add to the memorial that here lies my family. My grandparents and my mother. A mother who died giving me life. Who somehow got involved with an Azanite male and fell pregnant. I always thought that if I found out who she was that I'd feel a sense of closure. I dreamt about her and contemplated what she looked like countless times over the years.

Katey keeps throwing me odd glances and I'm sure she's worked it out. How could she not? It's probably why it didn't bother her when I asked if I could keep the photo or when I asked her to show me where they are buried.

James stands close to my side, showing respect. He has checked in a few times to make sure that I'm all right. I've appreciated his support even though he's dying to get back to Roxy. We've been gone longer than I thought.

'Thank you,' I say to the woman beside me. My mother's cousin. A woman who is part of my family and will never know.

'You're welcome, my lady. Thank you for bringing joy to my aunt after she lost Quinn.'

I can only nod stiffly, if I speak I may break down and weep. Meryl protected me and treated me like I was precious. She never let me be upset too long and when Medir Leon and Father did what they did, she fought against them constantly despite the danger to herself. I loved her dearly and reaching out to caress her plaque, I whisper my thanks.

'You were the only light in the darkness.' In Zaric, so that Katey doesn't understand, I say, 'I wish I had known that you were my grandmother. I wish I had known that I wasn't alone. I would never have left the lair.'

It hits me pretty hard that she probably did that on purpose. She risked everything for me.

'From the bottom of my heart, I thank you'

'I really appreciate you taking time out of your day,' I say, unsure what is wrong with my arm. It feels funny. I feel funny now that I think of it. There isn't much of a reason, I don't think. I search the sky and the streets. There are definitely more humans out on the roads now that the rain has stopped. Children are back on the streets, playing ball games and causing trouble. Groups of men and woman are sharing some food and drinks. One guy even has a small firepit barbeque cooking meats. The energy is electric, so why do I feel so weird?

Katey chats away about how it was her pleasure, totally oblivious to my uncertainty. We stayed at the cemetery for a while. I have a great deal to process, which I feel like is the only thing I've been doing since coming to the Darkwoods.

James and Katey walk ahead a little, chatting away. They both stop at a group of people, aged from my age to older than Katey. Everyone welcomes them with open arms. I just watch, standing back a little, ignoring the subtle glances. My hoody is hiding half my face, I don't want to frighten these people or have them stop their street party because of me.

Watching James and Katey together, a lightbulb goes on in my head and I put two and two together. They are related. A few aunts removed or something, which means that James and I have family ties too.

Holy shit. It must be why my beast feels at ease around him and why I loved Roxy so quickly. Dragon shifters are very primal in our understanding of family ties. We are loyal beasts. I guess that is why I could never comprehend why my father did what he did.

It's surreal to think of James as my family.

It's a lot though.

I deserve a holiday after this. I don't know where Azanites take holidays, or even if that's something that they do, but I will be taking one once all this shit is sorted. Maybe Wilder and I can go somewhere, far away. The shudder that starts deep in my core ends at my head and toes, I think of what Wilder and I could do alone together. I miss him so much.

Emmet said that he was going to send for him. If he got the message to come here, he should've been here already. His clothes are losing his scent.

I've worn them too much. My beast is getting antsy which could be why she stretches under my skin.

I try to connect with her and get nothing. *'I don't know what's wrong.'* Nothing. *'Wilder should be here soon, if that's what is making you so unsettled.'* Nothing.

Wilder told me on our road trip that I shouldn't fight her and allow myself to be one with my dragon. I have no idea what he meant until I was drowning in that ocean. She told me to allow her to take over. Honestly, I have no idea how I did it and I've tried every day since.

'Raff, come over here and have something to eat,' James calls over at me with a huge smile. The guy with the barbecue waves me over too. Feeling a little more confident, I start to move and then stop dead when a sound fills the world. A noise that haunts my dreams.

The screech of wraith demons.

Chapter Fifty Eight

'Oh my Gods,' I murmur, turning and seeing the dense cloud of black shimmering smoke.

The smell of sulphur permeates the air.

The sounds on the street dies. No one moves for a heartbeat as we all stare at the horror of what is fast approaching. It's still daylight and I curse my stupidity because there is no sun. It may be late afternoon but it is dark enough for the strongest of wraiths. Wraiths that have probably fed recently and have the power to withstand the in-between time of day and night. My Drengar warned me about this when I first met them. I tried to get away from them in a cemetery and only went willingly with them when I was told that I was still in danger from an attack.

The noise of wraiths screeching has me clap my hands over my ears. The sound seems to knock everyone out of their trance. Chaos erupts.

Children scream. Men and woman shout and yell for everyone to take cover.

People run around me, getting to safety while I watch in terror as the first houses in the street are attacked. Wraiths break off from the main horde. Their shimmering bodies are more corporal than I remember and with no effort they break through glass windows. Screams of agony follow and I can't look away. If these homes aren't fitted with the same glass as the lair, then these people will die.

A little girl screams and cries not far from me. She is shouting for her mummy and I react without thought. I run forward, my feet moving faster than any of these humans and I scoop her into my arms.

I push her head into my shoulder and tell her to close her eyes. She is sobbing but the brave kid does what I say.

James is at my side in an instant, the long sword in his hand. I want to tell him that it won't do anything. We need fire. We need the dragons.

'Raff, we need to get inside. Now.'

'I don't think being inside is going to help,' I shout over the noise of screaming and demons enjoying themselves. Pointing to the destroyed houses, I stare in horror as one after another, the other humans are eaten alive. A woman. A man.

Where are the Drengar?

Pulling my hood off, I watch as men and woman run toward the middle of the street, their faces set in determination. Two are holding massive weapons and they both flick a switch and fire erupts out the front. A fucking flame thrower.

Another woman runs close to us, her flamethrower turning on the moment she stops. I notice the odd tattoo on her wrist that appears to be white ink. Yet, when I do a double-take her sleeve has been pulled down. I push the absurd thoughts from my mind that it could be a rebel tattoo the moment she shouts at us to run. We have more pressing things to be thinking about right now. Like the damn horde coming closer, uncaring of the fire.

'Raff!' James yells and I turn to stare at him and see Katey curled up against the side of a townhouse, her gaze locked on mine.

'These people are going to die,' I say, drawing my attention back on James.

'Get behind us James!' One of the flamethrower guys shouts in warning that we need to move.

James seems to realise that we are going to die and I can only imagine that his thoughts are with Roxy. She is up in the lair. I have to believe that she is safe. Felix won't let anything happen to her.

'Take her, James.' I have to shout even though he is beside me. Death and destruction surrounds us. The demon noises are making my ears bleed. James hesitates but I force the little girl into his arms. 'Get everyone inside.'

'Raff—'

'James!' I yell, getting his attention. 'You must do what I say. You are pledged to me, so go! Get everyone back!' I'm being harsh but he needs to move. I pull a dagger from his belt.

'All of you, get inside!' I shout, my voice loud enough to penetrate the frantic noises around me. My skin bends and I know why half of the humans who have stopped to stare back off. The world has turned red.

James' eyes bug out of his head and he complies instantly.

My gaze travels over the humans watching, I just hope that what I have planned is going to work again. My Drengar had a theory of what these demons want most.

I take a deep breath and walk down the road towards the horde of demons. My heart in my throat and my stomach rolling. If I had anything in my stomach right now I'd be hurling my guts up.

Good thing I don't.

Moving with determination, I get as close to the horde as I can stand. I can see them clearly now. Their bodies flicker from solid to smoke-like. Some are white, others are black. All of them frightening. Distorted, long faces and teeth like razors, they shred through flesh easily.

A good handful at the front are solid now, meaning they've eaten their fill of energy from these humans.

It makes me so angry.

I formulate my plan. There is a path leading into the Darkwoods to my left.

Determined, I lift the dagger and throw one last look over my shoulder. No one listened when I told them to get inside. Hundreds of humans stand behind the ones with the flamethrowers watching me with a mixture of emotions.

James is shouting my name but he still has the girl in his arms so I know he won't follow me. It's exactly what I want.

'Come and get me you fucking bastards!' I roar in the human tongue. The noise coming from my throat is not something I have ever made before and I slice my palm deeply and watch as blood pools in my hand.

Lifting up the wound, I watch the blood drip down my palm and hit the road.

There is a heartbeat where I stand, bleeding, gaze locked with hundreds of wraiths who stop what they're doing in the most terrifying sight of my life. Silence falls.

They move as one. Tilting their heads, they shriek and I fucking run.

Chapter Fifty Nine

Dodging trees and low hanging vines, I sprint through the Darkwoods with my chest on fire.

The shrieking of wraiths haunts me as I run for my life. I run as fast and as hard as I can away from the humans who can't defend themselves. Instinctively I know that they are following my blood. It is what I expected after what we learnt in the human realm. They love my blood.

Trees crash down around me under the force of the horde of demons. Each time one falls, I squeal. My blood drips in a constant stream to the forest floor. I don't feel the pain of the wound. All I feel is my heart galloping in my chest and the building energy under my skin.

I try desperately to call to my dragon. To get her to make a sound like she did in the ocean to alert the Drengar of where I am. My mind is in a panic though, stopping all hope.

I run and I run, knowing that they are getting closer and wishing that I had more time. There is still so much to do.

'Astgeer!' A roar in my head has me cry out and trip. Stumbling, I lose a few minutes on my lead but manage to get my legs back under me. I can smell the sulphur now.

More voices enter my mind. Viktor calls my name. Felix snarls in my head. They want to know where I am.

'Wilder, they're after me.' I sound frantic and scream when another tree falls to my left, this one closer. They are nearly on me. The stench is making it hard to breath, which is making it harder to move faster.

'I'm coming Serafina. I will be there...don't...' I have no idea how I know but Wilder is fighting his own battle at the moment. It does nothing to calm me down.

'Wilder!' Praying to every Sun God that he is okay, I whimper.

My legs stop abruptly and I bend forward and then snap back against something solid, almost breaking my neck.

The entire world goes all fuzzy.

Confused, I look around and see only trees.

My feet don't move. They're not touching the floor.

What?

My mind feels as if it's covered in sticky honey. Every thought is slow.

My body feels weird.

Looking down, I frown at the sword-like object sticking through my gut. I blink once, twice and then slowly look over my shoulder at the wraith standing behind me. It's mouth opened in a snarl.

I scream until my lungs burn and then choke on something metallic that I cough up.

Blood drips from my mouth. Each breath is getting harder and harder to draw in and I swear the wraith smiles at me and then I am pushed forward.

I hit the ground and am overcome with agonising pain.

Turning onto my back with a groan, I hold my stomach on instinct, knowing that I am going to die.

'Wilder...I...love...I'm...'

'Serafina!'

I swear I hear his roar of anguish fill not just my head but the entire world.

Staring up at the wraiths hoovering a few metres away watching me, breathing becomes harder and harder. 'Fuck you,' I manage to choke out. Blood fills my mouth, threatening to suffocate me.

The pain is torture and yet even in my dying mind I know it wasn't the same as the dream I had. That agony was like my body was too small for my insides. It was as if I was going to explode. This, this is somehow different. Maybe even the pain is receding a little. I don't feel it much anymore as the edges of the forest darken.

Wraiths shriek and I blink over at them, refusing to cower or close my eyes to death. I won't die without some kind of rebellion.

Then they pounce and I throw a prayer for my Wilder and my Drengar. James and Emmet. Roxy. My nephews who I've only just met and my family back home in the human realm. In this moment before my death I realise that I have more than I thought.

I have people I love. Both beasts and humans. I'm lucky to have had them all.

Pain erupts in my leg and I look down and try to scream seeing a wraith bury its teeth into my calf. I feel the life draining from me.

All I can think is that I hope I can see my mother in the next life. Meryl and my grandfather.

The next noise that assaults my dying body isn't one I was expecting and I stare up at the red mass shrieking through the sky and brace myself for the ball of flame that barrels towards me.

Chapter Sixty

Falling in and out of awareness, I try to focus my eyes enough to understand what is happening.

A dragon stands over me and for some reason it's not the one I expected. The red beast attacks the demons with every part of its body. His fire engulfs the Darkwoods. Hot waves of power eliminate the threat with an efficiency of a Drengar who has done this time and time again.

The red dragon is rather beautiful. Deadly and frightening but something magical to behold.

The noise slowly calms and I float above the battle, my mind drifting. Dying is peaceful. There is no pain anymore which is what I tell the male shouting at me right now to open my eyes.

'Now, Serafina!'

I'm powerless to the demand and with an effort that comes from deep within, I crack open my lids with a groan.

'Being awake hurts,' I groan.

'I know it does, but you will stay awake. You will not die, do you understand me?' My father sounds frantic. I come to enough to just see him removing his shirt and then he is pressing it to my stomach. I cry out. 'I'm sorry. We will get you to a Medir.'

'You can't Dad,' I manage to say. Every move sends a fresh wave of agony through my limbs. 'They will discover I'm half human.'

Father scowls. 'I don't care what they find out. I'll kill them if they threaten to tell anyone.'

I can't respond, the pain is too great. I need to know though. I need him to help me understand. 'Did you love her Dad?'

'Who?' he doesn't seem like he is listening. He is now trying to wrap my wounds to probably transport me to the lair. I don't even know how far we are into the Darkwoods.

'My mother. Quinn Darling.'

He stops what he is doing and with red eyes that match his beasts skin, he frowns. 'How did...we can talk about this later, Serafina.'

'No, Dad, we can't. The wraith cut me right through.'

He seems to understand what I mean and then curses loudly. His roar lifts the dirt from the ground.

'Tell me, Daddy. Please,' I beg.

Hanging his head, the Lord of the Darkwoods nods. 'Yes. I loved her with every part of my soul. My dragon was obsessed from the moment we saw her. When she told me she was pregnant with you, it was the best moment of my life,' he confesses and a tear drips into my ear.

'You were?'

'Yes,' he states, wiping the water from my face. 'Of course I was. But then she died. A human woman can't birth an Azanite, Serafina. She died in terrible pain and there was nothing I could do to fix it. No Medir could help and I called them all in.'

I cry harder at the pain in his voice. My dad was in love with my mother and she died.

'You lived. I tried to protect you. I haven't been the same since she left this world. There is less colour. Less happiness.'

'Was she your mate?' I whisper, everything is hard now. My lungs are only taking in a little air and my hands slip from my wound. Like lead they sit beside my body, too heavy to move.

He nods. 'I was already mated to Celine but she isn't my *mate*, not really. Quinn Darling was, even though she was a human.' The Lord throws his head back and the sound that comes from his throat is all beast. It's a cry for help. A warning to all that they are needed. I don't have the heart to tell him that it's too late for that.

'Why do you fight the quest to find out if humans can be mated to Azanites, Dad? Our family has the answers.'

I don't understand and with his chin pressed into his chest he tells me why. 'I told you. Humans can't birth Azanites. We can mate with them but for what purpose. The first child they have would kill them. No Azanite male should feel the pain that I did, that I still do. It is not an answer to our races problem, Serafina. It's a death sentence to innocent humans like your mother.'

Reaching out to grip his hand, I look up at my heartbroken father. It is like I'm seeing him for the first time. 'I'm sorry.'

'Oh precious daughter, I'm sorry. I haven't been a good father to you. I was frightened that if you were discovered that they'd take you from me and that you'd become the subject of their study. Or worse. The hatred some have to this idea would mean you would've been in constant danger.'

Speaking is impossible now and Dad leans forward to keep our gazes locked. 'Forgive me for hurting you.'

My heart skips a beat and my lungs stop for a moment. Panic sets in. 'Da...'

Frantic, Dad grips my face. I can see he is trying to stay strong. 'I'm here. I have you. Keep your eyes open, Serafina,' he demands just as the world goes dark.

Chapter Sixty One

My body shakes when the ground below me does and I welcome peace.

My body lightens. The lead feeling evaporating to be replaced by a heat that is familiar and welcomed. It starts at my toes and buries deep into my soul, soothing every hurt as it rushes through my veins.

Death is not that bad. It smells like my mate.

Wilder.

Wilder.

Wait...

'Astgeer, open your eyes for me.'

'Wilder?'

'Yes, my heart, I am here now. Everything is all right. You are safe.'

'Am I?'

Everything is covered in darkness and I can't move or feel anything but the power of my mate. It envelopes me like a hug. Wraps around my body and cradles me in protection and love.

'Of course you are. Do you think I would let you leave this world without me?'

That has me smile even though I don't have a face in this floating world. *'I missed you. Please don't leave me again.'*

There is a deep throbbing heat coming from somewhere.

'I don't plan on leaving you again.'

I like the sound of that.

'Can you open your eyes for me, love?'

'I don't know.'

His chuckle surrounds me. Wilder is everywhere. In me. Beside me. Lodged right into my soul. A flicker of unease filters into my mind and I think having him looking so closely within my body should have me worried.

'Try for me. Feel the ground under my hands. Can you feel the leaves and dirt?'

Awareness creeps back into my senses and I do feel the crunch of leaves. 'Yes.'

'Do you hear the sound of worried talking and Felix demanding that I hurry up and heal you faster?'

Straining, I do start to hear some familiar voices. Lots of voices. I hear Felix telling someone that if I don't wake, he will be joining me in the afterlife.

It makes me laugh and the voices stop. Someone sighs.

'Do you feel this, my heart?'

'Yes,' I moan. A strong, calloused hand runs up my arm, across my neck and then my cheek. The sensation shoves me back into my body and I become aware of every muscle. Every bone and every way my nerves scream for Wilder.

'And this?' his sultry tone is enough to have me now fully aware and then I'm being kissed. Slowly at first, Wilder brushes his lips against mine. Whimpering into his touch, I open my mouth for his assault when the

need to be with him takes over. My beast seems to open her eyes and wake too and I give back as much as he is giving me.

I taste his fire. His breath is my breath. I don't know where he ends and I begin. When he pulls away, I finally find the power to open my eyes and when I do I'm met with the colour of obsidian.

Not able to believe that he is here, I reach out, very aware that there is no more pain and trace my finger along the white scar that runs down his left cheek and cuts across his throat. He is the most beautiful male I have ever seen.

'You're here.'

'I'm here,' he reassures me.

Throwing myself at him, I wrap my arms around his body and hold on tightly. He is here. He healed me.

He cages me in his mighty arms and I suck in his scent like an addict. Wilder has buried his nose into my neck and is doing the same.

'You scared me, love. You're never allowed to do that again.'

'I'm sorry.'

I refuse to let go even though I can hear the others exclaim their relief that I am okay.

'It's dark, we must get her back to the lair,' a familiar voice says and I peek over Wilder's shoulder to see Alistair standing with Viktor and Felix. It makes me so happy that they're all together again.

Relief floods my system and I become painfully aware of how drained and tired I am.

'The Darkwoods Drengar have the kingdom locked down but the prince is right. Serafina needs to be resting.' My father sounds like the hard-arse male again, long gone is the male who bared his heart to me.

I don't care, not right now, because I have Wilder.

'The human quarter, are they safe?' I mumble against Wilder chest.

'They are Lady,' James replies. 'You saved the entire quarter. The wraiths followed you.'

'Good.' I sigh, feeling better.

Wilder tucks me close to his body and rises swiftly, keeping me secure and unbothered as he does. His strength takes my breath away.

Carrying me with an arm under my knees and across my back, Wilder holds me like I weigh nothing at all. I snuggle in closer. My eyes closed. I don't want to face the night or what just happened. Being in his arms is all I need right now.

I think I fall asleep between being given over to Alistair while Wilder shifts and then his dragon cradles me within his paw. With Wilder around, I don't have to worry. I can let go and finally rest.

Chapter Sixty Two

'I'm okay, Wilder. I feel really good. Better than I have in such a long time actually,' I exclaim, grabbing his face so that he is looking at me. The moment we got into my rooms, he slammed the door shut behind us, scaring Otwin and Clarice half to death, and hasn't let me off his lap. I know he is mad, I just can't tell what at specifically.

We've been sitting here, my body on his, just holding each other.

The darkness is seeping in through the glass doors but nothing could scare me within Wilder's arms. I know that the danger is gone and even if we were overtaken by wraiths, he'd burn the world for me. The fact that he is here now is testament to that. Also, there are countless dragons flying in formation through the night sky. The Drengar of the Darkwoods are out in force after what just happened. No wraith would stand a chance right now. We could have used them down in the human quarter earlier. I will be asking questions later.

'Where were you? How did you get to me?'

'Alistair and I got word from your brother two days again. We were in the Cavelands on the other side of the Kingdom so I wasn't close. We started our journey straight away. We had stopped at the Blazelands at the border between the Darkwoods. My beast was restless tonight and I just knew that I needed to get to you. When we were ambushed by wraiths, I worked out why

my dragon had to find you. I tried to get to you faster. When I heard you call out, I nearly went mad. I should've gotten to you faster.'

My heart cracks under his tone. 'You saved my life, Wilder. You did get to me.'

'Not quick enough. You were dying, you had one foot in the afterlife, Astgeer. A wraith bit you. One of those filthy vermin tried to take your energy.' His chest rumbles with his dragon's rage.

I can't do anything but stroke his face and run my hands through his hair. I don't know why I'm doing it, it just feels right and it's like my beast wants it. She isn't whining softly in my head when I'm touching him like this.

'Let me just hold you for a moment,' he says and it breaks my heart. I frightened him. *'I nearly lost you.'* The anguish in his tone has tears slip down my face which he slowly wipes off.

'I'm sorry. I had to save all those people. There were so many wraiths, Wilder. The humans didn't stand a chance. So many would've died if I hadn't led them away. There were children.' I think of the little girl crying for her parents and shiver. I'll need to remember to ask James if she got to them safely and if Katey is okay.

'What did I say the last time you put yourself in danger?'

I can't help but smile at his grumpy-ness, at least it's a different emotion to the anguish that was hurting my soul. I'd rather him be his grumpy self than heartbroken or afraid. I'd do anything to ensure he never feels that again.

'What was I supposed to do? There were children, Wilder.'

He makes a gruff sound and looks away from me. He knows he has nothing to say to that and it has me bite my lip to keep from giggling. There is no way that he, or any of my Drengar, would let children die.

'If you insist on always putting yourself in these situations then we will begin your training when we head to my lair in the Blazelands.'

That has my smile slip and all my humour evaporate. I tense and find myself lost in those obsidian depths. 'Training?'

'Yes. Training. You have a natural talent that we saw in the human realm and you seem to have the will of a Drengar, so we will train you on how to defend yourself so that you never have to be in that kind of danger again.'

I sit up quickly and straddle him. My legs wrap around his back and Wilder's eyes flash red before settling back to black. His large hands grip the sides of my thigh and I can feel every inch of him but I'm too distracted right now. 'Really?' I ask a little giddy. 'Train like a Drengar. I can't shift though.'

'I believe you can do much more than you think Serafina. We saw you fire transfer in that carpark to save Felix's life, only the most gifted of Drengar are able to do that and you did it without thought or realising what you had done.'

Flashes of that moment assault my mind. Felix was nearly impaled by a wraith. I had dreamt his death only moments before I ran outside the motel and saw my nightmare becoming a reality. There is no way that I can explain what happened when I threw that dagger and saw it flickering with a strong blue flame. My fire.

Wilder's eyes are intense like he is remembering the moment too. *'Don't forget that when you were attacked in the car, you created a decent fireball that saved your life.'*

'I did,' I whisper, remembering that too. 'I was so shocked. I had never, ever done something like that before. I started a fire once when I was beating up some guys after they hurt Van but that was it.' I don't tell him what happened in the human quarter when I protected Roxy but Emmet's words replay in my mind.

Wilder's eyes narrow and I chuckle. *'See,'* he grumbles. *'Being a Drengar is not about how big your beast is or how we fly. It is about loyalty and bravery and the need to protect others. You are all of those things and more, my heart. I'm not saying I want you patrolling the lair at night. I'm saying that if you agree, I will begin to show you how to connect with your dragon and how to use her qualities to protect yourself, and others.'*

'I don't know if I can connect with her. I try, all the time.' I sigh and become aware of how his hands flex against my thighs. How solid and warm he is. My core clenches and I watch his nostrils flare. Sun Gods, the temperature increases. I'm instantly hot.

Wilder reaches up and runs his hand over my cheek and through my hair. I lean into the caress, loving the feel of his calloused skin. Closing my eyes, my mind stills in the best kind of way.

'I'm guessing it may have something to do with the fact that you are half Azanite and half human.'

'What!' I shriek, eyes no longer closed. Every muscle in my body tenses and before I realise what I've done, I am standing against the glass doors, away from him. 'What did you say?'

'I know, Serafina. I know everything.' His red eyes take me all in and the glass stops me from backing up further as he rises and eats up the space between us with his long strides.

Chapter Sixty Three

Deep down I know that I shouldn't be afraid, but the way Wilder is staring right now has my heart pounding and my skin crawling.

Raising a shaking hand, I stop him from getting any closer. He stops and not because I am stronger. His beast is watching me.

My mouth is too dry. 'How?'

Wilder's midnight hair falls to his shoulders. He normally has it bound at his nape with some leather cord. He looks wild. That square jaw and those piercing eyes, it is making me weak at the knees. I can't read his energy or the look on his face.

'I have suspected you were keeping something from me since the moment I met you. I didn't know what it was until tonight.' Frowning, everything is such a muddled mess in my head. *'I was inside you, Serafina. I had to call you back from the halls of the Sun Gods. I have seen your very soul when I healed you tonight.'*

My jaw hits the floor. Fingers sprawled over his chest, stopping him from touching me, I tremble. No nightmare can compare to the fear I have now. This is a true nightmare. One that will hurt more than being stabbed by a wraith. Right now, my very heart and soul is within his grasp. I'm so afraid of the answers and yet I still need to know. 'Do you hate me? Do you want to not finish this mating?' I don't know when the tears started.

Wilder's red eyes track them as they fall down my face. His jaw twitches. His brow furrows slightly. *'Why would I hate you?'*

'Because,' I sniffle. 'I'm an abomination. I'm a human and an Azanite. A shifter who can't shift. I'm...broken and useless and not worthy to be your mate.'

The growl that fills the room has me squeak in shock and then his body is crushed against mine. His hand at some point snaked around the back of my head to protect it from hitting the glass door. His other hand grips my waist, pulling me flush against his chest. Wilder holds me for a moment, our gazes locked as I wait to see his anger that I kept this from him. That I betrayed him.

Shaking his head, Wilder grumbles an audible sounds. *'Serafina DarkwoodsAzar you are my mate. I am yours in this life and the next. You, my heart, are the reason I draw air into my lungs. You are the reason that keeps me flying. Do not ever call yourself an abomination or broken. If you are broken, then my heart, I am broken. If you are happy, I am happy. If you are in pain, I am in pain. It is I who is unworthy to call you my mate.'*

I'm a mess. I'm crying so hard that if he wasn't speaking in my mind, I probably wouldn't be able to hear him. I continue to stare through my waterlogged eyes at the male who continues to put all the broken pieces that is me back together.

Wilder runs his hand over my face, my shoulder, my neck like he can't get enough.

The emotion in his tone as he continues does nothing to help me stop crying. *'You are a gift from the heavens. An answer to the dire circumstance that we have found ourselves in. You are incredible, Serafina. And to know that I am yours and that I have been honoured to care, protect and love you makes me thank the Gods. You will never say or think of yourself as an abomination because if you are one than I am one. Together, Astgeer, forever.'*

'Wilder.' His name is a plea. A prayer. I fly at him. My lips collide with his and I'm lost to sensation. Lost in the power of his embrace and the feel of his hardness against my body.

Lifting me easily into his arms, Wilder carries us to the bed. Our tongues dance, our hands explore every inch of each other.

'You are my mate, Drengar Wilder BlazeAzar Medir and it is I who is honoured,' I say in my mind with my mouth busy devouring his.

Wilder growls and it vibrates against my body, making me moan. I don't know where his body starts or where mine ends.

Detaching me eventually, Wilder throws me onto the bed and I bounce with a small giggle. It dies though when I blink up at the dominant predator standing at the foot of the bed, looking at me with those red eyes like I'm his next meal.

Holy fuck.

My core clenches and heat pools low. He is a god. A male so frightening and gorgeous that he can't possibly be real, and mine. It has me question how I could be so lucky.

Withering on the bed, it's getting hard to keep my breathing even. His stare strips me bare.

'If you don't want this, tell me now Astgeer and we will stop. You have all the power here. I understand why you were hesitating to finish our mating. If you need more time, you will have it.'

I think I fall harder for him and honestly, I didn't think it could be possible.

I answer by going up on my knees and pulling my ruined tunic off my head, actually it was his tunic. I don't focus on the blood on it. I am healed fully and I'm ready to commit myself to my mate.

Wilder's gaze eats me up. It has me ready for his touch. The coverings over my breast are the next thing I pull over my head and throw across the room. His growl fills my mind and I whimper in need. I've never been naked like this in front of a male. I thought it would be scary or that I'd be really self-conscious when this time came. I don't feel any of that. Not with Wilder. My soul knows him. My body craves him and my beast is no longer asleep.

Never once have I let my eyes fall from his. I love watching the way his face hardens at the sight of my nakedness. His red eyes flash back to black and then shine red. Both beast and male.

I'm just a puddle of heat at this point. 'I want this Wilder. I want you, forever.'

My words seem to snap whatever leash he was using to control himself because the next sound he makes has me begging for him to join me on the bed.

Chapter Sixty Four

'*L*AY BACK.'

I do what I'm told and the feeling of the furs against my oversensitive skin is exquisite. Never do I look away from the male watching me.

Wilder grabs at the bottom of my pants and I help him to shimmy them off until he throws them away and I'm left completely naked under his gaze.

Something flashes across his face. A flash of complete awe. It makes me feel wanted and loved.

'Beautiful,' he purrs and I have to squeeze my thighs together to relieve the tension forming in my core. His strong arms are on my ankles instantly and with a shake of his head, he spreads me wide so that he can continue to drink me all in. My face reddens until he says, *'beautiful,'* once more. That is exactly how I feel under his gaze.

'I want to pleasure you, Serafina. Feel you against my tongue. If at any point you want me to stop or if you need me to slow down, tell me.' Those black eyes flick to my face and he waits for me to agree before they glide back to the space yearning for his touch.

The bed dips as he kneels on the mattress and then he's between my legs. I scream his name. Beg for something, anything, as his tongue strokes through my centre. His beast is in my head, exclaiming it's pleasure at having his mate finally under him.

My legs shake and I wrap them around his shoulders and cry out his name when his hand comes up to work me to a frenzy. He enters me with one finger and then two, never stopping the way he devours me.

'Gods, Wilder!' I moan, deep and needy as the pressure builds and builds. 'Wilder! *Wilder!*'

'That's it, my mate. Let go.'

I come apart with an intensity that has my back bow off the bed, pushing Wilder harder against me. I come again at the new angle. I'm floating but this time I know I'm tethered to this world through the male slowly helping me to come down off my high.

Panting, I don't know if I could ever feel anything so intense again, I get my answer when Wilder lifts his head and our eyes collide. My heart swells and I giggle at the very arrogant and very male grin he throws me. It's the most boy-ish gesture I have ever seen from him and I love it.

'Wow,' I manage to say with my breathing so erratic.

That seems to please him. *'We've only just started, Astgeer.'*

Fucking hell. My body lights up once more and he knows it. I watch as he gets off the bed and strips his Drengar leathers.

My mouth pops open at the sight of him. He *is* a god. No one in the history of the world looks like that. Tall, covered in defined, hard muscle, I don't know where to look first. The eight pack or the thick arms with the muscles that come around to his pecs or the lines around his hips.

It's enough to have me nearly climax again. I need him. I need him now. There is a noise deep in my head that I know isn't him. The sound grows until it becomes audible.

His eyes are back to red. *'Your beast wants to play, Astgeer. Maybe later. Right now, we are going to finish our mating so that everyone knows that you and I are bound together.'*

Catching my bottom lip between my teeth, I blush and nod and ask him to please hurry.

Crawling over me, I open my legs to allow him to settle his hips against mine. He keeps most of his weight on those mighty arms, arms that I love to be caged in. With one on each side of my head, Wilder is all that I see.

His scent is so much stronger right now. I suck it in, loving how it fuels the fire in my centre.

Staring up at him, I marvel in the moment. All I feel is him. I'm nervous but couldn't feel safer.

'I love you. I only ever found love when I left Azanir, I didn't realise I could have it here too,' I whisper. The words seem too small for the feelings that I have for him but they're all I've got to offer. 'I had no idea where I belonged my entire life. Until I met you. You are my home, Wilder. I belong with you and I understand that now.'

His face softens. *'Forever, Astgeer.'* He enters me in one swift movement. I arch my back. Stars erupt behind my lids. His power flowing through me at the same time, ensuring that I'm okay. Adding to the pleasure raging through every muscle.

I forget who I am.

There is only Wilder and me.

Only pleasure and true love.

Chapter Sixty Five

The couple on the bed are deep in their passion. A human and a male Azanite. A Drengar by the size of him. I have to turn away, my cheeks aflame.

When he begins to profess is love and devotion is when I peek over my shoulder to watch the tender moment between the pair.

The male tells her that she is his forever. It's sweet and reminds me of my own mate.

Then he bites her on the shoulder and I'm left shouting for him to stop. He is going to kill her.

Eventually he pulls back, the male apologises and licks at the wound. She seems fine

until a wave of emotions flicks over her face and she screams a blood-curdling sound.

I'm falling and the world is on fire.

I'm outside under the night sky watching in horror as a dragon falls from the sky. My shriek is drowned out by the tell-tale sounds of demons.

Someone grabs me and I'm spinning.

Standing in a room with wood-panelled walls, I scream in rage. I can't be here. I need to help the others.

The world moves left and right, over and over. Rocking back and forth. My rage is boiling. I need to be somewhere. I need to go back.

A noise has me turn and then fall backwards just as a section on the far wall opens and a figure steps through. Just before I can see who it is, the world goes black and I know nothing will ever be the same again.

Startled, my eyelids fly open. The face of the male using his elbow and hand to prop up his head has the nightmare leave my mind instantly.

Wilder lays on his side, watching me. My cheeks heat. Everything that we did last night rushes back and my lip falls between my teeth as I try to hide the embarrassed grin that forms on my face.

'Good morning, mate.'

Mate.

'Good morning.'

Wilder uses the tips of his finger to wipe the hair from my face. Those fingers. The way he pleasured me with them has me almost choke on my own saliva. I've read books, even if I never really felt a desire to have sex before I met him, I knew what to expect. Or at least I thought I did.

I never in my wildest dreams thought that it would be like what I experienced last night. Wilder played with my body like an expert. He knew every button to press and how to have me screaming his name. I feel sorry for the others, we were not quiet last night.

The heat in my face grows.

'What?'

'I was just thinking that we probably should've asked everyone to stay somewhere else last night. They would've heard us.'

Wilder laughs and it has a bolt of energy shoot down my spine. I shiver in need. *'I already told them to leave when we got back to your rooms.'*

Smiling wide, I can't help but bury in closer to his heat. 'You are amazing.'

'I know.'

My laughter filters through the room. 'And modest,' I add and squeal when he grabs my hand and kisses my wrist. His teeth come out and graze against my skin and I think I come. He is pure perfection.

The act has me ask, 'do Azanites bite like…you know…each other…' Why am I embarrassed all of a sudden? After what he did to me last night, you'd think I could ask a simple question about sex.

Wilder's lips trail kisses along my arm, slowly and sensually. His tongue and teeth too. *'Do you mean during intercourse?'*

I nod and then realise that he isn't looking at me. He is too busy making me squirm. One of his hands is now resting on my bare stomach. 'Yes.'

'Yes, it is very common for males and females to feel the need to bite and claim each other with their beasts.'

'Their beasts?' I moan the last word, his fingers are now tracing patterns on my stomach, teasing me slowly as they get lower and lower.

'Hhhmm, our beasts are very playful and biting is how they complete the mating.'

Oh fuck, he is no longer teasing me and I almost forget what I was asking. 'You didn't bite me with your beast though.'

Why does that turn me on so hard?

Wilder's lips are now at my neck and flashes of a dream muddle my brain further. *'No, not yet Astgeer. You are half human. I wouldn't want to hurt you and last night I barely had control over my desire for you.'*

I groan at that. I love that I can cause him to lose control. It makes me feel powerful, something I have never felt before.

'Shall we lose control again?' he barely finishes his sentence before I pull his face down on mine and give him my answer with a consuming kiss.

Chapter Sixty Six

We don't leave the bed for most of the day. The only thing that got us up is the fact that we were both starving. I managed to win the argument to bathe before food and Wilder carried me to the bath before lowering us into the hot water and taking me three times.

When I got out and started drying myself, his growl filled the bathing room and before I knew what I was doing I was straddling him on the tiles, guiding him into my body.

We can't seem to get enough.

'You are feeling well, yes? You will tell me if I've caused you any pain or discomfort.'

Popping a grape in my mouth, I shove a piece of cheese into my already stuffed gob. I have to use my beast to reassure him for the hundredth time that I'm fine because my mouth is so full. *'Wilder, I feel your healing power in my body every few minutes. You would know if I was in pain. I am really hungry though.'*

He makes a deep sound and I quickly look up from the plate of food he piled high for me to understand what it meant. Red eyes, take me in and he's at it again adding more to my plate.

I stopped trying to protest when we first sat down in the sitting room and just continue to eat like I've never eaten before.

'You nearly died last night and then instead of letting you sleep, I ravished you. You need energy.'

'Wilder, you can ravish me any day,' I say with a mouthful of food so it comes out more like 'Wil...der...you...ca...rav...ish...me...anday.'

'It's also the mating. Males and females are locked in this state of frenzied desire in the beginning that we Medir's believe is our biological need to reproduce quickly.'

A piece of bread or meat or whatever is in my mouth now gets lodged in my throat and I cough and splat in the most unlady-like way. Wilder watches me intently from the couch across from mine.

'Reproduce?' I manage to get out through my coughing. Fucking hell, I didn't even think about protection or any of the things you're taught in health class about safe-sex.

Wide eyed, I stare at the male who hands me a glass of juice when I dislodge the piece stuck in my throat. Taking it, I knock half the contents back just to do something with my hands.

'It's biology, Astgeer. We are dragons, the need to mate and reproduce is very strong. You do not want to have younglings?' His question is curious, not judgy or anything. He takes more food, keeping his gaze from me as if he is respecting my need to gather my thoughts without his distracting eyes.

'I've never really thought about it. Well, actually that is a lie. I would love to have children,' I confess for the first time in my life. 'I've thought myself an abomination since I was small, Wilder. I never thought that I would find someone to love and I would hate for...my children to have the same trouble I have. Who would want my half human-half Azanite kids?' Wow, I got pretty bitter at the end there.

Wilder is no longer giving me space. Those obsidian depths are locked on me like the predator he is. *'It would be my honour if you'd have my children,'* he says calmly and without any trepidation. He uses the human word for younglings.

'Even if they can't shift like me? What if they are haunted with visions and nightmares like I am? What would your family say? The BlazeAzar's are one of the strongest families in Azanir, Wilder. Your parents would expect that their grand-younglings be full Azanite.'

'Serafina, do you honestly believe that I care about any of that?'

Shrugging, I don't feel like eating anymore which seems to upset my mate. *'Come here, my heart.'*

I uncurl myself from the lounge and step around the table to straddle him. Wilder pulls my body snuggly against his and makes sure that I am looking at him when he says, *'I wouldn't care what our young can and can't do. As long as they are healthy and have your stubbornness but my sense of safety. We both know that you don't think twice about throwing yourself into danger and I can't handle you and our younglings doing that at the same time, especially if we have daughters.'* He shivers visibly and I try not to smile. I'm being serious about my fears. They don't seem big issues now that I've shared them with Wilder.

Pressing my lips against his, I let our desire consume me and force the stupid voices in my head to stop being so harsh. Wilder loves me. Nothing else matters.

Not right now anyway.

Chapter Sixty Seven

Hugging Alistair, I reassure him that I'm perfectly fine. I get a small lecture of how important it is to keep myself safe and then stand sheepishly before Viktor. The male has his stern-face on and I hang my head and get the biggest 'talking to' of my life.

'We thought you were in your rooms! You promised that is where you'd be! How do you think Felix and I felt when we came back from training to your rooms empty and the shrieking of wraiths filling the kingdom? You cannot imagine the way that felt. It was our job to look after you and keep you safe! We made a promise to our wing-mate to protect his mate and you made that impossible by running off to the human quarter and putting yourself in danger.' I spy Felix behind the cranky male, his eyes are narrowed like he is mad but the way his mouth twitches tells me that he is trying hard to not laugh. The sight has me bite my lower lip to keep from giggling, which sets Viktor off even more.

'It is not funny, Serafina Darkwoods!'

'Oh man, he's using your full name, Raff. You're in deep shit now,' Felix states in mock horror and I can't help the laugh that burst from my mouth.

Viktor turns on the younger male with a look of death that sets everyone in the room off. Viktor bristles and huffs.

Knowing I'm being rude and that I fully deserve his arse-kicking, I throw my arms around his middle and hug him tightly even if he isn't hugging me back. 'I'm so sorry Viktor. I didn't think through my decision to leave or what it'd do to you or Felix. It was selfish. James came over and told me that he found information about Meryl and I became fixated on that. I had to go and find her. I thought she may have...' My throat clogs with tears and I bury my face into the big Drengar's chest when he finally wraps his tree-trunk arms around me. I'm sure he can feel my rolling emotions.

Viktor sighs. 'James told us what happened with your maid passing. I am sorry, Serafina. I know that she meant a great deal to you.'

At the mention of James, I peek over at the human standing quietly in the corner. Roxy nowhere to be seen. He catches me staring and shakes his head once and I throw him an appreciative head nod. I know he wouldn't betray me and tell them what we worked out about my mother.

Catching Wilder studying me, I realise quickly that he caught the gesture and I reassure him quietly in my head that I'll tell him later.

Pulling back, I step over to Felix and give him a big kiss on the cheek in apology and know that he has forgiven me. 'You get the cooks here to make me some more chicken nuggets as an apology and we're good,' he teases and I return to the couch to curl my body against my mates side.

The Drengar all seem very happy as they find a place to sit.

'So, you two finally...' Felix does a funny gesture with his hand that wins him a slap from the prince sitting beside him.

My laughter keeps Wilder from ripping the younger Drengar in two. 'You're dirty, Felix.'

'Not as dirty as I'm sure you two got last—ouch! That hurt!' Rubbing the spot on his arm where he's just been punched, Felix pouts.

'Stop being disrespectful,' Alistair warns, eyeing the human man who comes over and stands beside where I sit on the couch.

James watches everything with a trained eye. He knows these males from our travels.

'We leave you for five days and you end up stabbed by wraiths and with a new pledge, Serafina. I think I said we were all to stay out of trouble.' Alistair doesn't seem too impressed.

Wilder doesn't seem too shocked to hear that I have a pledge. He was very aware that I formed a connection with Roxy and her dad when we met them.

'That is not keeping out of trouble.'

'I don't think our Raff knows what keeping out of trouble means,' Felix replies for me with a wink in my direction. It's strange, I'm getting in trouble left right and centre but I feel completely at ease. Happy.

It definitely has something to do with the quiet male beside me, listening to everyone talk but it's also the others in this room. My Drengar. My pledge. There is something about the energy of having them all here that has me feeling grounded. If only my Van was here. Or Brent and Scott. Laney. With them here, I'd feel whole.

'So, you haven't had any luck finding the book my father wants?'

'No, we have Emmet Darkwoods helping though. He wasn't sure which book we meant.'

Wilder's eyebrow rises dramatically at Viktor's words. Damn, I forgot those two had history. 'He is actually not that bad. He knows of the King's plans and is on board with the whole finding out if humans are the solution to our race extinction problem.'

Felix dives in to explain further of what we learnt by speaking to my brother. Wilder distracts me with a simple caress of my face. Turning, I get caught in his predatory gaze. *'You are worried that your brother and I don't get along.'*

'How did you know?' Frowning, I lean into him as if trying to listen more closely as the others discuss our short time here in the Darkwoods.

'You think too loud.'

Eating my bottom lip, I try to work out what to say. 'He is my brother.'

His hand curls into my hair and through the wavy strands. It's the best touch in the world. *'He is your brother, Astgeer. I will build a relationship with him and any other family you desire.'*

'Even my father?' I blurt out, searching his face for any kind of negative reaction.

Wilder takes a moment before saying, *'even the Lord of the Darkwoods.'*

'We had a conversation when I was dying. He spoke about my mother with such sorrow and love, Wilder. I think she was his true mate and he is fighting this idea of humans and Azanites because he saw her die birthing me. He said that he'd never allow it again because no one deserves to feel the anguish he feels every day having lost her.'

Wilder catches a lone tear that slips down my face. Everyone stops talking instantly but it's Wilder who has my full attention. He frowns deeply and I can practically see his mind processing what I've just said. *'That gives me a great deal to think about.'*

'In what way?'

'Hey, you two want to share with the group?' Viktor snaps us out of our conversation and I only sit back because Wilder turns his attention back to the group.

A sense of unease forms in my chest.

'They are probably talking all lovey-dovey, sappy mate stuff,' Felix jokes and gets a grape thrown at his head.

'Anyway, as I was saying. Wilder and I discovered that the Cavelands are in a worse state than anyone could have imagined. Female numbers are nearly at zero. The last wraith attacked killed two and the need for answers is what is fuelling their acceptance to explore that mates can be found in humans.'

'Why had they not told the other houses what was happening?' Viktor grumbles.

'Because the Cavelands are filled with arrogant Drengar who barely talk to anyone,' Alistair replies and we all sit with our own thoughts for a moment.

'But we don't know if humans are the answer. I would hate for anyone to start coercing or heading to the human realm to find a mate and do something stupid.' Like my father warned, I want to add but don't.

'We are in a volatile stage of our existence that's for sure.'

There was also word from the capital that human rebels have been seen again trying to gain more information of their own.

'What kind of information?' I ask my mate, knowing that I'm going to hate the answer.

'What they have always been looking for, the answer to how they can become like us and gain the power of a dragon.'

Sun Gods, the issues just keep piling up.

Chapter Sixty Eight

'I should probably take you back to your rooms, it's getting late and the sun is going down really fast tonight. Wraith attacks happen within days of each other so we must take precautions,' Emmet muses and we both take a moment to look at the changing sky. It is getting pretty dark for the time. 'Your mate might come and disembowel me if I kept you out too late.'

'He'd probably be able to heal you though after he disembowels you, so that should be reassuring,' I joke and listen to my brother laugh a genuine sound of humour.

'Very true.' He chuckles and we continue our walk around the lair. There are a few Drengar out patrolling and all of them stop and bow at my appearance. News spread fast of what happened. Even Clarice and Otwin have been extra fussy. I've never had so many pastries and honey delights sent to my rooms before. Word that I saved the human quarter has been met with a great deal of embarrassing bowing and thanks.

'I still can't believe what you did. See what I said, no regard for safety or danger.'

Rolling my eyes I reassure him that I've gotten my arse kicked enough my Drengar.

'Good.'

Sighing, I have to explain myself a little. 'I couldn't let them die, Emmet. And I didn't see a Drengar come to their rescue either. What was with that?'

'I don't know,' he admits angrily. We've already had this conversation. 'I will be looking into it.'

I have to leave it with him and drop my anger over what happened. I still haven't seen our father to question him. Emmet told me he left the lair right after the incident and hasn't been back. No one seems worried that he's disappeared, it seems he does that a lot. Gets in a mood and leaves. I feel like I understand why.

He is a male Azanite who has lost his mate. I don't know how he is still functioning. If I lost Wilder, I wouldn't be able to breath. He is my life, in every way.

Holding his leather jacket around my shoulders as the beast under my skin starts to pull at me to get to my nest and my mate, I find myself looking around the Darkwoods for what is making me uncomfortable.

'And the book?'

Emmet makes a deep sound in his chest. 'Haven't discovered anything. I was going to speak with Father but he's off on one of his moods. I'll discuss it with him when he gets back.'

'Okay.' Something doesn't feel right. 'Emmet, I wanted to say thank you for being friendly with Wilder before when you came to my rooms.'

'He is your mate, Serafina. We can all be civil.'

The way he says civil has me smile. It sounds like he wants to be anything but. 'Thank you,' I say again, knowing that it's not going to get better overnight. I appreciate that they are trying.

'Come on, let's head in. We can talk more in the—'

The shriek of wraiths cuts him off and I squeal and jump into his side when he grabs me and pulls me into the protection of his body.

Emmet is calm and assertive as he barks orders to the handful of Drengar who begin to roar into the growing darkness. One by one they shift until all I see is dragons lifting off into the sky, ready to face the demons that haunt our kind.

Emmet swears colourfully in Zaric and begins to pull me toward the lair.

'Serafina! Where are you?' Wilder's demand comes like a roar in my head. I flinch and explain that I'm with Emmet. *'Good stay with your brother, I am coming for you.'*

Nodding, even though he can't see me, I don't question the way Emmet drags me up the hill towards the lair's entrance. He's practically carrying me at this point.

A mighty roar of a dragon shifter catches my attention and I look up just as Wilder kicks off the balcony high above us and then scream when out of nowhere wraiths drops from the sky, right on top of him. Hundreds of them.

'Wilder! *Wilder!*' My scream shakes the world. Emmet swears again. More and more dragons appear from the lair, flying to protect my mate. Alistair. Felix and Viktor amongst the first to get to him and I uselessly stare, gaping at the battle that rages above my head.

'Wilder.'

'It will take more than this to kill me, my heart. Now, get inside!'

The shrieking and the flames, they mix together in a symphony of rage and death. Wraith bite into flesh while the dragons flames and teeth rip them apart.

It is chaos.

'Serafina, come on, I have to get you inside. Now,' Emmet calls, tugging on my arm.

Running with him, we both come to a screeching halt when four wraiths appear in our path. I squeal and am thrown behind Emmett's back. I smack into his solid body and see stars.

Blinking them away, I watch as Emmet pulls back and releases a ball of fire from his mouth. His body contorting against me as more and more wraiths fall from the sky to surround us until he shifts completely.

I swear every wraith is looking at me.

Emmet's dragon now stands with me against his massive leg, protecting me with his body and his fire. Wraiths disappear to be replaced by at least two more.

Clapping my hands over my ears at their shrieking, I search the sky, more concerned with what is happening with Wilder. I've never seen so many wraiths before. Even the other night in the human quarter can't compare to this. There are thousands of demons and it appears not enough dragons.

Emmet steps forward when a group of smoky demons materialise and slam into his side, causing me to fall on my arse.

The trauma of what happened the last time I faced these demons has me frantically looking for a way back to the lair. It's impossible. There are battles raging everywhere. Sky and land.

A strange movement in the trees catches my attention and my already rolling stomach drops into my butt when what appears to be a child with red curls sprints into the trees to my left.

Roxy. 'Roxy!' I scream and jump to my feet.

Emmet roars into the night and I have to dodge the line of fire that erupts from his mouth taking out hundreds of demons.

I almost trip as I break the tree line, searching frantically for the little girl. What the fuck is she doing out here? What if she's been hurt? Where is James?'

The darkness is too heavy and I stumble over something on the floor and spin when I hear a sound that has my heart stop.

Staring, wide eyed up at the sky, I watch as Felix spirals down from high up in the night, his body is covered in smoky demons. Fear grips my throat and is unlike anything I have ever experienced before.

'Felix!' I shriek watching as he collides with the side of my father's lair. Stone flies at the impact and the body of the dragon continues to spiral as it gets closer and closer to the ground. Wilder is shouting in my head. I can't see him anymore. 'Felix! No!' He hits the dirt with a noise that will haunt me forever. 'No! No!' I go to run back to the lair, to help somehow. To see if he is all right. I dreamt this. I saw this. No. No.

Felix. My Felix. *'Wilder! Felix is—'*

That's when I feel the hands grab me by the shoulders, startled, I squeal and spin around to see who it is.

The world goes black.

Chapter Sixty Nine

Groggy and feeling sick, I can't catch the groan that escapes my lips. Everything is throbbing from my toes to my head.

Opening my heavy lids is a mission, they refuse to open and it takes everything I have to force them apart.

What the fuck happened?

And where the fuck am I?

The world tilts back and forth, side to side, in a constant movement that has me unable to push myself up off the cold wooden floor.

On my hands and knees, I dry heave. I feel like I've been eaten by a wraith.

Wraiths.

Wilder.

Felix.

Fuck. I need to get back. Felix wasn't moving. He was being eaten by wraiths. I need to make sure that he is okay.

I try desperately to connect with Wilder. All I get is silence. It does nothing to calm me down.

The panic forces my mind to work properly again and the fuzziness evaporates to leave me squinting in the harsh firelight coming from the sconces along the wall.

What is this place?

Everything looks familiar but I can't seem to piece together where I am. Wood panelled walls with no door in sight, a small window to my left, the place is bare. Not a single item of furniture. The motion is relentless and I heave again, hating the feeling of being so disorientated.

Trying to stand, it takes my poor mind a ridiculous amount of time to understand why I can't. The relentless jingling has me finally looking down at the thick silver chain locking me to the floor.

I finger the cuff it's attached to on my waist frantically. I'm locked up. 'No!'

I pull and pull and get nowhere. The chain doesn't budge. Refusing to believe that this is happening, I try over and over to get free. 'What is this? Help! Is there anyone there! Help!'

I've been chained up like an animal. This can't be real. I scream in anger and rage at the fact that someone has done this to me. That I can't connect with my mate. I need to get back.

That's when I remember.

My dream.

This is when, I spin just as the wall on the far wall opens.

My heart escalates to an unhealthy rhythm when a tall man, dressed in black pants and a black tee steps through into my cell. I smell his lemon bodywash and that over-used musk aftershave first. Those familiar symmetrical features and that light brown styled hair make me freeze.

It takes me too long to understand what is happening.

'Raff,' Miles greets me with a small, arrogant smile and a nod of his head. There was a time where I called this man my best friend. He betrayed me. He is a human rebel and helped in my capture by the man who steps into the room after him.

'It is nice to see you, Raff. It has been too long,' Joseph says like he is genuinely happy to see me. 'I bet you're shocked to see us. Were you hoping that I was eaten by the wraiths? I'm much harder to kill than that,' he doesn't wait for me to answer. He never came across as a man who needed two people in a conversation, he seems happy to talk enough about himself for two.

I stay quiet, assessing the situation. I'm back with the human rebels who believe that I can somehow help them to get the power of an Azanite. Joseph kidnapped me. Drugged me. Hit me. Promised pain and death if I didn't comply. He doesn't have the sacred text of Azanir to open now, so finding out what he wants is important. He believed he needed my blood before, what the fuck is his twisted theory now?

'We are so very glad to have you join us again. You see, we originally thought that we needed your blood in order to find our answer, but do you know what I recently found out from my rebel friends in the Darkwoods?'

My insides turn to liquid at the smirk he throws me. He's confident and cocky.

'I found out that you may be the key after all to the secret of the Azanites. That you can help us to become like you. Half human and half beast.'

Fuck. I try really hard to keep my emotions calm and off my face. To not react.

Miles grins at whatever he sees on my face and I growl a deep sound that has his eyes bug out of his head.

I will not be prisoner to these people again. I will not be used for their twisted quest for power.

Felix needs me. My mate and my family need me.

I lose my mind.

My beast rumbles in my head and I test the chain again, this time with every ounce of strength I can muster. I pull and pull, hearing the crack and creak of the wood under my feet.

My roar matches that of any Azanite dragon.

I'm not the girl they caught all those months ago . I have learnt that I have power. I am the mate to Drengar Wilder BlazeAzar Medir. I am the daughter of the Lord of the Darkwoods and the friend to many.

I snarl, loving the way the two men step back.

Joseph calls out something that is drowned out by my snarling. I pull and see the wood crack and then I stop when a new man steps into the room.

My anger dies as I try to process who I'm staring at.

It can't be. He isn't a rebel. He can't be! He would never betray me—right!

'Van?' I whisper. My dragon whines in pain.

My foster brother, the man I love more than life itself, smiles sadly at me. He is here. He is a rebel. 'Hi Raff.'

No.

THE FINAL BOOK IN THE

SHIFTERS OF AZANIR SERIES

COMING SOON

ABOUT THE AUTHOR

A L Rojo is an author, educator, wife and mother who lives in Sydney, Australia. From a young age, she understood the power of getting lost in a good book. After giving herself permission to explore her creativity, she found that she loved writing novels that focus on strong female characters, love, spice, and the wonderful complexities of life. Her goal is to simply create worlds where anyone can escape into, for however long they may need. She says that along this journey she has left behind a piece of herself in every character she creates.

To get the latest updates, follow A L Rojo on:

Website: www.alrojo.com.au
Facebook: A L Rojo
Instagram: alrojo_writer